Clayton's Star

Book 4
The O-Line Series

Jillian Jacobs

JILLIAN JACOBS

Published by Green Moose Productions
Copyright 2016 by Jillian Jacobs

ISBN: 978-1-942313-12-0

DEDICATION

To: My shining star, Jeremy

ACKNOWLEDGMENTS

To the sensational five! My beta-girls: TC, Lisa, Anya, Mom, and Jennifer.

CHAPTER 1

Outside a conference center located off a major highway in northern Ohio, Sheridan Bennett rubbed her temples and breathed in a mix of late-spring showers and wet asphalt. While sparkling glasses, inane chitchat, and uncomfortable shoes were part of every fundraiser, tonight's curious stares and repeated requests for "selfies" had become a bit overwhelming. However, she'd smiled through it all in order to show appreciation to Lieutenant O'Malley—a man who'd led her and her sisters through their darkest hours. Her gratitude toward the burly old man was the reason she'd attended tonight's, "Go Blue" law enforcement fundraiser.

"Good evening, Sheridan."

Heart thrumming a terrified beat, she shifted slightly and studied the man who'd spoken. Noted his smug visage, the brush of white through his dark blond hair, and the few wrinkles now evident around his mouth and eyes. His casual black suit fit his trim frame. Though, he'd likely stolen the whole ensemble.

"What's the matter? Party not high-brow enough for a famous actress like you?" He spoke in a smoother than silk tone that lulled you into complacency before striking like a snake.

This man, who was featured on the FBI's most wanted list, stood on the other side of the ornate fountain at the center of the circular drive—at a police fundraiser, no less. Reckless. Brazen. And one hundred percent her father, Jack Bennett.

Unable to run in her teal evening gown and sky-high heels, Sheridan considered the distance to the hotel's front door. Ten feet? Twenty? Calculations were too complicated when every muscle in her body was tensed for flight, and if necessary—fight.

After waiting years for his return, Sheridan looked forward to showing him as much kindness as he'd shown her and her sisters. A bullet from her Sig Sauer P224 would work nicely. Unfortunately, the gun sat nestled in her purse, which was still inside on the table.

Drawing on all her acting skills, she considered the scene and became her own director. Still, her heart hadn't yet received the calm-down memo so she released a long, shaky breath.

"I see I've shocked you. Good." Her father smirked. "Figured I was due to teach my little girl another life lesson...among other things."

While remembering those horrific lessons, Sheridan narrowed her eyes and eased closer to the hotel's doors. The fountain's trickling rhythms had soothed her for a time, but now the entire sculpture served as a massive hindrance. As she inched around the pool's outer edge, she kept her gaze locked on her long-lost father. "What game are you playing this time?"

"What? No welcome home hug? Haven't you missed me?" He held both arms open wide. "No? I can tell by that look you haven't concerned yourself with my welfare. Well *I* find myself very interested in my dear daughter. Made quite the success of yourself. Been keeping tabs, you know." He winked and flashed a false smile. "Got all your articles up on the fridge."

"You can shove those articles where the sun don't shine, *Jack.*" Sheridan halted her slow pace toward the door. No longer a naïve fourteen-year-old girl, she'd lived every moment preparing for vengeance against this man. "Leave now, because I won't give you a dime."

"Oh no, dear, that will never do. As you say, I had hoped we could have a nice little chat about your abundance of funds…and my lack of them." He quieted as a young couple came out of the building and walked toward their car.

Sheridan considered screaming at them to run but sudden sounds or movements might cause the slithering psycho to strike.

"Good evening." Her father smiled at the couple then, with one hand, he mimed a gun shooting at the back of their heads. Laughing, he turned and met her gaze. "Now where were we?" He scratched his chin. "Ah, yes. Money and our family reunion. I was thinking your sisters could join us."

Red-hot fireworks erupted in Sheridan's brain. "A family dinner would be lovely. I would be more than happy to serve you a bullet right between your fucking eyes."

"Such rude language." He leaned back, placing a hand on his crisp linen shirt.

"You haven't seen rude." Sheridan clenched both hands into fists at her sides.

Her father sauntered two steps closer and jabbed a finger in her direction. "And you seem to forget that as your father I deserve to be spoken to with respect."

"I haven't forgotten anything." Out of the corner of her eye, she caught a flash of red on his arm almost like a laser-pointer…or a…

The beam traveled across his cheek before stopping right between his eyes.

Oh no!

"Get down." Sheridan lunged, but her father was just out of reach. She cursed as her left hip absorbed the brunt of the fall. Tiny rocks grated across her elbow and hand.

Concrete chunks splintered off the fountain and peppered her hair. Fighting through her fear, she braced both arms over her head and searched the area for the shooter.

Her father had dropped behind the fountain and, using one

index finger, he pounded on his cell phone.

The rifleman must have one hell of a suppressor. She'd barely heard the gun's crack and pop before the fountain area around her father exploded into pieces.

"Brilliant." She yelled at the source of all this chaos. "You're here for five minutes and already bullets are flying." Jaw tight, she kicked off her shoes and considered the distance between the fountain and the conference center's automatic doors. Although outrunning a sniper was a risky—and stupid move. And the man firing from above had to be a professional, because each shot was aimed squarely at her father.

A motor rumbled to life in the parking lot.

Tires squealed and then two bright lights barreled closer, blinding her.

Sheridan screamed, sure she'd end up liquid goo against the fountain.

The van screeched to a halt, inches from her leg.

Her father scurried toward the vehicle and jumped into the open side panel.

Two muffled cracks reverberated through the air.

Her father screamed and clutched his ankle, blood spilling between his fingers. "Go! Go!" He yelled as he wrenched the van's door shut.

Sheridan lifted her head an inch above the fountain's edge and watched the van careen out of the parking lot.

Shaking uncontrollably, she remained crouched by the fountain. What the hell had just happened? One minute her father had appeared, and the next everything had gone to shit so fast her head still spun.

"Damn you, Jack Bennett." Sheridan bit her bottom lip, drawing on the pain to shake her out of her stupor. She had to move. Had to warn her sisters. Had to shake off her complacency. *He* was back.

"Sheridan? Is everything all right?" Clayton Kincaid called

from just outside the conference center's entrance.

A muscle-heavy security guard stood like a sentinel at his side.

Oh no. No! They couldn't be out here. Not with a trigger-happy sniper on the rooftop somewhere, waving around his red beam.

Was Clayton's employer, Harris Investigations providing security for this event? How much had they seen and heard?

She glanced up and saw the security cameras along the portico's ceiling, both pointing in her direction. "Great."

"Our guy in the security booth said a van almost ran you over. Why are you out here all alone?" Clayton barreled toward her, straight into the sniper's sights.

"Wait. Stop. Don't come out here!" Terror tore down her spine as that damn detective stepped out into the open. "Go back inside."

"Sheridan, you're shaking?" Crouching beside her, Clayton nudged a concrete chunk off her shoulder. "What happened?"

A breeze blew a trace of cedar and citrus. His scent. If she breathed in enough of him, could she remove the stench of her father's visit? Stop focusing on Clayton's cologne in the middle of a deadly situation. *Idiot!*

She tugged him onto the ground beside her, hopefully out of any lurking sniper's sights. "I think the guy in the van was drunk. Yeah, he scared me, but I'm all right now."

He brushed off the sleeve of his black tuxedo jacket before clutching her shoulder. "Are you sure?" He frowned and glanced up at the fountain. "Did he hit this fountain, because there's concrete everywhere?"

Sheridan sighed. Trust the ex-police detective and now private eye to ask questions she didn't want to answer. Plus, Mr. Kincaid was just as distracting in a formal suit as he was in his swimsuit. Not that she'd noticed his very fit body, square jaw, perfectly trimmed dark brown hair, or his striking aqua eyes, which may or may not have influenced her purchase of this teal dress after she'd spent far too many mornings swimming beside him at Excel gym.

She peered into those eyes now and fought against a wish to fall into his arms and find comfort and guidance. Stupid, especially after her worst fears had just played out before her like some prime-time crime show. She stood alone. Always had. Always would.

"Listen, I came outside to get some fresh air, trying to shake this headache." Acting the part, she rubbed her temples. "Like I said, the guy was likely drunk."

Clayton arched a brow. "While that may be the case, we still have all this debris from the fountain."

"There's more debris over here." The security guard, Tony if the embroidered nametag on his shirt was to be believed, stood in the spot her father had vacated.

Distract and vacate! "Clayton, can you help me stand?" Saying a silent prayer that sniper-man had left, Sheridan lifted her hand.

Clayton rose and helped her to her feet.

"Thank you. I'm going back inside." She peered around him and noted the security guard was studying something on the parking lot's surface. Bullets? Blood? She needed to leave before every cop in the building charged outside, and she became the top story on *Hollywood News.* "You guys have this under control, so I'll go get cleaned up." She dusted off her dress. "Bye."

"Wait a second." Clayton grabbed her elbow and then twisted open both her hands. "I don't believe you. Your hands are all scuffed up, and your entire body is shaking. Plus, you've studied the parking lot like you're searching for someone. What's going on?" He clutched both her shoulders. "Why are there concrete chunks all over? What hit the fountain?"

"Release me." She flicked a glance at his hand. "I appreciate your concern, but I'm fine."

"Sheridan."

That single word. Her name coming from that masculine, clean-shaven mouth, tagged with his blue eyes pleading for the truth, almost stopped her. Almost.

"I need to go." She shifted free from his touch. A touch too warm and far too soothing.

Now wasn't the time for comfort but rather for action. An adrenaline rush only lasted so long. She needed to step away from Clayton Kincaid before she burst into please-help-me tears over her father's return…because she wasn't helpless. Not anymore. She had resources, training. Eight years ago her father had taught her a life-altering lesson. She'd be damned if he made her a student again.

Clayton Kincaid didn't belong in her nefarious world, because she offered nothing but misery in return. Wasn't that clear by her father's brazen approach in the middle of a police charity event? His homecoming would spawn nothing but hardship for however long he chose to torment her this time.

Yeah, this time. But, she was more than ready.

This time.

CHAPTER 2

Since meeting her at an author event a few months ago, Clayton Kincaid had considered a lot when it came to Ms. Sheridan Bennett, but her being a liar wasn't one of them. And yet, wasn't lying her career? On the big screen she became someone else—the femme fatale or the quirky girl next door and everyone adored her. But who was she really?

Back inside the bustling event, he kept her shiny, blonde head in sight as she weaved through the crowd, oblivious to those snapping photos when she passed.

What the hell was she doing here anyway? Not just at this Manchester police fundraiser but also in Ohio of all places? They kept bumping into each other, which had him wondering if perhaps fate was giving him a hint. A hint he'd gladly take if he thought she'd accept. Yet everything about her said, look but don't touch.

"Hey, Kincaid." Tony, the security guard nudged his arm. "I found a couple of these out in the lot." He opened his palm and inside rested two spent casings from what looked like from a SV-98 Russian sniper rifle.

Clayton had only seen these in textbooks during his Ranger training. The gun wasn't for sale in the United States, and was used by Russian law enforcement and counter-terrorist forces.

"Well, this blows the whole 'drunk driver story' all to hell."

Clayton picked up the empty shell. Unsure whether to follow this lead or follow that lying blonde beauty back to her home and bend her over his knee. "Show me where you found this." He yanked at the stupid bowtie practically strangling him and followed Tony to the parking lot.

Damn it! Hadn't his instincts been screaming? And instead of relying on his training and assessing the scene, he'd blindly rushed to Sheridan's side. But now he had time to reassess. Now he wasn't blinded by the hard beat of lust that always raged in her presence.

"I found a couple shell casings here." Tony waved a hand over an area in the lot then peered at the roof. "A few more were in the bushes against the building there." He pointed to landscaping along the side of the building.

"Can we access the roof?"

"Sure." Tony cracked his knuckles.

"All right, head up there. See what you can find. Be careful. The shooter might still be around. We might need to evacuate everyone." Clayton faced the fountain. "I'll check around the fountain, and then head inside. I have some questions for Ms. Bennett."

Tony took off toward the rear entrance used by employees. A camera was mounted outside the door for the safety of staff leaving late at night. Clayton would check the footage as the shooter had likely used that exit.

Right now, he circled back to the water sculpture. Sheridan hadn't been shot, but had someone else? And who had been in the van? Shaking his head, he rolled up his sleeves and studied the ground where she'd been lying on her side. He picked up a sliver of a broken fish, working the piece between his forefinger and thumb. Had she been the shooter's target?

One of the fish statues had exploded and water poured out the remaining plastic tube, causing all the others fish mouths to dribble. He slipped off his black socks and rented dress shoes before climbing into the fountain. Grumbling a few choice curse words as the cold water hit his feet, he waded closer to the sculpture. His feet brushed against coins tossed in with starry-eyed wishes. He'd likely toss in a few wishes for Sheridan's safety as the dangers of tonight became more and more evident.

"What do we have here?" A bullet was lodged in the inner structure. Likely a warning shot, as this was higher on the fountain, not down where she'd been crouching. "Unbelievable. Does she think she's in the middle of a movie scene? Who the hell is shooting at her?" He mimed her voice, "Oh, no Clayton, I'm fine." After taking a few photos with his phone, he squeezed out his pant legs, grabbed his shoes and socks, and charged back inside, barefoot.

A few months ago at his boss, Rachel Harris's author event, he'd given Sheridan hell about not having a bodyguard. She'd smiled and pulled a tiny, Glock .380 from her purse. He'd asked if she knew how to use it, and she'd challenged him to meet her at the shooting range.

A challenge—that summed up Ms. Bennett. He loved a challenge, and could see himself loving the hell out of this one.

Back inside, he wasted crucial minutes searching for the wayward woman through the crowd of friendly officers and local dignitaries. Right now, he needed someone familiar with Bennett who could offer real answers and talk some sense into her stubborn head. Why would an international star gallivant around Manchester without any protection? Not to mention lie about being the target of a sniper at a police fundraiser.

"Clayton." Constance Grey, his friend and date for the evening clutched his arm. "Where have you been?"

"Sorry." He peered into her blue eyes, which were a different hue than Sheridan's, lighter and carrying a hint of annoyance. They also had a similar hair color and style, slightly wavy and falling just past their shoulders. However, Sheridan was a natural blonde whereas Constance had an array of light colors throughout, aided by her stylist.

He and Constance had grown up together as their families were close. He'd dated her in high school, but that had ended when she'd balked at his career choice. He cared for her, but had made clear they would never again be lovers—she disagreed. "Constance, a drunk driver was out in the parking lot. He's caused some damage to the fountain, so I need to work on locating the vehicle before another accident occurs."

"Let the center's security handle it." She waved manicured fingers toward the ceiling. Her tall, slim frame was encased in a long-sleeved black dress. New and designer. Facts he knew because, on the way here tonight, she'd told him all about her shopping excursion.

"Harris Investigations is working with the center's security team. I explained this."

She sniffed and looked away. "Your mother and I were discussing your work schedule the other day. She misses you by the way. Says you haven't been home much since Michael—"

"Constance, please don't." Clayton fought against the wash of pain flooding his system upon hearing his younger brother's name. "I have to work. Here are the keys to my Expedition. I'm sorry, but I have to speak to Lieutenant O'Malley."

"All right." She took his keys. "See, I can be understanding."

"Sure. Yeah." He raked a hand through his hair. "I know you can. Thanks again for coming tonight."

She kissed his cheek. "Anytime."

He eased back. "Let me know when you're leaving, and I'll have someone walk you out."

Constance smiled and then weaved her way through the crowd. She stopped and spoke to his boss, Rachel, which would be an entertaining conversation since Rachel called her Clingstance. Though he regretted abandoning his date, he was tasked with the safety of tonight's participants. Pulling his phone from his pocket, he texted Rachel and asked that she follow

Constance to his SUV at the end of the night.

His phone immediately pinged with a reply.

Why?

"No time for explanations, Rach," he mumbled before tucking his phone back in his pocket.

Sheridan had arrived with the O'Malley's so Clayton scanned the crowd for the burly Irishman. Lieutenant O'Malley and his wife were pillars in the community and didn't have any children.

When giving her large donation earlier, Sheridan had mentioned how the O'Malley's helped her through a rough childhood—a comment that had spawned all kinds of questions in his mind.

The Lieutenant stood alone by the bar, his cell phone plastered to his ear. Behind a set of bifocals, the keen-eyed cop scanned the area. His thick black hair was peppered with gray, and his brawny frame filled out his suit, though the pants were a little long.

Clayton eased closer and leaned against the bar beside him, blatantly eavesdropping.

"What? Your father was *here*?" O'Malley's eyes narrowed. "Did he say why he's come back...I see...Where are you?... absolutely not...I'll check the perimeter and the fountain...you'll have to come in...You know what to do?...Set your alarm. I'll be by later." He ended his call and then slammed his whiskey glass against the bar.

"Lieutenant." Clayton straightened and held out his hand.

"Ah, Kincaid, nice to see you." O'Malley shook Clayton's hand and shifted past him. "Excuse me. I need to step outside."

Clayton gripped the older man's shoulder. "Sir, I was outside earlier with Ms. Bennett. I'm not sure what happened, but she was visibly shaken."

O'Malley met his gaze and then nodded. "Did you happen to see anyone? A man?"

"No." Why he would ask that specific question? And what

JILLIAN JACOBS

had O'Malley meant when he'd asked, 'Your father was here?' Did he mean Sheridan's father? Clayton rubbed his chin and glanced out over the crowd, searching for the missing blonde once more. "I discovered a bullet lodged in the fountain out front. And a security guard found spent casings from what I believe was a SV-98."

"Show me." O'Malley led the way outside, barely waiting for the automatic doors to open before he strode toward the fountain. He circled the entire fountain before bending to pick up a piece of concrete. "Any indication of where the shots originated?"

"Following the bullet's trajectory, I'd say the shooter was up high, firing from that rooftop there." Clayton pointed to a portion above the conference center. "I sent Tony up earlier. He should have something for us."

O'Malley adjusted his glasses and heaved a sigh. "I've known Sheridan for a long time." He settled on the fountain's ledge, rubbing his thick hands together. "She's already been through many hardships. I don't want her to relive..." He shook his head. "Thing is, if we notify everyone inside that we're looking for someone shooting at Sheridan Bennett...if indeed she was the target, and I'm not convinced she was...we'll have every news van in the world on the scene in two hours flat. Attention she doesn't want or need." O'Malley sighed again. "Think you can investigate this on your own, Kincaid. Keep quiet while you do?"

Clayton frowned. "As you said, she was shot at, sir. Her privacy is a non-issue. Plus a drunk driver was on scene."

"Not drunk. Fleeing bullets more likely." O'Malley stood and braced a leg against the fountain's edge. "You've never had your privacy breached, have you? Not like Sheridan does or will if this story comes to light." The Lieutenant raised a caterpillar-like brow. "I'll make some phone calls. You look into these bullets but keep quiet about what happened."

"I'm not comfortable with that decision." Clayton couldn't dismiss the sheer terror he'd seen in Sheridan's eyes nor the way

14

her entire body shook as she'd laid beside that fountain. "She needs someone to look after her."

"Isn't that what you're doing?"

"Who was shooting at her?"

"Again…I don't believe she was the shooter's target." O'Malley shoved both hands in his pockets. "Stay close to her for now."

Wincing, Clayton bent and dislodged a small rock from his bare big toe. Patience had never been a virtue, and aggravation was quickly turning into raging fury. Why was O'Malley holding back pertinent information? Didn't the man want her safe? "Sir, a van tried to run her down, she *was* shot at, and you're holding back. Why all the secrets?"

"Sheridan's secrets are not mine to tell."

"Would they be yours to tell if she was lying here with a bullet between her eyes?"

"Careful, Kincaid." Eyes narrowed, the Lieutenant held up a hand. "The girl is always in danger. From her past. From her very public job. But she's the bravest little thing you'll ever meet. And she chooses not to live in fear. Instead she does everything she can to protect herself and her family."

"Sometimes that isn't enough."

"I know." O'Malley's shoulders slumped. "I'm getting old, son. Considering retiring. But Sheridan's one job I can't quit."

"I won't quit either. I don't give a damn what Ms. Bennett believes. She's not safe."

"No, she isn't." O'Malley clapped Clayton on the back with his beefy paw. "Sheridan is like a daughter to me, and I don't give my blessing easily, so don't fuck it up. But know this, if you choose to investigate her, you'll keep her past a secret or you'll deal with me."

Clayton nodded, and though more curious than ever, he refrained from asking more questions that wouldn't receive answers. No problem, digging through people's lives was what he did for a living.

"We on the same page, Kincaid?" O'Malley held out his hand.

Clayton shook it. "Agreed...for now."

"Good." O'Malley gave him a hearty squeeze before releasing his hand. "How's the family?"

As they headed back inside, Clayton answered the man's mundane questions. Then he promised to keep O'Malley updated and veered toward the security office to review the video surveillance.

The vision of Sheridan's wide blue eyes and huddled body would fuel his investigation, one he'd have to work on without his boss, Rachel. Although, he'd include both her and his other co-worker and ex-Ranger compatriot, Scotty, if necessary.

To his mind, Ms. Bennett had always been a person of interest. And now he had a reason...and a blessing to get to know her very, very well.

CHAPTER 3

The next morning, Clayton held up a finger when Rachel knocked on his open office door. "Constance, I need to wrap up this call." He tapped his cell off speaker mode and lifted the phone to his ear. "Rachel's here. I'll talk to you later."

"We'll do lunch on Tuesday since our evening got cut short."

Instead of arguing against her assumption that his schedule would be clear, he said, "I'll call if I'm available."

"Clayton, is everything okay?" Constance asked with a sniffle.

Multiple layers existed in her question. Layers he refused to address while at work. Everything wasn't "okay" because she kept expecting more than he could give.

Sighing, he rubbed a hand along his nylon workout pants and glanced at his boss. He'd thrown on comfortable clothes after heading home from the fundraiser earlier this morning. Lack of sleep and too many questions had his patience on a thin edge.

"Listen, Constance, I really need to speak with Rachel. I'm sorry, but I've got to go." He hung up, which was in a way rude, but she'd called first thing this morning, carrying on about her plans for the day. Not once asking about his dilemma last night, which in hindsight was probably a good thing.

"Digging in her claws, is she?" Rachel smirked, tapping her

knuckles against the doorframe. "I warned you not to take her last night." She sipped from her mega-mug of hot tea.

"Not in the mood for an I-told-you-so, Harris."

She grunted and plopped her pixie butt in one of his metal-framed office chairs. Her straight dark hair fell just past her shoulders and framed her pert nose and brown eyes. Rarely sitting still, his energetic boss bounced her knee up and down. Her skinny jeans fit her athletic body well, and she'd topped everything off with a long-sleeved cotton shirt stitched with the Harris Investigations logo above her left breast.

"Investigating anything today?" He waved a hand at her shirt. "If so, not very covert."

"Changing the subject?"

"What subject?" He furrowed his brow. "My personal life is never a subject."

Rachel huffed out a laugh then swore when a fly landed on her arm. "Dang it. I never had flies downtown."

"Why are you in my office swatting flies? I have work to do. Shoo." He flicked a hand toward the door.

She lifted her middle finger while loudly slurping her tea.

He bit back a grin. Once he'd joined Rachel's firm, they'd moved out of her uncle's downtown office and purchased this building located in a seedier neighborhood on Manchester's southeast side. They'd spruced up the place, walling off four office cubes and adding a slightly-bigger-than-a-closet break room using his old college fridge that hovered on the verge of death, although the constant thrum soothed, at times.

Quiet for a moment, Rachel sipped her tea then dropped the empty mug on his desk with a loud clunk.

He narrowed his eyes and tapped a pen on his wooden desk. Maybe he should throw it at her. She wasn't generally the type to chitchat. Something must be ticking in her shrewd mind.

Rachel leaned back in the chair. "Working on the weekend…hmmm…trying to impress your boss?" Smirking, she raised a brow then glanced behind him. "Did you make coffee?"

"Yes, I made coffee."

"How long have you been here?" Popping out of the chair, Rachel scooted behind him, and then lifted the coffee pot before studying the contents. "I'd say since about what…four?"

Clayton rubbed both hands across his face. "What are you some coffee whisperer who thinks they can tell employee hours by what's left in a pot?"

"No, but I can tell you've been here for a while." She leaned her hip against his desk and ruffled his hair.

He shrugged. "I'm organizing files…catching up on paperwork."

"Uh huh." Rachel grabbed her mug and filled it to the brim. "Ah, coffee. Bronco prefers tea, but sometimes you need jitter-giving goodness."

"How's Big B doing?" Moving the topic to Rachel's pro-football player boyfriend would keep her interest off him. Plus, he was curious about the big-guy. He'd grown close to Bronco after helping him and Rachel with a case last year.

"Bronco's good. Off to camp on Thursday." She sighed. "He gets worried about the Marauders dropping him. Silly man."

Clayton shrugged. "Happens."

"Shut it." After slapping his arm, Rachel headed for the door, but stopped and glanced over her shoulder. "Bronco playing for another team will *not* happen, because I am *not* moving. Period. And since you're a ball of sunshine this morning, I'm out." She saluted him then disappeared around the corner, likely heading for her office.

Releasing a breath, he reached for his lukewarm coffee but halted with the cup halfway to his mouth as the annoying presence once more stood in his doorway.

"For the record, I know 'organizing files' is code for, 'I'm doing something I don't want you to know about.'" Rachel tossed up air quotes with her fingers. "If you need help, holler, I'll be in my office alphabetizing my cases." She stuck out her tongue.

He did throw the pen this time.

She ducked then pointed her finger at him. "You're a detective now. Lie better."

"Fine. And by the way, that coffee is leftover from yesterday."

"I can't hear you."

"Why did you answer?"

"If I die from coffee poisoning, I'll send Bronco after you."

"Can't, you'll be dead."

"Will I?"

Clayton shook his head. Rachel could drive a man crazy. He had nothing but sympathy for the Marauders left guard and...yes...admiration. Rachel was one hell of an investigator and friend. Not that he'd ever tell her. But hell, she knew.

She was wrong though. He hadn't lied. Since the crack of dawn this morning, he'd shifted through his cases in order to determine how much time he could spare on Sheridan Bennett.

He'd watched the conference center's security camera footage at least six times. An older man had been by the fountain at the same time as Sheridan. Although, he'd kept his back to the cameras as if knowing they were there. After Sheridan and the man had a short conversation, they'd both hit the pavement. Moments later a white service-type van roared into the picture before shooting out of the parking lot. The vehicle's plates were registered to a sixteen-year-old kid's new car. Obviously stolen.

The look of pure hatred in Sheridan's eyes when she'd conversed with the older man made sense when Clayton added together O'Malley's short phone conversation and all the research he'd done into her background.

The man in the video had to be her father, Jack Bennett. He appeared on posters just like his movie star daughter, only his face was featured on the FBI's most wanted list. His crimes included fraud, larceny, murder, drug trafficking, child trafficking, and more terrifying than anything, he was wanted in connection with the Korzakov crime family. As if her father's crime-riddled past wasn't bad enough, Clayton had also learned that Sheridan's mother had died of a heroin overdose.

How had Sheridan risen past a childhood embedded with such negative influences? *Very intriguing.* Changing a path that dark and dirty took a lot of inner strength. She'd started modeling locally then was discovered by a big house. After a few years, she used her earnings to take acting classes. Her first film had been a hit. Further investigation via YouTube revealed a plethora of interviews from film promotions to award ceremonies to people just stopping her on the street. Each video was viewed by thousands of fans. She even had fan-made social media sites.

He cringed at the thought of that much scrutiny. At the personal invasion of her space and her life. Something he could never have in his line of work.

Clayton tapped a mechanical pencil against his desk. How could he protect her from such a wily man? Jack Bennett had evaded the FBI for years. Had O'Malley contacted anyone at the fed's Ohio branch? He'd check in with the Lieutenant later.

One sure way to discover if a new player was in town and affiliated with the Russian mob was to speak to someone with mafia ties. A someone Rachel knew quite well.

Shoving away from his desk, Clayton took the six steps to Rachel's office. After knocking on her open door, he waited for her to look up from her laptop.

She tossed her reading glasses onto her desk and met his gaze. "What?"

"I need to talk to Erik."

She frowned and glanced away before opening a folder. "He's back in witness protection."

"No. He isn't." Clayton knew this for a fact, because Erik had recently helped another Marauder player out of a sticky situation.

Rachel sniffed, eyes glued to the single paper in the folder. "It's not a good time for Erik to be seen."

"So he won't be."

"Why do you want to talk to my brother?"

"For a case."

"I know all your cases. None require speaking to Erik."

"This one does."

She leaned back in her chair and studied him for a moment. "There's no other way?"

Clayton shrugged. "Other ways take time." If Sheridan's father was approaching her at police fundraisers, then he was desperate for something. Likely cash. Every minute the man remained in town posed a danger to the Hollywood beauty. Erik could shed some light on Sheridan's father's involvement in the Korzakov crime family since he was brought into the family as a child. But now...Clayton had no idea what kinds of illicit deeds Rachel's brother was involved in, either for the FBI or himself. Erik's whole situation was far too murky to investigate.

"I'll see what I can do." Rachel returned her attention to her computer screen.

Clayton nodded before heading back to his office and brewing another pot of coffee. Typically he only drank one cup, but this morning required focus.

He thumbed through the photos on his desk and found one of Sheridan's estate taken by some tabloid a few years ago. She'd custom built her home in a wooded area, just outside of Manchester. No one had ever been inside. When interviewed, she never discussed any relationships with men. Rarely mentioned her sisters.

He tipped his hat at her ability to keep everything private in a world that exposed everything. But since she worked so hard to keep her secrets hidden, that only meant she had many to reveal.

And investigating secrets was his job.

CHAPTER 4

"Come on, Legs. One more set."

Late Tuesday afternoon, Sheridan sweated through her exercise bra while lifting weights as directed by her personal trainer, Elston Charter. After a nerve-racking weekend, she appreciated the intense workout. For such a short guy, only five-eight, he barked at her like a feral Great Dane most days. Today, he'd forgone his more colorful attire and sported black gym shorts and a sleeveless gray tank top. His blond hair styled perfectly atop his gorgeous face, while hers dripped with sweat.

Ten squats later, she lifted the weight bar onto the rack and wiped her face with a towel. Closing her eyes for a moment, she shook her head, staving off the dizziness from Elston's brutal exercise regime. Seeing her father again had ruined her appetite. Not eating added to little sleep, plus the strain of moving her older sister, Laney into her home had pushed Sheridan to her limits. After informing Laney's adoptive parents, the Masers' of the safety issues inherent with the return of their biological father, she'd brooked no argument before moving her twenty-five-year old special-needs sister into her home. A home Sheridan had designed with enhanced security features, including a safe room and escape tunnels located in her garage and basement. Each year, she reviewed her security system and updated as needed.

Since the police fundraiser, Sheridan hadn't seen her father. But that hadn't stopped her from running through emergency procedures with her sisters and logging hours at the firing range. O'Malley had stopped by the house late Saturday night and promised extra patrols in the area. Once again, he'd ordered her to chop down a few trees for security reasons, but those living creatures had been on this earth far longer than her, and she couldn't bring herself to remove a single one.

Thoughts of those sturdy trees had her realizing her mind had drifted far off course. This is what her father did—had her so frazzled she couldn't focus on taking care of herself, which didn't bode well for the safety of her sisters.

"I'm done for the day, Easy E." Sheridan snapped Elston with her towel. "I should get home to Laney and Jenny."

"Only half-way done, Sher. We need to get in the rest of your reps or it throws off your training schedule."

After taking a swig from her water bottle, she shot Elston a glare. "A schedule. A predetermined agenda on how my life is supposed to be?" She half-laughed. "If only."

"Not into it today, are you?"

"Nope."

"Rough weekend?"

"Yep."

"Man troubles."

"You tell me. You're the expert."

"Why, yes, love. I am." He winked.

This is why she loved Elston. He could make her smile, just by breathing or talking, or giving her hell. He'd whipped her body into shape, even though her "people" thought she should use a well-known trainer. Forget that business. She'd hit the jackpot years ago with this feisty fella.

Hoping to make amends for her sour attitude, she grabbed his hand. "Come on. I'll buy ya a smoothie."

Pursing his lips, he rolled his eyes but followed, keeping his hand in hers.

They walked by the basketball courts where shouts and taunts came from a group of muscular and sweaty men.

Sheridan generally didn't pay attention to such things, but today she did a double take. "Elston, do you know anything about that guy?" Fiddling with her ponytail, she nodded toward the gym. "The one wearing the green shorts with the white stripe." *The one glistening with sweat and looking absolutely amazing while doing so.* Words she would not repeat aloud. Ever. To anyone.

"Why?" Elston raised a blond brow. "Are you interested?"

"What?" She sniffed then wiped her face with the now-damp towel. "You know I don't date. I've just seen him around." She cleared her throat. "And I saw him at the fundraiser this weekend, that's all."

Elston released her hand and leaned against the open door. "He's prime, isn't he?" He fluttered a hand back and forth in front of his face. "That my dear is Clayton Kincaid. And even though you say you're not interested, I'll tell you about him anyway. Like a brave and good little boy, Clayton went off to the military, where I believe he became a Ranger. Then he was a Manchester cop. Now he's an investigator." Her overly-excitable trainer nudged her shoulder. "Are you looking for a bodyguard? Cause, I'd certainly let him guard mine."

"Really, Elston." Sheridan gasped. "What would Rick think of your perusal of other men?"

"I can look, you know. No use pretending these gorgeous green eyes can't see." He struck a pose, holding a hand against his cheek.

"You're such a goof." Sheridan scanned the assembled players, but her gaze kept tracking back to one nicely toned, dark-haired figure.

Elston rubbed a finger under her bottom lip. "You've got a bit of drool."

Sheridan slapped away his hand and laughed.

Clayton's torso *was* drool-worthy. So very defined likely due to the swimming and all his other…exertions. He played hard, yelling at his teammates as he dashed up and down the court.

"Kincaid's a good sort. Was always kind to me in high school, and I crushed a little. Hot jock with all the best of everything—nice clothes, nice face, nice family. I think he lost his younger brother recently though. Bit of a scandal."

"I didn't realize he attended your alma mater." Sheridan pulled her gaze from the lively game.

"Yes, my young one, he was a year ahead of me."

"So, he's probably what then, twenty-nine or thirty?"

"I imagine."

"So, what happened with his brother?"

"Well, love, his brother played for my team and some rowdies at a bar didn't take too kindly to him visiting the same establishment with his boyfriend. So, they took the fight outside and he died."

"That's insane." Sheridan whipped around and stared at Elston then glanced at Clayton again, who now stood on the line preparing to shoot a free throw. "Were they close?"

"Very."

A wave of dizziness struck again and she swallowed down a very real fear that she could suffer the same fate. Losing Jenny. Losing Laney. Danger was too close, and she had no idea when her father would emerge again. As a child, she'd almost lost Jenny. But instead, she'd lost a piece of herself. A piece so damaged nothing could ever repair it.

"Come on." Sheridan bumped Elston with her shoulder. "We've gawked enough for one day." Turning to leave, Sheridan couldn't help but sneak one last peek at Clayton. He ran backwards down the court and when he caught her eye, he winked.

She smiled in return, sure her cheeks were bright pink after being caught ogling the man.

"Oh, yeah." Elston smirked. "You're not interested *at all.*"

# # #

"Next time we play, we'll spot you twenty." Pearson jeered from the bench. "You guys suck."

After the game, Clayton remained only half alert as insults were hurled back and forth. Unsure how he'd managed to play when his concentration had been hindered by Sheridan Bennett hovering in the doorway beside Elston Charter. Since the police fundraiser, he'd thought about her a lot and dreamed about her more. Not that those dreams would ever come to fruition. Heaving a sigh, Clayton packed his gym bag and headed toward the exit.

His thoughts were jarred back to reality when Scott Pearson, his red-headed fellow ex-Ranger and now Harris Investigations employee, elbowed him in the ribs.

"What's eating you man? You were awfully rough out there today." Scotty bounced the basketball as they walked out the open doors toward the locker rooms.

Clayton was saved from responding when he heard raised voices coming from the free weights area.

"What the hell's going on over there?" Scotty changed direction and started toward the commotion.

Upon hearing someone shout, 'faggot', Clayton hustled to catch up with his friend. Rounding the corner, he saw a tall blonde braced between two very angry men. Clayton stopped beside Scotty and assessed the scene.

"Harper." Elston jabbed the man's chest with his index finger. "Sheridan has told you and told you. She's not interested. Back off!"

"Oh? What? Is she interested in you then? You realize"— Harper turned to Sheridan—"he only likes cock."

"Okay, that's it." Sheridan shot her fist straight toward

Harper's chin.

Elston lunged. His forward motion knocked Sheridan off course, and she tumbled backwards against a weight bench.

A loud hollow thunk sounded as her head bounced against a twenty-five pound weight set on the bar.

"Sheridan!" Clayton raced forward, helpless to save her from what he feared was a life-ending injury. "Someone call an ambulance!" Luckily his focus was on her alone or he'd rip Harper to pieces for his words against Elston. Harper knew better than to talk that kind of trash, but apparently the man needed a reminder. One he'd be all too happy to deliver.

"Look what you've done." Elston yelled at Harper, shoving against the man's chest. "I'll kill you."

"Scotty, get Elston away from Harper now!" Clayton knelt beside Sheridan, lifted her into his arms, and then gently ran a hand along the back of her head.

She moaned when he touched an area above her left ear.

"Oh, thank God." He settled against the weight bench, supporting her head in the crook of his elbow.

"Conway." Clayton called to the gym's owner, who had arrived during the melee. "Call an ambulance. I think she may have a concussion."

Her headband had fallen over her eyes. Clayton brushed it back, taking a moment to run his fingers through those thick blonde strands. Rachel would laugh her ass off if she saw him now. Her petite self, jumping up and down, shouting, "I knew you were hooked."

With a wince, Sheridan lifted her lids. Pain and confusion evident as she squinted her sky blue eyes. Eyes that suddenly widened, and then she sat up.

"Wh-what are you doing?" Touching the side of her head, she gasped.

"Stop." He pulled her close against his chest then answered in a low, even tone. "You've hit your head. Lay back."

"Elston got in my way." She grumbled before closing her eyes.

Clayton ran a hand up and down her arm. He rested his chin on her head, savoring the moment, as it may never come again. Sweat and the scent of roses filtered through his nose, an enticing combination. "You likely have a concussion. You went down pretty hard." He clenched his jaw, wishing he hadn't seen her fall. His heart still hadn't started beating correctly.

"I doubt that, likely just a big bump." She reached up and ran a finger along his neck. "You're all sweaty."

"Yes, that tends to happen when you run up and down a basketball court numerous times, Slim." Her single finger had him thinking of other activities that could get him sweaty—with her. "I had Conway call for an ambulance."

"What?" She twisted and met his gaze. "I don't need an ambulance. I'm fine." Huffing out a breath, she slumped in his arms. "Plus, I don't need the 'paps' twisting and turning the story until it doesn't even begin to describe what really happened."

"Paps?"

"The paps-smear-azzi." She enunciated each portion of the word then frowned and touched her left temple. "They could write novels with the fiction they create."

"Paps, or whatever you said, creates an unpleasant visual." Though Clayton *had* wondered how many stories about her were true, as he'd stood in line at the grocery store staring at her face on magazine covers. Not to mention all the research he'd done over the weekend. "You *are* going to the hospital."

She closed her eyes. "I've been through worse. Believe me, this is nothing. I'll go home, take some aspirin, and be good."

"Quit being so stubborn." Elston plunked down at Sheridan's side. "Clayton's right. So, no arguments."

"Are you all right? Did he hit you?" Sheridan braced a hand against Clayton's shoulder and tried to sit up.

"I'm fine, love." Shaking his head, Elston lightly pressed her back down. "What were you thinking going after him like that?"

"I'm not going to stand there and let him talk that way just because he's pissed I won't go out with him." She fisted Clayton's shirt in her hand. "I'm going to bust his jaw so he can't run his mouth anymore."

"Sheridan, leave it alone." Elston leaned over and patted her cheek. "I've had worse said about my sexuality."

"Not while I'm around."

Clayton tipped her chin, catching her gaze. "Leave Harper alone." He brushed a thumb against that full bottom lip. "If he bothers you again, tell me and I'll handle it."

"Leave Harper to you?" Sheridan scoffed, and then poked a finger against his chest. "Who the hell do you think you are? This is *my* fight, and I'll solve it *my* way. I'm sick to death of men like Harper who think just because I've played certain movie roles that I'm promiscuous in real life. Ever heard of a body double? Not only that, I'm playing a character. I do not get paid for sex." Her voice rose and each word was punctuated with a sharp jab against his chest by her manicured fingernail. "I don't even have sex, and if I did, I'm certainly not having sex with a disgusting jerk like him. And one other thing..." She whipped toward Elston, hair flying into Clayton's face. "Ow, ow, ow not good to rant with a head injury."

"No, it's not." Clayton brushed her hair over her ear. "Now that we're all clear on your sex life, we're going to get your head checked out."

"Listen to me, Kincaid...."

"And here's the EMT's now."

CHAPTER 5

Metal links clinked together along the top of the emergency room curtain. Temples pounding, Sheridan opened her eyes and frowned at the man shoving himself into her space—literally and figuratively. "I appreciate you sticking around, Clayton, but you can go now."

Smiling, he approached the bedside. "First off, I've been working with security on how we can get you out of here since two media vans are already out front. And secondly, it's better for Harper if I'm stuck here at the hospital. I need to cool down a bit." After raking his fingers through his hair, he sighed and gripped the side railing. "I have…issues with intolerant people. He'll never speak to Elston like that again, and I guarantee he won't be bothering you anymore."

"Ooo Aquaman's come out to play, has he?" She raised a brow, which shot a shard of pain through her aching skull. Biting back a wince, she met Clayton's gaze. "I can handle myself. I am not some weak fish who needs a trident-carrying superhero to protect her. And I didn't need to come to the hospital because now this story will be blown out of proportion in the media. The last thing I need right now is paps following me around." She pinched the bridge of her nose. "People rarely bothered me at Excel gym and now they might join just to see me. I don't know why I leave the house sometimes."

"Must be tough living under that kind of scrutiny." Clayton bit his bottom lip, likely fighting back a smirk. "And Aquaman? What's that about?"

Ignoring the shot of whatever pulsed through her body at the sight of him gnawing on that full lip, she straightened against the unyielding hospital pillow. "Aquaman because you swim all the time. And living under the public eye is troublesome, at times, yes." She narrowed her eyes. "Don't you dare say 'oh you're famous that's what you get' because I'll chuck this pillow at your head."

"I had no intention of saying that." He grinned. "Even though it's true."

"Harper's jaw isn't the only one I can break, you know?"

"Slim, I'll let you plant a facer on me anytime."

"A facer, really?" If he kept smiling, he'd get a facer all right. Who did he think he was, some 1920's private eye? Next thing she knew he'd be calling her doll face, or doing something equally ridiculous like covering up his very fine form with a trench coat. "I'm dying over here." Sheridan rested her forearm over her eyes and sighed heavily.

"No cameras in here, Slim." Clayton chuckled as he squeezed her knee. "Don't need to act out your death scene."

Frowning, she opened one eye. "Listen, it isn't okay to get all up in my personal space. Hands off."

"I'll stop by your place tomorrow and check on you." He kept his hand on her knee and brushed his thumb back and forth.

"That's not necessary. I'll be fine." Sheridan shifted her knee out from under his hand. Casual touching had never been her thing. Her sister, Jenny was the one who went around hugging everyone, but then again her life had been sheltered from the evils of this world.

"I've got time around noon." Clayton stroked his chin with his forefinger and thumb. "Do you like Chinese?"

"I believe I said it's not necessary." She sniffed then drummed her fingers on the bed covers.

"Noon it is." He nodded before leaning down and kissing her cheek. Then the man patted her head as if she were an injured puppy, turned on his heel, and walked out the door.

What the hell?

Aquaman needed to take a few steps back and check himself. True, he had helped today, but she didn't need him kissing her or patting her damn head.

With all she'd endured during her childhood and after fighting for each acting part, she'd developed thick skin and a thick skull. Four painkillers would alleviate any of today's lingering discomfort, not dark-haired investigators with caring eyes who stood tall against homophobic jerks.

"What am I supposed to do about you Clayton Kincaid?" Shaking her head, she stared at the ceiling's square tiles, trying not to linger over the soft press of Clayton's lips. The big screen's hottest actors had kissed her—deeply and madly during very intense sex scenes, but none had caused a riot of feelings like Clayton's little peck.

She did not want to feel things. The love scenes in her films were mechanical, all laid out move by move. Relationships with men came with certain expectations and Sheridan would never, could never, physically meet a man's most primitive needs.

But today a tiny yearning broke past her battle-scarred heart. For one moment, she'd allow herself a smidgeon of curiosity, using her head injury as an excuse to dream a little.

How would his strong arms feel wrapped around her body? What would've happened if his lips had strayed from her cheek to her lips? If he'd taken her face in his hands and deepened the plunge? Would her heart beat? Would birds sing? Hell no! Aquaman couldn't erase all the damage done by the two people who were supposed to love her the most. Two people who had taught her to distrust everyone and everything.

Experiencing an intimate moment with Clayton would never happen and surprisingly, that hurt more than a little. Closing her eyes, she breathed deeply and exhaled slowly. She knew better than to wish for more. So Clayton "the Aquaman" Kincaid would be forgotten.

A tear slipped down her cheek. With a flick of her hand, she wiped it away, removing proof of softer emotions. Tears were for the weak, something she'd never been allowed to be. Her father had seen to that...as had her mother.

Though she lived her life in the spotlight, no one would ever see the broken woman beneath the façade.

No one.

CHAPTER 6

Clayton studied the light brown brick monstrosity before him. Sheridan's home had to be at least 6,000 square feet. The attached three-car garage had dark brown doors that matched the shutters. Mature trees surrounded her entire estate, however the road leading to her house had cornfields on both sides. An old farmhouse had been here before she'd mowed it down, which in some way explained all the trees, but she'd likely hired landscapers to plant the fully grown evergreens along the drive.

Though he'd grown up in a home similar to this, he still felt out of place. He'd made it this far, but he wasn't sure how much farther he wanted to go—for this case or for Sheridan. Not that she'd ever be interested in a regular guy like him. Plus she lived in the spotlight, and he was an investigator. Private investigator. Emphasis on the private, but something kept him moving forward. Probably his dick. *Stupid.* Rachel needed to send him on an assignment in a different country. Not that he'd go.

Before he'd pulled into Sheridan's drive, he'd passed through a code-secured gate. Jenny had buzzed him through. While driving up the lane, which was approximately sixty yards or half a football field long, he'd noted a couple cameras mounted in the trees. A metal spiked fence encompassed the property, as well. Her home seemed well fortified, but he'd review her security system soon.

Having stalled long enough, he hopped out of his SUV and proceeded to the front door. A fragrant mix of ginger, garlic, and sesame oil wafted up from the bag crooked in his elbow. He lifted his fist to knock but a pretty petite redhead opened the door.

"Hi. I'm Clayton Kincaid." He smiled at the young teen standing in the doorway. "I brought Chinese food for the head case...I mean patient." Laughing, he waved the bag in front of the girl's nose.

"Food pays the toll." She shifted to the side. "Come on in."

"You must be Jenny." Clayton stopped in the entryway and glanced around the open expanse. Stairs rose to the second level on the left, and a sitting room on the right was decorated in deep fall colors—dark greens, burnt golds, and deep maroons, highlighted by cabin-like wood framing on the walls and ceiling.

"I *am*, Jenny. Nice to meet you." She nodded and shook his hand. "Let's get you to the kitchen."

The cheerful girl's eyes were a familiar shade of blue. She stood perhaps three inches shorter than Sheridan, but her height fit her small frame.

"So, how's the patient doing today?" Clayton set his brown paper bag on the cream-colored marble countertop.

"She needs tea." Jenny waved a tea bag before his eyes. "She hasn't been out of bed yet, but resting is probably a good thing."

A timer of some sort beeped.

Jenny turned and poured water into a coffee cup from a high-tech silver kitchen appliance. "If it takes a hit to the head to get Sheridan to rest, then maybe I'll knock her out once a week."

Clayton huffed out a laugh. "I imagine she does have a pretty full schedule."

She dunked a tea bag up and down in the cup.

"Tell me about you? What grade are you in?"

Jenny leaned against the counter, still bobbing that tea bag up and down. With a tilt to her head, she said, "Is this where you try to be my buddy? Feign interest in my life to get to Sheridan? You know my sister doesn't date, right?"

Little sister was just as protective. *Interesting.* "Yet. Your sister doesn't date *yet*. Might as well be clear from the beginning." A sure grin spread across his face and he winked. Point made, he removed the containers from the bag.

"I see. So you're going to be *the one*." Jenny bent two fingers in the air, simulating quotation marks. "What makes you so sure?"

"You want the run down?"

"I'm listening."

"Tell you what, I'll give you my qualifications if you'll get out forks and plates."

"Yeah...I mean, you can go ahead and say what you want, but Sheridan won't date you."

In answer, he merely raised a brow, and then pointedly glanced at the cabinets.

After rolling her eyes, she threw up her hands and mumbled what sounded like, "Whatever."

"Where should I start?" Clayton munched on an eggroll then wiped his mouth with a napkin. "How about...I'm twenty-nine years old. I'm not in a serious relationship although I've weathered a few." He studied the thinly sliced vegetables in the eggroll as he considered what else to add. "After graduating high school, I went into the military and became an Army Ranger. When I finished my service, I did the college thing for a few years before the Manchester PD hired me. My family is great, although I lost my brother not too long ago. Don't want to talk about it. So, please don't ask. I'm working for Harris Investigations now. Great job. Great boss." He opened a packet of duck sauce and drizzled it on his eggroll before tipping it in her direction. "Want one?"

"In a minute." Jenny dropped three plates on the counter. "That's it? Because nothing you've said has convinced me you're good enough for my sister."

"Serving this country and being a cop didn't earn me any points?"

"Okay, maybe two."

"Tough crowd." Clayton licked sauce off his finger. "I'll shoot straight with you, kid. I find your sister very beautiful. She escaped a troubled past and built this life." He waved his eggroll around the kitchen. "I admire that. And I'm very curious how she managed it all on her own. I'd like to know the woman behind the big screen." With a shrug, he took another bite, studying the girl before him. "I understand why you're so protective. You've only had each other for a long time. I hope to change that."

Jenny pursed her lips as she opened each white container. She popped a piece of broccoli in her mouth before meeting his gaze. "Quite a notch on your bedpost if you bedded Sheridan Bennett."

"Little girl, the notches on my bedpost are none of your concern." He wagged a finger, trying to lessen the steel in his tone.

Jenny opened her mouth to say something, closed it, and then opened it again.

Clayton raised a brow. "Go ahead and say what you're thinking."

"I love my sister." She shifted a carton back and forth on the counter. "She is my world, so know this"—she jabbed a fork into the lo mein—"I may be a 'little girl,' but I will kick your butt if you hurt her. She's been through enough, and while I know she says she doesn't want or need a man in her life, I disagree. If you think you're the man for the job, well then, I wish you luck, but understand this, Aquaman, I'll be watching you." She arrowed her fingers up to her eyes, and then pointed them at him. "Her tea is ready. Come on, we'll take it up to her grouchy self." After jerking her thumb toward the stairs, she grabbed the tea and headed up.

"So you're using the Aquaman name too? Must mean she talks about me since you know who I am."

Jenny glanced over her shoulder. "She wouldn't want me telling you this, but she may have mentioned you a few times. Says you look real nice in your trunks."

"Is that so?"

"Didn't hear it from me."

Wasn't that interesting. Sheridan Bennett had checked him out. He didn't dare think of how she looked in her swimsuit or more than his ego would inflate. Though, he'd always wondered why she wore shorts with her suit. Maybe she had some sort of insecurity. Odd because she had no problem showing her body in movies, but...hadn't she said something at the gym about a body double? Why would she need a body double? And why was he thinking about this now?

Shaking his head, he followed Jenny up the stairs. The cream colored carpets were plush under his feet. He memorized the second floor's layout. Four bedrooms, a closet, and likely a spare bathroom. Unfortunately, he hadn't had a chance to scope out much of the lower level.

Her home had been professionally decorated, yet at the same time the vibe reminded him of a cabin locked deep in the woods. Why was Hollywood's biggest bombshell living in Northern Ohio? Just one more piece of a very complicated puzzle he meant to complete.

# # #

A flowery scent drifted from the mug Jenny had handed over after making him promise to be good and leaving him outside Sheridan's door. With his free hand, Clayton knocked, but in order to make clear he wouldn't be dismissed, he walked in without waiting for her response. "Hey, Slim. How are you feeling today?"

Gasping, Sheridan gathered her sheets together by her chest. "Did my sister let you up here?"

"Yep."

"I could have been naked, and you just barged in here like you own the place."

"Yeah, I did." He shrugged. "You knew I was here. This place has cameras everywhere which I'm sure are linked to an app on your phone, so don't act all scandalized."

While naked would have been nice, her mussed hair and a sleepy-eyed gaze were sexy as hell. Damn if he didn't want to rip off the sheets and join her, but he settled for sitting on the bed's edge.

Her room's decor was a lot more…flowery than he expected. Roses covered her bedspread, decorative pink and lace pillows surrounded her make-up free face. No clothes or shoes littered the floor. Green candles sat atop a huge dresser beside bottles filled with whatever secret potions women used. Apparently, Ms. Bennett had a softer, maybe even romantic side. "Where would you like this very hot tea?"

"I'll take it." She reached for the cup, took a sip, and then set the steaming brew between her legs, resting it precariously on top of the comforter.

"Is your head better today?" He wanted to touch her, so he did by placing a hand on her knee.

"Yes, I've only got a slight ache today. You didn't need to trouble yourself." She moved her knee from under his hand, causing her tea to slosh over the rim.

"I don't mind troubling myself. I brought lunch, and I'll bring you a plate." He jerked his thumb toward the door. "Is there anything you don't like? I got a bit of everything at this Chinese place by my duplex."

"No. I'm fine. I'll just drink my tea." She pushed her blonde waves away from her face and sipped. "Thanks for stopping by."

Her blatant brush off wouldn't work. "Have you eaten today?" Biting back a grin, he raised a brow while waiting for her answer. "Sheridan?"

"I'm not hungry." She sniffed.

"Have you taken your pain meds?"

"I took them last night."

"It's good I'm here to fetch you some food before you take some more then."

"Oh yes, rescued by Aquaman." She laid a hand upon her chest. "All my fairytale fantasies have come true."

"Not *all*." Grinning, he made a blatant perusal of her body.

Her jaw dropped. Then she squirmed a little. "Jenny is taking care of me. I don't need you or your wandering eyes." She flicked the fingers of one hand in his direction. "Go, please."

"I'm hungry and you need to eat, so let's start with you telling me where you keep your pain meds? Then I'll bring you up a plate with a dab of everything."

"In case you hadn't noticed, this is a bedroom, not a dining room."

"I'm very aware of the bed in the room, Slim." Clayton waggled his brows.

"Oh, I'm sure you're familiar with all sorts of bedrooms, hotel rooms, back alleys."

Clayton lightly took her hand in his. "Your pain meds. Where are they?"

"Ahh..." Sheridan screeched. "There's no getting rid of you, is there?"

"Nope."

"Fine." She gestured toward a room off to her right. "They're on my bathroom counter."

When he released her hand and stood to retrieve her meds, he heard her quietly mumble, "I don't like pea pods."

Clayton shot a glance over his shoulder and laughed. Though not really sure why he was so amused, only that her entire dismissive attitude followed by her little pea-pod-pout struck him as funny—and adorable.

"Right." Chuckling, he headed for the bathroom. "No pea pods. Got it."

"I fail to see why my not liking pea pods is so hilarious."

"I am at a loss as well, Ms. Bennett."

After grabbing her medicine, he shot her a wink before leaving the room.

Smiling over her blue-eyed glare, he tromped down the stairs and wondered again how far he could realistically take this relationship. Wondered how long their little chats would stay amusing? And thought about how warm she would be beneath those rose-covered sheets. Her skin had a creamy hue but what about other parts of her body? Hidden parts. Would they be rosy and pink? Would they rise to his touch and beg for more? "Get your head out of your ass, Kincaid," he grumbled. "You've lost your mind."

On his way down the hall, he stopped when his phone buzzed in his pocket. Pulling the cell free, he leaned against a side table topped with a moose statue

The notification was from Constance, asking if he'd come by later because her car was making a funny noise. He'd go, but later. In the end, a woman like Constance was probably the better choice—the quiet, out-of-the-spotlight choice—but she didn't create the same heady rush he felt around Sheridan.

And yet, had he truly decided to pursue the blonde movie queen? Did he even have a choice at this point? Hadn't O'Malley just today asked him to stay diligent? She needed someone to care for her, watch over her, and protect her from threats like her criminal father and Russian gangsters.

She challenged him in ways he'd never felt before. And for the first time since he'd lost his best friend and brother, Michael, he experienced a modicum of hope. The woman had him down here picking pea pods out of veggie chicken for fuck's sake. He wouldn't do that for any other woman. He wanted this, wanted her. Game on.

CHAPTER 7

Two days later, Sheridan flipped through her phone messages and checked the time. Exactly five fifty-five. Clayton always arrived at six a.m. And, of course he would be on time. One more thing to add to his annoying list of attributes, which included a killer body, cocky smile, and one thing she'd do well not to forget—clear blue eyes that saw too far beneath the surface.

She was no water girl waiting for a hero. Hadn't she drowned many years ago? "So then why are you doing this?" She rubbed her temples.

Poolside at the Excel gym, she swirled her protein powder in her mug of warm water. After taking time to recuperate from her injury, she'd resigned herself to eating small meals and drinking lots of water. Though, due to her genes, she'd never had trouble staying thin. One of the few welcome attributes passed down from her parents.

Listening to a message from her agent pitching another romantic comedy had her considering spending some time hitting the punching bag later today. Last night, she'd tossed script after script onto an overflowing no-go pile. Hadn't she already proven she could act in meatier roles by winning the Academy Award two years ago? Why send her fluff? She'd sacrifice making money on mediocre films for a quality script any day. She didn't need excessive amounts of money. Not now. Although, knowing what life was like without a dime to spare was not a memory she'd ever forget.

She smiled as Clayton pushed open the men's locker room door that led into the pool area. Afraid of being caught staring, she pretended to study her phone, while checking him out from beneath her lashes. A white towel rested across his tanned broad shoulders and he held a green gym bag in his hand. He had two or three different pairs of flip-flops he shuffled between. None were locker-room gross, either. And his body…

Shew, girl, don't even look. Just friends. Nothing more. A mantra she'd do well to remember. Relationships were difficult enough to develop due to her high-profile job and her background.

During his lunch visit, he'd only stayed to eat then left her to rest. He'd been honest in his intentions, too—and that mattered a lot. Plus, she sort of liked him, which was completely asinine. But why not pretend they could be friends if only for a little while? Though with her father lurking, Clayton's safety was a serious consideration. She'd be better off never speaking to him again, yet for some reason that just seemed kind of rude…and maybe she would miss him a little. So insane. She'd finally boarded the crazy-train. Too bad there was no ticket off, because she knew it'd crash in a fiery heap someday. Friends only. She'd staple that post-it note to her heart.

Uncharacteristically nervous, she grabbed her bag, hopped off the bench, and perused her phone. On her way to the women's locker room, she "accidentally" bumped into his arm. "Oh, hey." She tossed her phone in her bag then cleared her throat. "Sorry, I was distracted there."

"S'okay. How are you?" He stretched, highlighting that long lean body. "How's the head?"

"Good. Yeah, all good. So…um…thanks again for…uh…the Chinese food the other day." She lightly punched his arm. Geez, did she need a script for real life conversations now, too? "Anyway, I'd like to return the favor. So, I thought…You see, on Sunday nights Jenny's friends gather at our house, and I feed them. Do you want to come?" She paused, and then grimaced when she noted she was ringing her hands together. *Damn it!* "Are you musical at all? There tends to be a lot of dancing and singing and general craziness." She laughed, which came out more like a giggle. Next time, she'd dig up an article on how to ask a friend to dinner without sounding like a bleating goat.

"No, I'm not musical." He grinned, and then tossed his bag over by the bench. "So, you're going to cook?"

"Yes, I am a fantastic cook."

Clayton tipped her chin with his finger. "You're tough, talented, and you can cook? Will you marry me?"

Jolted by his words, she blinked. The finger beneath her chin ensured she couldn't look away. "If that's your attempt at a marriage proposal, it's pretty pitiful. I want the whole down on one knee with a romantic poem written from the depths of your heart. And a mongo diamond." She huffed out a laugh, because that would *never* happen. Total pipe dream.

"You want me down on my knees?"

His voice deepened and tingled along her skin. Then the flirt trailed his finger across her lips.

This conversation had gone from cool innocence to blazing fire in seconds. Not good. Time to turn the tide. She stepped back from his touch, her feelings, and the general sex vibe suddenly surrounding them by going into her avoidance-by-turning-everything-into-a-joke mode. "Tell you what. Come by tomorrow and if there's a preacher present then the answer to your weak proposal is yes. If not, then sorry…answer's no. Anyway,"— she shook her head—"I'll give you my personal number, but first you have to take a solemn oath, ready?"

"Wedding vows and solemn oaths. I'm liking the direction of

this conversation." Smiling, he tugged the towel from around his neck and threw it on top of his bag.

"Let's move on." Sheridan rolled her eyes. "You want my number you say the oath, I, Clayton Kincaid do solemnly swear that I will never give Sheridan Bennett's very private number to anyone else, nor will I tell anyone I have it."

"I give you my word." He braced both hands on his hips. "I'm not repeating your oath."

"This is my private number for family only." She lifted his hand and placed it against his heart, ignoring the smooth warmth of his skin as her fingers brushed against his chest. "Oath taking is required."

"Sheridan." He trapped her hand under his. "You'll just have to trust me."

She nodded. The heat and essence of him was thumping to life all sorts of crazy thoughts and heated dreams. Why the hell was she flirting with this man, let alone inviting him to dinner? "Listen, I don't trust anyone. If we're going to be friends, I need you to take my privacy very seriously."

"Okay, okay. If speaking your oath will ease your mind, I'll say it. I, Clayton Kincaid, being of sound mind and body..." He waggled his brows.

"Oh, please. I just threw up a little in my mouth."

He laughed. "I swear I will not share Sheridan Bennett's number with anyone. How was that?"

"It'll do." She jerked her hand out from under his then flicked her fingers at his bag. "Get out your phone, please." She watched the play of muscles across his back as he dug through his bag. At this rate, she'd need another dip in the pool.

He turned and handed over his cell, but at the last second pulled back his hand. "What kind of oaths do I get?"

"You're an outrageous flirt. Sell your situation"—she flicked a hand at his crotch—"to someone else. I'm not buying." Sheridan grabbed the phone out of his hand and programmed her number into his contacts. "Come to the house around six." On her way to the women's locker rooms, she turned around and walked backwards. "I *should* get a minister just to see if you'd really marry me."

"Well, that'd be one hell of a *situation*, Slim." He smiled—a cheeky, cocky grin. "Go ahead and try it."

"Maybe I will." She stuck out her tongue.

"I could do a lot with that tongue and my…situation."

She halted at the corner of the entrance. "Stop saying situation." She glanced around even though no one else was at the pool so early.

"You really gonna cook?"

"Yes." She scoffed. "Why?"

"Well that just puts me in a deeper…situation."

"Oh, sweet baby geez." Refusing to continue, she flounced off, leaving him and his ridiculous situation behind.

When had she ever enjoyed this sort of banter with another person? Never. Ding, ding, ding, that was the correct answer.

"What are you thinking, Bennett?" Eyes closed, she leaned her forehead against the cool metal locker. Her clearly smitten heart was thoroughly betraying her no-can-do body. "Don't do this to yourself or him." She huffed out a laugh. "And now you're talking to yourself in the ladies' locker room. But you know…damn it, you know that train's just going to wreck. It always does. No matter how much you wish otherwise."

Her father was still in town, which meant the only 'situation' she could concern herself with was her sisters' safety and her own.

CHAPTER 8

Keys gripped firmly in hand, Sheridan shifted her gym bag on her shoulder and studied the parking lot. Her father hadn't made another appearance, but she always remained situationally aware. Dear Lord, that word again. Still, who knew when someone would pop up? Either an over-eager fan, a photographer, or much more headache-inducing—the FBI. Some days she really did rethink her stance on having personal security, but someone that involved in her business wasn't ideal. Not with her secrets.

Speaking of people in her business, FBI Agent Daniel Denver was leaning against a dark sedan parked next to her baby—a Mustang Shelby GT350. She parked away from lesser vehicles when she drove her mean girl, but Denver was apparently oblivious to the necessity of treating her car with the appropriate awe.

Denver was propped beside her car because of her father. Yet every time she saw the agent, she clamped down the real fear he would arrest her. That he knew the truth of what she'd done so many years ago, but that was impossible because the only other witness was dead.

Sporting a poker face, she ambled over. "Agent Denver." Sheridan nodded. "I see you're out enjoying this lovely early-summer weather." Politeness rolled off her tongue when she'd prefer to rant and rave, because rather than a real concern for her safety, he'd come for information on her father. If the Feds kept that tight of reins on the man's location, why wasn't he already in their custody? She didn't understand how they worked sometimes.

Agent Denver had a serious hard-on for her father. Around five years ago, her dear old-dad had manipulated and stolen everything from Denver's wealthy aunt. Since then, the agent would pop into her life, drag her somewhere for questions, and then annoy her with his subtle jabs and insinuations that she would end up just like her father. Hell, she couldn't blame him as those thoughts crept within her own mind at times. Still, she'd hired lawyers to stop his impromptu visits, so now he would "run into her" in public places.

"Ms. Bennett." He nodded then eyed her quickly. "You're looking well."

He looked the same—black suit, red tie, buzz cut, dark hair, brown eyes, and a sturdy frame that was likely all of five-seven.

"In answer to your as yet unasked question, yes, I have seen Jack Bennett. He wants money. I don't intend to give him any."

Lifting his lenses onto the top of his head, Denver straightened. "We need to discuss what happened at the fundraiser."

Bullets, imminent death—the usual when her father was concerned. "If you know about that night then you know as much as I do." Trusting others with her life, her safety, and that of her sister's wasn't happening. Ever.

"Did you see the shooter?" Denver pulled a notepad and pen from his front jacket pocket.

"No."

"What about the getaway vehicle? Did you see the driver?"

"No."

"What were you doing outside?"

"Breathing."

"Not helping yourself here, Bennett."

"You're not supposed to question me in parking lots, Denver."

"We'd like to talk to you about some options."

"No."

"Why not? You haven't even heard them."

"Don't need to." Sheridan opened her car's trunk and tossed in her bag. "No way am I'm using my money in some fake scheme to draw my father out so you can swoop in and save the day." Sheridan met Denver's gaze. "He's eluded you this long, and I really don't want to be standing holding an empty bag while ya'll are trying to figure out how he outsmarted you."

"He's in deep with the wrong people." Denver tugged on his tie, squinting against the early-morning sun. "People that won't hesitate to come after you."

"People are *after* me every day." Sheridan shrugged. "Comes with the job."

"I'm in law enforcement and getting shot at comes with *my* job. *You* star in movies and get shot at by fake bullets. The ones in the hotel parking lot the other night were real .308 caliber bullets from a SV-98 bolt-action sniper rifle. Those don't just injure you, they end you."

Sheridan fought back a shiver at his raw words. Maybe she was in over her head. This power play with her father had begun in a grungy hotel eight years ago. That night had ended in tragedy, and she'd vowed he would never win again. Since he'd disappeared, she'd become smarter, stronger, and a lot deadlier. She'd readjust her strategy and research this new threat. Denver might be a pain in her ass, but she'd be insane not to heed his warning.

"Are we through here, Agent Denver? I have places to be." She raised a brow and jingled her keys.

"Do yourself a favor, hire a couple bodyguards." Denver handed her a business card. "Call these guys."

"I have a collection of these at home." After taking the

embossed black card, Sheridan tapped it against her palm. "If you know my father's here, why don't you arrest him?"

Denver dropped his sunglasses back over his eyes. "We hadn't received actual confirmation until just now."

"Glad I could be of service." Sheridan scoffed, shading her eyes with her hand. Her father was a side project for Denver. He was far from his Nevada base. He'd likely picked up on O'Malley's investigations into the shooter. The FBI agent kept an eagle eye on anything out of the ordinary happening in her world.

Denver crossed both arms over his chest. "We both know your father will reach out again."

"I'm anxiously awaiting his return. Believe me."

"We need your daily schedule." He studied the parking lot. "If we know where you are, we'll be able to get someone to you quicker when you call in his location."

"As if you don't already have access to all my information." She spun her key ring around her index finger. Plus, who was this we, he kept referring to? Did he have a new partner in his investigate-Sheridan-campaign? "Don't put people on me. You can keep an eye on my sisters, because that's where he'll strike." Exasperated and a tad bit frightened, she whipped open her car door, more than ready to leave.

"Sheridan." Denver had the audacity to touch her car door. "If you see him again, call immediately. You can't handle your father alone."

"Please remove your paws from my car. She doesn't like to be manhandled." Knowing she sounded like a diva and not caring, Sheridan rubbed her temples, wishing she'd worn her sunglasses before coming outside. "I am aware of the dangers my father presents, Agent Denver." With a glare that could cut steel, she met his gaze. "I understand more than anyone."

Hadn't she lived the first fourteen years of her life in complete hell? Hadn't she survived on her own? Running a shaky hand through her hair, Sheridan leaned against her open car door.

"Understand this, everything Jack Bennett does—every action he takes—*is* a game, and he plays two steps ahead. But I'm already there. Waiting." Tilting her head, she flashed a fake smile. "You and your little team of agents aren't the only ones with eyes on the streets." That said, she settled into her car and tugged on the door. "You want to talk again. Call my lawyer."

Denver took two steps back. "I'll be in touch."

Sheridan slammed shut the door and started the car. As the hard beat of Rob Zombie's "Living Dead Girl" filled the cab, she sang along with the words. Music soothed the soul, and hers raged with every dark emotion—fear, anger, doubt, and a whole load of resentment.

Whatever came next, whatever her father planned, was no game. When Jack set the board, he made sure the bout became a twisted death match.

She needed information. Fast. And an edge. An ace.

Why did her father need money? Who did he owe?

All these thoughts spinning through her mind added up to one fact—these people hunting her father knew who she was and likely already had people watching her, which also meant they were watching her sisters.

She refused to be that scared fourteen-year-old girl again, standing before her father and facing a decision that had too high a cost no matter which option she chose.

This time she had to win. But the only way out would add another dark mark to her soul or end in her death.

CHAPTER 9

When Sheridan's front door opened Sunday night, Clayton took a step back. The woman standing at the threshold had gold hoops in her nose, a tattoo on her neck, and what the hell was all over her face? Beside her was a short, dark-haired woman wearing a T-shirt from one of Sheridan's movies and navy blue capris, holding greenery of some sort.

"Hey, Clayton." The black lips spoke.

Odd combination—goth makeup and piercings contrasted with blonde hair and fair skin. Plus, she wore soft pink sweatpants and a T-shirt with Disney dogs on the front.

"I'm glad you could make it." Sheridan smiled, revealing a row of perfect white teeth. "Come on in." She raised a brow then laughed and waved a hand by her face. "I'm sorry. It's the makeup, right?" She shook her head. "I had to run to the store, because I forgot a couple things. This"—she cupped her chin—"is Scary Sherry. I'll wash off this makeup in a minute. Anyway, this is Laney, my older sister."

"Hello, Laney." Clayton shifted his wine bottle to his left hand and stretched out his right. "Nice to meet you."

"Hello." She held out the greenery and a fake flower fell to the floor. "Can you help me with my wreath?"

"Sure, what's wrong with it?"

Laney glanced at Sheridan. "My sister put it on the front gate,

53

but then yesterday when she took me to work it was out in the street all smashed. And last night when I was sleeping the alarm went off."

"An alarm?" Clayton turned to Sheridan. "What is she talking about?"

"An outer perimeter alarm went off. Likely a deer out for an evening stroll." She met his gaze. "Laney needs her sleep so I told her not to worry."

Clayton nodded. "I see." Laney may not need to worry but he would. They'd be discussing her security systems and this new information later. For now, he faced Laney again. "Let's see what we can do about this wreath."

"All my stuff is on the kitchen table." She took his hand. "Follow me."

Sheridan simply smiled as they passed.

For someone so involved in the Hollywood scene, Sheridan didn't live or act like a diva. Once again, he wondered what he was doing standing in the spotlight surrounding a famous actress, because he had no control of the on/off switch. And that bright light was glaring ridiculous hopes and fantasies across his mind, featuring him and her in heated scenes, starting with him covering those painted-black lips with his own.

He needed to stow those thoughts for now, because her sister needed his help. Once in the kitchen, he settled at the table. "How can I help?"

"Wipe the dust off the leaves, please." Laney handed him a paper towel, and then showed him how to gently wipe off the ivy leaves. "Are you Sheridan's boyfriend?" She gathered two pink tulips in her hand and met his gaze. "She doesn't have a boyfriend, but I do."

"That right? What's his name?"

"Charlie."

"Oh yeah."

"Don't get her talking about Charlie." Sheridan entered the

kitchen, her face clean now, though her lips were a deep red, likely from all the scrubbing. "She'll wax on and on about how great he is."

While completing his duty, he watched Sheridan cut into an avocado. Limes, freshly chopped tomatoes, and cilantro sat beside a big bowl. Bags of taco chips and an onion waited in the grocery bag. A huge crockpot on the counter was likely the source of the cumin filling the air.

"Dinner smells great." Clayton glanced at Laney. "Does your sister always cook like this?"

Laney pursed her lips. "We have to eat healthy because Sheridan is an actress."

"And do you like your sister's movies?"

"Yes. Do you want to watch one?"

"I've seen them, but thanks for asking."

"You're welcome. Here"—she handed him a purple tulip—"can you twist this onto the back of the wreath?"

"Sure."

He and Laney worked in harmony for a while, chatting together, with Sheridan occasionally adding in. She seemed more at ease today. In her element.

"Where's Jenny?" Clayton finished adding a red tulip.

"She's downstairs." Sheridan set a handful of napkins beside a stack of paper plates. "They'll start singing and playing soon."

"I like music. Do you like music, Clayton?" Laney started singing a country song he'd heard on the radio the other day, but he didn't know the title or artist. She had a lovely voice. Soft. Innocent. No wonder Sheridan fought so hard for her sister's. They were both as sweet as could be.

"How about this Laney?" Clayton held up the finished wreath. "I think we did an excellent job."

"Let me see." Sheridan rounded the kitchen island, wiping her hands on the towel she'd thrown over her shoulder. "It's beautiful. Great job." She leaned down and kissed her sister's cheek.

"Kiss him too, Sheridan. He helped."

Sheridan sniffed then actually did as her sister requested, her warm lips pressing against his cheek.

Then Laney kissed him, too. He laughed and wrapped an arm around her shoulder. "Thanks, sweetheart."

Music...actually what sounded more like live music sounded from beneath them.

"Sheridan, can I go down now?"

"Sure. Tell Jenny the food's ready."

"Okay. I'll take my wreath and show everyone."

"Good idea."

Laney exited the kitchen and opened a door in the hallway that obviously led to a basement.

"Is your basement fully furnished?" And when could he go down and investigate? He'd like to have a general idea of the house's layout.

"I'd say three quarters finished." Sheridan headed back behind the island and opened a bag of chips. "I have a storage area down there too."

"Laney's sweet."

"Yeah, she got out young."

"Out of where?"

"Oh, you know, the Bennett house of horrors." Sheridan picked up her wooden spoon and stirred whatever was in the crockpot.

"You're very good at evading questions about your past."

"Yes, I am." She grinned, tapping her spoon against the side of the pot. "Thank you for helping, Laney."

"No problem. Let's talk about this alarm that went off last night."

"I already explained it."

"I understand why you lied to your sister, but that won't work with me." He braced his elbows on the table and folded his hands together. "I've been investigating what happened at the police fundraiser."

"What?" Spinning to face him, she glared before leaning against the counter, arms folded across her chest.

"I know your father was there. I also know someone was shooting at either him or you. You're in a lot of danger." He sighed and leaned back in his chair. "Did you know your father is wanted in connection with the Korzakov crime family?"

Her gasp was answer enough.

"Not good, Slim. The Russian mafia doesn't let anything or anyone stand in their way." Clayton raked his fingers through his hair, considering how much more he should reveal. "I know you had a rough childhood."

She huffed out a laugh. "You have no clue about my childhood."

"I know you were in and out of foster homes starting at age fourteen." He grabbed a leftover tulip and tapped it against the table. "I know your mother was a drug addict, and your father is wanted by the FBI. I also know how hard you've worked to take care of yourself and your sisters."

"Well, listen to you. Isn't that a fascinating history on the life of Sheridan Bennett? Believe me, you left a lot out." She yanked open the fridge, grabbed a water bottle, twisted off the lid, and downed half. "You forgot the fact that I barely graduated high school, and I didn't go to some fancy college. You're right. My mother was a drug addict among a lot of other things. And a little edit to your story, the person responsible for the other half of my existence is not worth mentioning. Ever."

"All right. I'm only trying to help." He lifted a hand, palm up. "Quick question, did you get video footage of last night's intruder?"

She kept his gaze for a moment before turning away. "Food's getting cold."

"No, it isn't." He rose from his chair, stepped in front of her, and took both her hands in his. "Let me help you. Trust me."

"Ah, yes. Trust. It'd be nice if I could have that luxury." She pulled out of his grip. "You just listed my entire background and yet you still expect me to open up?" She shook her head. "I believe you said, 'rough childhood' that doesn't even begin to describe what I went through. I bet your mom and dad love you, right? I bet you had birthday presents, homemade cookies, and a clean bed every night. I didn't. So no, I don't want your help, and no I don't trust you." She dropped her gaze. "Even if I wanted to I wouldn't know how. I didn't get all those lovely life lessons. I got pain and misery. That's all I expect from anyone, and you won't be any different."

"Wow. Judge and jury."

"I don't like when people dig into my past. I'm barely refraining from kicking you out right now."

"You can kick me out if you'd like, but I'm not going to drop this case."

"Case? I haven't hired you to investigate anything. Not me. Not my father. Nothing."

"I will not stand by while you're in danger." With his index finger, he tipped up her chin. "I'm being straight with you, and I wasn't asking your permission."

Sheridan narrowed her eyes. "You want my permission to die, because that's what happens to people who go up against my father."

"Does O'Malley know about last night?"

"Yes. He knows, because I trust him."

"Good. See, you *can* trust someone, so we'll get there."

She huffed out a half-laugh and shook her head. "You're unbelievable."

"Thanks." He winked then stepped back, figuratively and literally. He'd pushed her enough. Time to lighten the mood. Tomorrow he'd call the Lieutenant to discover what the man knew about the alarm incident.

"I'm going down to get the crew." Sheridan flicked a hand toward the basement door.

"Good. I'm hungry."

She met his gaze. "Please stop digging into my life. The world needs Aquaman a hell of a lot more than it needs Sheridan Bennett."

"I disagree." Her comment said a lot about her feelings of self-worth. Not good—but a huge glimpse into the inner workings of her mind. He wanted nothing more than to wrap her in his arms and tell her she *was* needed, by him, by her sisters, by all the fans she entertained. But her whole body said back-off, so he kept his distance. "Go get your sisters, Slim."

She took two steps toward the door then turned and faced him. "The way you were with Laney...that matters to me. You were very kind. Sometimes people act odd or seem uncomfortable, but you were real, and that means a lot. I may not trust you, but I appreciate how you were with her. So, thank you."

He didn't respond. Couldn't. The fact she'd expected him to treat her sister with anything other than kindness baffled him. Yet, she had said she didn't expect much from people.

One minute she railed at him, the next she was thanking him with tears in those beautiful blue eyes. He'd survived another round and would keep fighting until the final buzzer sounded. At that point, he'd either have earned her trust or he'd walk away with a broken heart.

# # #

"This is the best guacamole I've ever eaten." Clayton scooped more dip onto his tortilla chip.

Dinner was over and the last of Jenny's friends had left minutes ago. Sheridan had asked Clayton to join her in the basement in order to discover more information on her father and the Russian Mafia.

The basement was fully furnished, with a small area toward the back sectioned off for storage and a hidden escape route should it prove necessary.

Clayton had settled in the corner of hunter green velour couch that faced a huge flat screen TV. A kitchen area was built in off to the side, with a full size fridge fully stocked with snacks and drinks for Jenny and her friends.

"You almost ate the entire bowl by yourself." Smiling over the fact he enjoyed her cooking, Sheridan silently patted herself on the back as she plopped onto the couch beside him. "I think everyone else was afraid to eat any, or you'd bite off their hand."

He shrugged and took a long swig from his beer bottle.

The fact he'd investigated her past still rankled, but she wasn't overly surprised. Kincaid was like a basset hound after a scent. Too bad his findings would lead to a field filled with land mines. Explosions. Death. The usual carnage when her father was involved. This she knew because, upon receiving the funds from her first film deal, she'd hired an investigator to look into her father. A month after the private eye delivered his information, he was killed in a hit and run. A suspicious hit and run. A Jack-Bennett-killed-the-poor-man hit and run. Clayton needed to understand her father was like the Joker in Batman, living off chaos and pain, never caring who got hurt and woe to those who tried to stop him. She'd never hired another investigator after that. She already had enough blood on her hands.

"Clayton, if you're done eating, can we discuss my father's involvement with this mafia family? Who are they?"

"The Korzakov's." He wiped his mouth with a napkin. "They smuggle heroin, guns, women. They're into Cybercrime. Terrorism. Contract killing. Psychological torture, like obtaining your phone number and distributing it on fliers advertising sexual services. They'll threaten death or the loss of limbs. Firebomb your house. Kidnap your sisters. Lovely group of people."

Sheridan's stomach started to churn. Tacos and discussions

about her father did not mix. "Regardless of what I said earlier, I do appreciate your concern. However, what you just said…that right there is the exact reason you need to stay away from me."

He shook his head. "I won't. I—"

"Stop." Sheridan lifted a hand. "Please, stop. I've built a fortress around myself, and I *will* keep you out."

"Here's the thing, Bennett. It's too late. I'm in this. No way, can you handle this situation yourself, and I'm not abandoning you to these people."

"I'm not giving you a choice." She shot off the couch and pointed at the basement door. "Get out."

Gaze on the carpet, he rested both elbows on his knees then clapped his hands together before lifting his ocean-blue eyes once more. "I can't."

"Clayton, I'm trying to do the right thing here. My life is too dangerous for you. The only person I can risk is myself. Please, just go."

"I let my brother go, and I'll be damned if I do the same to you." He averted his gaze, hands now locked together in a tight grip between his legs. "Michael came to my room when he was fourteen and told me he was gay. I'd known all along, but figured I'd let him tell me when he was ready. He was confused and scared, but I told him I'd always love him no matter what."

"Clayton, I know this sounds cruel, but this story you're about to tell won't change my mind." Sheridan bit her bottom lip to keep from crying. Emotional blackmail wouldn't work. "Your parents have already lost one child. I won't be responsible for them losing another."

"I kept Michael as safe as I could during high school, but then I left for Ranger training. He did well on his own, never hiding who he was. He studied law, graduated then got a job with the public defenders office. Once there, he fell in love with Alec, another attorney. Alec had already worked in the office for a few years and was disliked by my colleagues who didn't appreciate him putting criminals back on the streets."

Sheridan grabbed some tissues off the wood side table. "Here, since you're determined to do this." She handed him the box. "I'll sit by your side, because I understand the need to release some pain." A practice she'd never do herself, because her stories were buried too deep.

"Thank you." Clayton grabbed a tissue and crumpled it in his hand. "I was working a case on the outskirts of town, following a lead. My brother called and asked me to meet him for lunch. I couldn't because I was waiting for my guy to leave his house, so I asked Michael if I could meet him later. He agreed, of course. He was like that, sweet and always kind."

Sheridan scooted closer to Clayton on the couch and took his hand. "Did you meet him?"

"No." Clayton drew in a long breath. "He went to lunch with Alec. Unfortunately, they were celebrating a case they'd just won when a group of Manchester cops walked in...I've never been convinced their appearance was a coincidence, but anyway, a verbal altercation ensued. Michael, who was ever worried about others around him, asked to take the fight outside." Clayton shook his head and met her gaze, agony evident in his eyes. "Six against two. They never had a chance. My brother took a blow that knocked him against the brick building. He struck his head." Clayton touched his left temple. "Michael went down and never got up again." He closed his eyes, and tears leaked out the corners. "I wasn't there. And he died."

"I'm so sorry." Sheridan wrapped him in her arms. "I hate that you endured such a thing. I hate it. Please don't cry." She swallowed the lump in her throat and lightly kissed his lips. "Don't. Please don't."

Clayton pulled her against him and buried his face in her hair. "He wanted to meet there because he and Alec were getting married. He needed me, and I chose not to go. I'd promised to always stand at his side. I even knew the outcome of his case, but

I never considered he'd be in danger. I missed all the signs."

Sheridan eased back and met his gaze. "Those men are to blame. Not you."

"You can say that to me after everything you've done to keep your sisters safe. I wasn't there when he needed me, and I'll always blame myself for that."

She understood more than she could ever reveal, because she *had* saved her sister from death and would continue to do so until her last breath. "All right. You're right. I can't tell you how to feel. Thank you for telling me."

"So now you understand."

"No, see, I said nothing would change."

He placed both hands on her shoulders. "I won't lose someone I care about. Not again." He ran a finger down the side of her neck before tracing her lips in a feather light brush.

She shivered. "Clayton, please. I-I'm not sure this is wise."

He wrapped a hand around the back of her neck. "Wise isn't what you feel in moments like these, it's all danger and heat and blaring emotions, so why not get burned?" His lips hovered an inch above her mouth. "Fuck wise."

Sheridan felt his hand tighten in her hair as he lowered his mouth to hers, taking command. She savored this moment, as it was her true first kiss—not part of a movie script.

With each stroke of his tongue, his expertise ensnared her, drew her deeper into a hope and dream that could never be, but for now in this small, reckless moment she would take for as long as it lasted.

He softened his exploration, enticing her, encouraging her to follow his lead. A master teaching a novice. With dueling tongues and heated moans, the kiss spun on—hot and urgent as he led her down an unwise path. But who could resist as he claimed more?

Easing back, he gazed into her eyes. "God, you're so beautiful and that mouth…" He shook his head before slanting his mouth over hers again.

Urgency building, his tongue rasped across hers, creating a friction that seared through her body. His need blatantly evident in the rigid column pressed against her stomach. *Oh no!*

She jerked back. "Wait…Clayton, we can't do this." She cupped his cheek. "I'm sorry. I can't…I realize I'm giving off mixed signals, but I can't pursue this."

While her body wanted to move with his, to invite him in, to explore and learn, she couldn't take this any further. She had to break away while her mind remained lucid. None of this was fair to him—or to her. The thought of losing this connection, of no more moments like this, ripped another tear across her tattered heart. Shivering, she brought her arm to her chest, holding her rioting emotions close. "I can't have this kind of relationship. I'm sorry I got carried away, but…it's best if we remain friends."

Clayton brushed her hair over her shoulder. "I want us to be friends, too."

"Thanks." Sheridan breathed a sigh of relief.

"Friends…*and* lovers." Clayton grinned as he massaged the bend of her neck. "Something's building between us, Slim. Something I plan to explore. I'd prefer keeping our relationship as private as possible though."

"No. Privacy doesn't exist in my life, and my body…I-I mean my world is…is not set-up for a relationship. It won't work." She rubbed her damp palms against her sweatpants. "Clayton, you can explore this with someone else. Aren't you dating that woman you were with at the police fundraiser?" Sheridan tried not to remember the flare of jealousy she'd felt upon seeing him with another woman, especially when the night had ended with a stark reminder of why that emotion was foolish.

"Constance?" He ran a hand up and down her back. "She's a good friend."

Since Sheridan wanted nothing more than to settle into his touch and have him caress her everywhere, she shot out of his arms, avoiding temptation. "Is Constance aware you aren't serious?" Indignation seemed a far safer emotion than lust. This thrumming desire was too new, too raw, and too frightening.

"Sheridan, my relationship with Constance is—"

"Clayton." She slashed a hand between them because nothing he said could change her reality. "In my life I have room for my sisters and my work. I'm often away shooting movies for months at a time. I'm not present or available on any level." She held back a grimace at the deep truth behind that statement—a horrid and scarred truth. "I shouldn't have kissed you like that, and I'm sorry if it…if you believed it could mean something more." Heart aching, she rubbed a hand against her chest. "I can't be who you want."

"I'm not sorry." He gipped her hips and tugged her closer. "And I'll work very diligently to show you who I want."

"Clayton. Stop." Sheridan shoved free then paced in front of the couch. "You don't know me." Good God this was painful. His lips so red and plumped from their kisses, his hair disheveled. The thought of never seeing him like this again, or imagining him in this state with another woman, hurt and that alone was enough to steel her spine. If she already felt this ache in her heart, then she was in too deep. Time to step way, way back.

Clayton squeezed her hip. "I know you are a lot more than what's on the outside. You're loyal and strong. Your family is your heart and you support the things you believe in. I understand why you've developed that hard outer shell, but on the inside you need support, and I will be that."

"No. You won't *be* anything. Everything between us ends tonight." Sheridan fought to keep her voice strong as she considered him actually discovering just how disgusting her past truly was, just how dirty and filthy. He could never know. Never. Seeing pity or revulsion in his eyes would break her, and she'd already given up on finding all the pieces of her shattered heart.

He met her gaze and spoke in that deep voice, "You felt the same thing I did when I kissed you—the intensity, the need to just lay back and let our bodies take control. That isn't something I can find with another woman, Slim. I'm not walking away. I've explained why, now all that's left is for you to believe me."

She already believed, already wanted to soothe his pain over losing his brother, and because of that, she had to cut Clayton loose. She couldn't add his death to her overburdened soul. "I want you to leave. You've shared your story, and I-I'm sorry for the pain you've endured. I understand why you think I could be your redemption, but I don't want to be. I've never asked that of you. So don't put me in that position. Find your solace elsewhere."

He held her gaze for a moment then nodded. "Fine. I'll go but I'm not leaving." He headed for the stairs.

"That makes no sense, Kincaid."

"Nothing ever does."

Wasn't that the truth, because as she followed him to the front door, she felt stupidly grateful he wasn't abandoning her and that made no sense at all.

CHAPTER 10

Rachel sauntered into Clayton's office the next morning, her green and white Manchester Marauder coffee cup steaming with some sort of tea. "Sheridan Bennett."

He stopped typing his report on a man guilty of insurance fraud and met Rachel's gaze. Discussing Ms. Bennett when he hadn't fully recuperated from last night wasn't on his list of duties today. He'd been kissed and kicked out, but after a sleepless night he'd still come to the same conclusion—Sheridan needed his help. He'd never spoken of his guilt over Michael's death with anyone and he was glad she'd been on the receiving end of his confession. "Rachel, I'm in the middle of this report. I don't have time to hear about you and Bronco's movie choices."

"Nice try." Rachel cracked a grin. "She's why you were here the other day at the crack of dawn. After I heard of her accident at the gym the other day, I did a little digging."

Damn. She'd likely heard the entire story from Elston since he was her trainer, too. "Put the shovel away, Harris." Clayton turned back to his computer. "Go dig in someone else's sandbox."

"Her little bump on the head was national news. I wonder what they'd do if she stubbed her perfectly manicured toe?"

"Rachel, I've got to finish this report so…" He waved a hand in a circular motion, egging her on because he already knew what was coming. "Did you wish to discuss something *work* related?"

"She's high profile."

"I'm aware." He eased back in his chair, folding both hands at his waist.

"*You* are a *private* investigator." Rachel sat her jean-clad ass down in what he was coming to think of as her chair since she'd used it so often lately.

"Again, I know this. I also know Elston should stick to talking reps instead of telling tales."

Rachel's brow lifted. "Leave Elston be and listen for a second. People are beginning to recognize me because Bronco's in the spotlight as a pro football player. Standing out in a crowd isn't a good thing in our profession. It's why we hired Scotty to take on cases I can no longer do, remember?" She sipped from her tea. "I get that Sheridan's beautiful, intriguing, mysterious, and you want to save her from whatever's going on and based on her past it must be bad…but consider very carefully how much your life will change. I don't regret having Bronco in my life. At times, I wish the damn man wasn't so…big and the fact he hangs out with that social media whore, Jason Stafford, doesn't help."

"First off." Clayton leaned forward and raised a hand. "Don't be trashing my boys. Second, I'm keeping an eye on her. That's all."

"Oh, you've got your eye on her all right, among other things." Rachel snorted before springing to her feet.

The intercom on the outside door of their secured office buzzed.

"Must be a walk-in." Rachel patted the gun on her hip. A habit he'd noted she'd do in unsure situations. "I'll check it out."

Clayton saved the file he'd been working on since he could no longer concentrate on stringing words together. Rachel was right, not only that, Sheridan had said she wasn't interested in him. And yet…she'd kissed him back, starved, hungry, a tad unsure. He could've devoured her last night, settled her back on the couch and made love to her forever. But he'd pushed her enough.

Many famous people had relationships with unknowns and were able to keep their privacy. Sure their relationship would be front-page news for a few weeks, but after that people would stop caring.

Rachel knocked on his open door. Behind her stood two men in suits.

"Agent Denver and Agent Pike from the FBI are here to see you." Rachel eased to the side to let them by. "I'll let you get to it, but Kincaid, that case we talked about earlier, perhaps you'll see my point now." She nodded at the men before heading to her office and slamming shut the door.

FBI agents. Interesting. Sheridan *was* in deep.

Clayton schooled his features and rose from his chair.

"Mr. Kincaid, I'm Agent Denver and this is Agent Pike. We'd like a few moments of your time."

"Sure. Please come in."

Pike's brown eyes were direct but also bloodshot as if from lack of sleep. His gray suit hung on his body. Perhaps he'd lost weight recently, and his hair was mussed with some sort of product in a poor attempt to replicate a more fashionable style. Likely in his early forties, perhaps the man had recently gone through a divorce and was delving into the dating game. Agent Denver was short in stature, sported a buzz cut, and a fake smile. His attire was more crisp, apparently the more fastidious of the two.

Clayton eased out of Sherlock-mode and offered coffee.

Pike agreed and settled into the metal chair in front of Clayton's desk.

Agent Denver remained standing and paced behind the chair.

"Mr. Kincaid, we're sorry to interrupt your day, but we've come across some information and need to act on it right away." Pike set his coffee cup on Clayton's desk.

"We understand you are friends with Sheridan Bennett."

Denver halted his pacing and faced Clayton.

"Yes. I know Sheridan." Clayton tapped his phone against his palm. They were keeping a close eye on her if they knew of his involvement. Still, their relationship was and would be private.

"We wondered...has she mentioned her family at all, specifically her father, Jack Bennett?" Denver inquired.

"No."

"We have reason to believe her father is in the area and that he will contact her."

Clayton wouldn't divulge her father had already contacted her at the police fundraiser. They likely already knew, so he'd play along. "Why would he contact her?"

"Money, Mr. Kincaid." Pike rested both elbows on the arms of the chair and then pressed both index fingers under his chin. "Her father is indebted to some very dangerous people. He was working for the Korzakov family then escaped after engaging in a very dangerous game with Korzakov's sister, Maria."

"I see." Crime families didn't care how they got paid just as long as they did. They posed a more dangerous threat than her father, especially if they decided to have Sheridan cover his debts.

"Sheridan's father is a treacherous man, Mr. Kincaid. Very clever. We'd like to bring him in, but we're holding off. We're hoping Otari Korzakov will accompany his sister here." Pike continued, obviously playing the good guy while Denver hovered. "We'd like to arrest them all at once. We need to play this very carefully. Sheridan has refused to work with us. She feels it is a family matter, and she can handle Jack on her own, but with the Korzakov's involvement...well frankly, she's out of her league."

Clayton nodded, he'd already decided to stick by her side, but after this visit, perhaps he needed to come clean with Rachel and bring in more men. The entire thing was a powder keg on top of a fireworks factory.

"Stick close to her," Agent Pike said. "Determine if she knows anything about her father's whereabouts and his plans while here. You've established a relationship with her…and I'm not ashamed to say we'll use that to bring her father and this crime family to justice."

Clayton shifted his gaze to Denver.

The man nodded before resting his hands on the back of the spare chair and leaning forward. "Sheridan should remain unaware of our conversations as she doesn't hold us in the highest regard. We'll leave our business cards, and as you garner information, please pass it along."

"Wait." Clayton lifted a finger. "Give me a minute."

Essentially, they were asking him to spy on Sheridan. Hadn't she had enough duplicity in her life already? He'd planned on keeping an eye on her, but this was something else. This was purposefully invading her life to help the feds close their case. This was, in a sense, lying about why he was with her. Could he separate the professional from the man? And if she began to trust him and believe in what they had together, would everything fall apart if she found out he was aiding these agents?

Clayton tossed his phone on the desk. "I don't like lying to her, but at this point, her safety matters most. I'll do it, but only if this is a reciprocal agreement." He stood and crossed both arms over his chest. "What did Jack do to Korzakov's sister? Break her heart?" He glanced at Pike, seeking confirmation.

"All the evidence points to that, yes."

"Fucking hell." Clayton raked his fingers through his hair. "These Russian mobsters punish in creative and horrific ways. What are you doing about Sheridan's safety? If we warn her, perhaps she'll cooperate."

Denver sank into the spare chair and drummed his fingers on the steel arms. "She won't share all she knows. Using your…relationship is the right path for now." He pulled a thumb drive from his pocket and tossed it on the desk. "We'll leave this as it contains all the relevant background information." He stood and nodded at Clayton. "Thanks for your time." He handed over his business card.

Pike did the same and said, "We'll be in touch."

Clayton rounded his desk and shook their hands. "I'll work on my end. You work on keeping her safe."

Pike nodded. "We've got eyes on her, son." He clapped Clayton's shoulder then followed Denver out the front door.

Clayton turned and stared at the thumb drive on his desk. What kind of world had he entered? Villainous fathers, bombshell blondes, nefarious gangsters, federal agents. He clenched his jaw against the real fear creeping down his spine. If not for that, he'd think he'd stepped onto a 1920's movie set.

He'd trained for danger. Faced death as a Ranger and as a cop. Fear was a good motivator. Kept things real. Anyone who said they weren't afraid in situations like these was a liar.

His phone pinged with a text alert. From Constance.

Are you available for dinner?

Perhaps he should meet with her, explain once again that he couldn't be more than friends. Her non-stop texts were driving him insane. Though, he understood wanting someone you couldn't have. Sheridan might never be fully his, but he'd protect her. As he'd explained last night, he wouldn't let another person he cared about stand alone. Sheridan was right, he did seek resolution in his brother's death even while understanding he'd never find it.

Regardless of his reasons, he'd jump in anyway. Ms. Bennett's world had just entered a red zone. Nothing, not even her Hollywood highness, would interfere with his plans to keep her safe, even if those plans were implemented in a slightly underhanded way.

Although, was it underhanded to work with the FBI when he'd warned her? Was it deceitful to help a friend who was too blind to see that others did care? That others wanted her safe? He laughed and shook his head. She was the devious one, because she'd already snuck off with his heart. *Fan-fucking-tastic.*

CHAPTER 11

Sheridan stepped out of her BMW X3 SUV and into the humid July air. She wouldn't bring her Mustang to this run down restaurant on Manchester's southeast side.

Sweat instantly formed on her upper lip, although from the mid-evening heat or from fear over stepping across the threshold of her aunt's place, she couldn't say.

Aunt Duplicitous, also known as her father's sister, Vera LaSasso owned this bar and grill. Sheridan wouldn't be here if her schedule didn't have her out of town for the next two and a half months. Her agent, Bobbi Knightley had informed her of the repercussions if she were to pull out of the movie so close to filming. Jenny and Laney would follow her to California but they'd return before she finished shooting. Hence her reason for standing outside this faded black door, gripping the warm metal handle. She needed information.

Breathing deeply, she opened the door. Smoke instantly filled her lungs. Her aunt didn't believe in following no-smoking laws.

On her way to the bar, Sheridan erased all emotion from her face. She'd learned very early to become someone else, to escape her true self. Sometimes she wondered if she didn't have some sort of multiple personality disorder. Yet, that helped with her acting roles, so…whatever. Done musing about her mental problems, she stepped up to the bar. Clayton would likely strangle her if he found her alone in such a place. She'd tried not to think about their kiss or his frequent, how-are-you texts. She'd compartmentalized their relationship, but everything she felt kept oozing out of the box.

The smoke stench had her practically gagging and brought her mind back from ridiculous thoughts of Aquaman. She'd have to find a way to scrub her lungs after leaving—and maybe find an anti-Clayton wash.

Her aunt's ex-husband and Sheridan's illustrious father had often run scams together. LaSasso was part of whatever could be called the mafia in this part of the world, maybe he was with the Korzakov's. Who knew?

Vera hadn't minded her husband and her brother's unlawful endeavors. In fact, she'd enjoyed the perks. Then her husband traded her in for a younger woman, leaving both Vera and their son, Ryan behind.

Ryan had walked away as a teen, choosing not to recognize either parent. Sheridan's only cousin didn't forget—or forgive.

"Hey, Vera. Business looks good." Sheridan nodded to the flaming red head stationed behind the bar, cigarette dangling off her bottom lip. Then she leaned against the bar's sticky surface noting the smell of cheap whiskey emanating from the wood.

Vera lifted a drawn-on red brow then slammed shut the cash register drawer before murmuring something to the bartender.

"Business is always better if people know *you* frequent the place." Vera stubbed out her cigarette in an empty ashtray then waved at a barstool. "Have a seat."

"Sure, let the show begin." Sheridan flashed a fake smile. "If you want your celebrity niece to be seen by everyone so you can bank on that for the next couple months, then I'll need a...shall we say, sitting fee."

"Figured you'd be by." Vera lit another cigarette, even though there were No Smoking signs plastered all over the bar. "Give me a minute."

Her aunt headed for the kitchen. No doubt alerting the wait

staff that Sheridan Bennett had entered the building. Soon, she would be inundated with people wanting to take her picture, so when Vera returned, Sheridan got straight to the point. "Why is my father here?"

Vera blew smoke out the side of her wrinkled mouth. "Only thing I know for sure is that your father's been back in town for a few months. He left though. Got shot. Said he'd be back once things cooled down."

"That's it?"

"How's Ryan?" Vera arched her brow.

Sheridan knew this side-step. Time to pay. And even though she hated giving any part of this woman's son back to her, she knew Ryan would be okay with her trading information. "He's fine as far as I know. Still overseas, last I heard."

"Got any pictures?"

"Got any more info?"

Vera smiled and used a bar towel to wipe an imaginary spot off the counter. "Jack and some kid's been working a few things, trying to come up with fast cash. Little brother's got himself in deep with the wrong people. They've been by looking for him." She sniffed. "Not a pleasant visit."

Sheridan flipped through pictures on her cell phone until she found one of Ryan then handed it over. "You said, some kid? Who is he?"

Busy studying the picture of her son, her aunt didn't answer right away.

"Vera?"

"Don't know… he's a beautiful bastard, isn't he?" She shook her head as she held Sheridan's phone in her hand.

Sheridan refused to be drawn into a conversation about Ryan. He didn't want his mother, or anyone else for that matter, knowing his business. Once he'd discovered the double-dealing deeds of his parents, he'd cut them from his life.

Seeing the way Vera looked at Ryan's picture did evoke a

wash of sympathy though. People made mistakes, trouble was, some kept on making them. "How are you doing, Vera?"

"Restaurant keeps me busy, but it's hard to find good help anymore."

As Vera liked to go on about her restaurant and all her health problems, Sheridan stayed another hour. In the midst of her colorful tales, Vera was frequently interrupted when the restaurant staff and a few curious customers sidled up for photos and autographs.

Thoroughly exhausted and jaw aching from wide smiles, Sheridan heaved a sigh and hopped off the barstool. "Thanks, Vera. Good to know Jack's out of town."

"Be careful." Walking her to the back door, Vera grabbed her arm. "These people your father crossed are very dangerous. And, that young kid helping him is a nasty piece of work. I'd steer clear."

Sheridan nodded. "Sure."

If only that were possible.

# # #

As Sheridan stepped out the door, she breathed in muggy air, which did nothing to eradicate the smoke coating her lungs.

Rolling her shoulders, Sheridan leaned against the restaurant's back wall for a moment before walking to her SUV. Who was the poor young guy helping her father? And just how injured was dear ole dad? The sniper had got him good in the leg, but people like her father never stayed down for long, they kept creeping and crawling back.

Mentally exhausted from dealing with Vera, she'd head home, have some peppermint tea, and call O'Malley. Maybe he could offer some insight on where her father might be hiding. If Jack had gone to a hospital, he might've checked in under an alias, but they could use the type of injury to find out where he'd been.

A long shot, but one worth taking.

Halfway to her SUV, she scanned the parking lot then skidded to a stop. Across the street a blond guy was standing next to a van, staring right at her.

A huge kid, both tall and beefy. Young though, maybe seventeen or eighteen.

The white van had bullet holes in the side panel.

Bullet holes.

Oh shit!

While meeting his gaze, she narrowed her eyes when a weird sense of recognition shot down her spine. Although, she couldn't say why. Prepared for a confrontation, she picked up her pace, removed her Remington .45 from her shoulder holster, and racked the slide, sending a bullet into the chamber.

Could this creep be her father's minion? Damn it, why did her father have to interfere with her life? He may need money, but he would never get a dime. She'd tried to outsmart him before and an innocent child had died. This time she'd be stronger and smarter—at least she hoped.

While keeping an eye on the blond stranger and a finger on the trigger, she cursed when she arrived at her vehicle.

Both back tires were hissing as they slowly flattened.

"What a jerk!" Stomping to the front of the SUV, Sheridan kicked the bumper upon seeing the front two were slashed, as well. She glared at the blond asshole. "What is your problem?"

He smirked, shot her a salute then hopped in his van and left.

There were no words.

"Stupid blond jerk minion. Going around slashing tires like some psycho in your creepy ass van." Shoving her gun in her holster, she yanked her phone from her back pocket and took a couple pictures as the blond menace drove away.

Glancing around the barely lit, empty lot, she again reconsidered her stance on having no bodyguard. "Get moving,

Bennett." She jogged across the lot and pounded on the employee door. She'd rather make her calls inside than out here with tire-slashers running around.

Her personal cell rang with a number she didn't recognize.

"Hello?"

"Why, hello, dear. How is my sister faring this eve?" Her father's voice slithered across the line.

Sheridan shouldn't be shocked that he'd obtained her personal number, after all her Aunt had called a few weeks ago.

"My sister never did know when to keep her mouth shut," he continued. "She's like your mother that way. Speaking of your dear departed mother, her birthday is next week. Did you remember? How was it she died again? I always thought the timing of her death was rather convenient...for you."

Sheridan refused to venture down that path. She clenched her cell tighter in her hand. "I'm sure you'll have a chance to ask her soon. And just so we're clear, I'm not giving you a dime."

"That sounds like a challenge. I'm willing to play, are you?" He tisked tisked over the line. "You do tend to lose whenever the stakes are high."

Sheridan disconnected the call then banged on the restaurant's back door. After a few choice curse words, she was about to shoot open the stupid lock when the door suddenly opened.

The dishwasher looked her over. "H-hi."

She offered a tight smile. "Excuse me." She darted inside and headed to the bar, ready to deliver a vicious verbal beat down to her aunt over the woman giving her number to Jack-ass Bennett.

Damn it! Now she had to change her number.

And try as she might to keep fear at bay, she still shivered as his taunts about her mother struck home. No matter what he may think happened, he couldn't know truth. Only two people were in the room that night. And only one had survived.

CHAPTER 12

Clayton had agreed to meet his informant on a fraud case at this restaurant because Sheridan's Aunt Vera owned the joint. Now that his meeting was over, he'd sit at the bar in order to get a sense of whether the woman would help or hinder the investigation into her brother.

Wiping his hands on his pants rather than using the smoke scented paper towels in the bathroom, he coughed and headed toward the bar. A tall, cold bottle of anything sounded good right about now.

"How dare you?" A very familiar voiced shouted from behind the kitchen door.

"What in the world?" He pushed open the door, but stopped just inside upon seeing Sheridan with her finger in the face of an older woman.

"How else did he get my number then?"

He'd seen her upset before, but right now, her face was bright red and her eyes were narrowed into slits.

"*You* are a liar." She hurtled the words at the woman.

"Sheridan...I-I didn't do it." A woman with a bad dye job— likely her aunt, lifted both hands between them.

"Save it!" Sheridan's bellow shook the rafters in this rickety joint. "I don't believe you."

After glancing up to make sure the roof wasn't caving in, Clayton noted the .45 in Sheridan's hand, which rested at her side. One thing he'd learned as a cop—high emotions and guns never mixed.

"Hey, Slim, how about you put the gun away." Using an even tone, he raised his hands, palms up and stepped further into the room.

She shot him a glare before jabbing her aunt's shoulder. "Be very careful, Vera. I can withhold all kinds of information too." Then without acknowledging his presence, she turned on her heel and walked toward the employee exit.

"Damn it." He charged after her, grabbing her shoulder just as she stepped out the back door.

"Are you following me?" She spun and shoved against his shoulder.

"Hey, now. I only get rough in the bedroom."

"You're ridiculous." Rolling her eyes, she turned and flounced off.

"Stop. And calm your shit down." He gripped her arm. "What are you doing carrying around that gun? Do you even have a license to carry in public?" He levered his six-three frame above her, his blood practically boiling in his veins. "Why are you running around town like you aren't a famous movie star someone could abduct or God knows what else?"

"I can take care of myself."

"Can you?" Using a quick maneuver, he removed her gun from her hand, and then checked the chamber before stuffing it in his waistband. "How about now?"

She heaved a sigh before shaking her head. "Clayton, please don't do this."

"Then how about I do this." He braced a hand under her chin, bent, and kissed her hard, drawing her body fully against his. He drove his tongue deep, claiming and owning. Dirty, hot, out of control, he devoured her sweet mouth and eased all his anger with each thrust of his tongue.

She whimpered a little before gripping the back of his neck.

A moment passed before he realized, his face was wet...from her tears.

"Sheridan, look at me." He drew back and cupped her face between his hands. "I'm sorry, but you drive me crazy."

She bit her bottom lip and then released a half-laugh, half-sob. "I need to leave."

"I'll take you home."

"No." She laughed again, half-hysterical this time. "I need to leave this place. Just pack everything and run. I can't be here anymore, you know?"

"I do know." He ran a hand down the back of her head, soothing her hair and trying to soothe her. "Where would you go?"

She bent and gripped her hair in her hands before shooting back up and backing away. "Nowhere. That's where. I have to stay, because I have contracts, costars, responsibilities, sisters, bills. Sheridan Bennett is a business. So, no matter how far I want to fly away, I'm stuck." She waved her hand toward her SUV. "For real stuck. Some blond jerk slashed my tires, so now I have to call a friggin' cab or car service or whatever they are."

"What?" He marched over to her vehicle and bent to check the damage. "Who did you say did this?"

"Some blond creep."

"How do you know? Were you here?" Jaw clenched, he rose from his crouch and grabbed her shoulders, giving her a small shake. "He had a knife, Sheridan."

"Stop jostling me. I wasn't here until after he went all Freddy Krueger." She flipped her phone out of her back pocket. "May I please have my gun back? I'm calling a cab, because honestly I'm over this day."

"You're not calling a cab." He grabbed her phone and tugged

her to where he'd parked his vehicle in the front of the building like a normal person.

"I need a tow truck."

"I'll handle it."

"You'll handle nothing." She jerked to a stop. "You've already done enough handling tonight."

"You didn't mind." He let a slow grin light his face as he gave her a blatant once-over.

"Stop it, Pervo!" She poked a finger against his chest. "I like, seriously, on a level unknown to man before now, do *not* like you...not at all."

"Slim, you love it when I get under your skin."

"Unknown. Level." She emphasized her words by flattening a hand up by her head.

"I'm sure we'll hit those unknown levels soon."

She groaned and rubbed her forehead, mumbling something he couldn't quite hear but sounded like, "stupid innuendos."

"What are you doing here anyway?" Once more, he grabbed her hand and trekked forward. "Who is that woman inside?" Feigning ignorance seemed the best course for now, because Ms. Bennett wouldn't want to hear he'd already investigated Vera LaSasso.

"Where's your stupid car?"

He wrapped an arm around her waist and squeezed. "Avoiding my questions makes me more curious."

She shoved him away. "She's my aunt. Geez, not everything is some super mystery."

"What'd she do to make you so angry?"

"You really want to know?"

"Yes."

With a Cheshire-grin, she turned and met his gaze. "She asked too many questions."

"Is that right?" He barely refrained from swatting her smart ass.

At his Expedition, he braced a hand against the passenger door and crowded her. "Play this smart and let me in."

"I can't."

"Can't or won't?"

"What's it matter?" Sheridan clutched his arm. "Please, just go back to your world and stay out of mine."

He shrugged. "I'm offering my bodyguard services for free."

"You don't understand. He's probably already seen you with me."

"Who?" Clayton narrowed his eyes. "Your father? Is he connected to this blond guy? What vehicle was he driving?"

"Yes, my father, and yes, the blond guy was driving the same van as the one at the fundraiser. Are you happy now, Mr. Investigator? Have I answered all your questions?" She rubbed her temple and huffed out a breath. "Listen, my father's gathering information, looking for weaknesses. And bingo, that's you. But I can't let him use you to bend me to his will, because...damn it...I'd do it."

"Isn't tonight proof enough that'd we'd be stronger together? We're both working toward the same end. You want me safe, then keep me close." He pulled her into his arms. "Trust me."

"I know you think I'm crazy, but my father has used people I care about against me before, I can't go through that again." She rested her forehead against his chest. "Don't make me."

"Okay, Slim." Clayton rocked her back and forth then kissed the top of her head. "Let me take you home, and we'll worry about everything else tomorrow."

"No." She eased back and met his gaze. "I've worried about you enough. I'm leaving soon anyway, so let's use that break as the end of things." She sniffed and studied her feet for a moment before lifting her gaze once more and bracing a small hand against his cheek. "I appreciate what you're trying to do, but please stop. People like you need to exist. Need to thrive. For a short time my world was a better place because you were in it, but that's all I get…because…" She bit her bottom lip. "It's just…actresses are a dime a dozen, but true heroes like you are irreplaceable." She rose on her tiptoes and lightly kissed his lips before opening his SUV's door and sliding in.

Wasn't that just the way of things. Shaking his head, he shoved both hands in his front pockets. Kissing him as if they were starring in the dramatic ending of some melodrama gone wrong.

Like hell. He'd break through her resistance, one way or another.

CHAPTER 13

Sitting on the edge of the gym's pool, Sheridan thumbed through her emails. In order to avoid Clayton, she'd come in the afternoon and completed her laps. Her swimsuit and workout shorts were practically dry after sitting in this slightly muggy room for over thirty minutes.

Her emails were full of important details regarding her upcoming film schedule. Social events. Flight facts. But the information wasn't sinking into her overloaded brain. Worry pushed everything else out.

Yawning, she covered her mouth. Rereading her script at 2 a.m. last night hadn't derailed her thoughts either. Everything kept spinning over and over in her mind: her father, the blond creeper, the mafia, her sisters, and Clayton.

He'd texted a few times, but she hadn't answered. Removing him from her life was the smart move. Relationships with men were impossible not only because of her current predicament but because of the very real horrors of her childhood. She'd known this and should have stopped him before he'd given her a taste of intimacy, because now her chest felt like an empty cavity, as if everything inside had dried up and drifted away with the wind.

The hairs on the back of Sheridan's neck prickled as a dark haired woman entered the pool area and paused a moment before two ominous looking fellas joined her from the men's side. The woman was short in stature and a bit plump, her chin-length bob had streaks of white, giving her a distinguished air. Her multi-colored swimsuit covered her hips with a short skirt. She had a brief conversation with the men then walked directly toward Sheridan.

A warning chill shot down her spine. She could run, but she wouldn't get far with guard one and guard two blocking the entrance to the women's locker room.

Guard one wore a black T-shirt and a pair of Bermuda shorts. Guard two was a tad bit older, wearing a collared shirt and a pair of khaki pants. He reminded her of a Russian boxer she'd watched once in Vegas. Straight ash-brown hair, tight jawline, and a prominent, slightly off-kilter nose that widened at the end.

An elderly couple and a pregnant woman were milling around the pool so hopefully guard two wouldn't get trigger-happy. He looked a little twitchy.

Stopping beside Sheridan, the older woman kicked off her designer flip-flops and settled next to her, dropping her pale legs into the pool.

"Good morning, Ms. Bennett." The older woman spoke with an accent that screamed *Russian*. "I see you are just as beautiful in person."

Sheridan's heart thundered. Hopefully the woman would get to the point of her visit before Sheridan's over-burdened organ said, "I'm done. Too much stress. I'm out."

She met the woman's shrewd brown-eyed gaze. "Thank you."

"Isn't that something?" The woman smiled. "I join today and the first person I see is famous actress." She turned and nodded at her bulky bodyguard.

Sheridan's stomach sank. This woman had to be part of the Russian mafia who wanted her father and her money. Keeping her gaze on her phone, Sheridan hit the voice memo button to record any threats. She cleared her throat. *Show no fear. Stay strong.* "You'll enjoy the gym. Pool's a nice temperature today. I hope you have a nice workout." Sheridan pulled her legs from the water, grabbed her flip-flops, and stood.

"You will stay, Ms. Bennett." The woman spoke in a tone that brooked no argument. "My name is Maria Korzakov. I am visiting for a short time." Maria faced her and pointedly glanced at the spot Sheridan had just vacated. "Please sit. I wish to tell story."

Sheridan glanced at the exit again, and then at the pregnant woman before sighing. Sometimes she had to pick her battles and this one she'd already lost. She lowered to her knees, much easier to pop up and run if necessary.

"You listen, yes?"

Sheridan nodded. "Yes. As long as your guards stay where they are, I'll stay where I am."

"Ah, my men." Maria waved a hand. "Pay them no mind. Now, my story." She stared out over the pool for a few seconds then said, "I marry young to please my family. This man, he die, and I was alone for a long time. Then I meet a man. He is so charming and kind. I fall in love, but he is not true to me. He is liar and cheat." She swished her legs through the water. "My family had trusted him, worked with him, but one day he disappear with something very dear to me. My mother's stone. A six carat diamond, one of the first stones to come from the Mir Mine in the late 1950's. He also take an emerald bracelet. A gift from my father."

Sheridan blew out a breath. Great, her father had hurt this woman and stolen her jewels. Now *his* jewels were on a chopping block. *Lovely visual, Bennett.* Could she convince this woman that her father had ruined her too? Or would her past mean very little to a Russian mafia queen bent on revenge?

"Would you like to see a picture of my jewels?" She beckoned guard two.

"Ma'am, I'm sorry for the pain my father caused you. He stole something valuable from me, too." Sheridan took the woman's hand. "Jack Bennett erased my innocence, my trust, my hope. I don't know anything about your stone, and I won't pay for his sins. If this visit is supposed to serve as a threat or to frighten me, consider your job done. But know this...I already live in fear. I've already seen death, so whatever debt he owes, please understand, I cannot and will not pay it."

Maria glanced at her guard who was now at her side. "My phone, please then return to your station."

He frowned but handed it over.

Placing her phone at her side, Maria cleared her throat then faced Sheridan. "Women see things differently than men. My brother wishes to see you, but I do not feel his interference is the best course. I can see you speak truth, but I cannot stop my brother forever. The Korzakov honor is at stake. He holds that above everything, do you understand?"

Releasing the woman's hand, Sheridan swallowed the lump in her throat. "I cannot give you back your stone or unbreak your heart. My money will not make amends for those things. If your brother chooses to bring me into this battle, please know, I will not go easily."

"You would." Maria sniffed and then pointedly glanced at the pregnant woman across the room.

"Please don't do that." Sheridan held up a hand. "Don't threaten innocent people. That's beneath you. I know you're hurt and maybe you think lashing out at me is a way to lash out at Jack, but I've dealt with that mindset before."

"You look like him."

"And I hate the way I look." Seeing Jack Bennett's blue eyes looking back at her every morning disgusted her. The shape of her face and her cheekbones were all Bennett. She did have her mother's mouth. Not that having her genes was any better.

"Ah, but you are one of the most beautiful women in the

world. Do not disregard something others covet."

"People only see the outside."

"I see the inside." Maria gripped her hand. "You are strong. A fighter."

"I've had to be." Sheridan met the woman's gaze. "You are not the only one tracking my movements. Agent Denver is probably preparing to storm the building at any moment."

Maria laughed. "Yes, he is a funny little man."

Sheridan stood, very much over this frightening exchange. "Nice meeting you, but I'll be on my way."

"My brother doesn't care who is on your side." Maria glanced up at her. "He only see dollar signs next to your name."

"I earned those dollars, and I won't let anyone take what's mine."

"Words are easy." Maria shrugged a shoulder.

"I've used more than words before, so know this, I'm ready for whatever comes my way."

Maria studied her then nodded. "I've asked my brother to stand aside. I am responsible for my own life and do not wish him to interfere." She soothed her short bob with a hand.

"I don't quite understand the purpose of your visit, other than an attempt to frighten me. I don't control my father's actions, and he certainly doesn't control mine."

"Help me stand." Maria lifted a hand.

Sheridan helped the woman to her feet.

"If your father contacts you, I expect you to notify me immediately."

"And you'll do what exactly?" Sheridan leaned back on her heels. "I'd rather not have to watch my back for the next twenty years, waiting for your brother to come after me because my father dishonored him."

"What do you think happens to people who cross the Korzakov family?"

"They die." Sheridan shook her head against visions of

torture and death. "I understand that, but if you love Jack, can you destroy him?"

Maria sniffed. "I did love him, but he made me look like fool. I defended him, stood by him, and he betrayed me."

"He does that." Sheridan nodded.

"Not anymore." Maria snapped her fingers. "Vitali! Card!"

Vitali, aka guard two, hustled forward and handed Sheridan a business card.

"You will call." She took Vitali's arm. "I will stay to swim."

Vitali led her to the pool's stairs.

Sheridan took a deep breath and blew it out slowly, willing her body to not crumble to the floor. Now that she'd been dismissed, she turned the card over in her hand. It was white with a single number in the center, nothing else.

Unsure if her legs could carry her to the exit, she stretched up on her toes then rolled her shoulders. What kind of an idiot broke the heart of a mafia leader's sister? Her father was going to cost her money after all. Before she left for California she'd hire a security team. But she didn't have much time to research the best men. She'd have to call Clayton. *Wait, scratch that.* If he heard what happened today, he'd get involved.

She'd do the next best thing and speak to Rachel.

Hopefully the woman could keep quiet about her request. Because if Sheridan knew anything it was that sibling's never listened to each other. Korzakov had also been made to look like a fool and if Maria thought her brother would let that stand just because she'd asked him to...well she was very, very wrong.

# # #

Clayton checked his phone on the way to his place for a late lunch. Sheridan had ignored his text again. She believed she was protecting him, but that wouldn't stop him from barreling through her door tonight. After two days of no contact, he was going back in.

He slammed his Expedition into Park and headed inside. Fast food wasn't on his radar. He did what he could to keep his body healthy. Most times he baked chicken or pork chops and ate that for lunch, but he'd had to monitor a woman suspected of insurance fraud early this morning, so he didn't have time to pack his regular meal. Something he'd blame on Sheridan as worry over her had kept him tossing and turning the past couple nights.

His duplex was nothing like Sheridan's home, but his place served its purpose. Two bedrooms—one served as an office, a kitchen, living room, one bathroom, and a couple closets. That's all he needed. He sat at his desk and powered up his laptop, preparing his notes for the lawyers on what he'd observed this morning.

While waiting for the computer to boot, he headed to the kitchen. He slapped a pork chop between two slices of wheat bread and froze with the sandwich halfway to his mouth.

Tossing his lunch on the counter, he spun around, hand already on his gun's trigger.

Erik Pavel leaned against the kitchen entryway.

"Good way to get yourself shot, Pavel." Clayton lowered his weapon then grabbed a couple paper towels and sat at his kitchen table. "I'd like to know how you got past my security system, but I doubt you'd tell me."

The man was dressed in a high dollar suit and looking so much like his sister, Rachel with his dark hair and brown eyes. He'd disappeared from her life at a young age, but she'd never stopped looking. In the end they'd found each other, but were still distant in many ways because of who this man had become. Erik's abductor had raised him deep within the Russian mafia, so his stony gaze and poker face came straight from living a dangerous life.

Erik had declared he was done with that life. However, for reasons only he knew, he kept a toe in the business, which made him a good ally when one needed info from the streets.

Though Clayton had been trained as a soldier, he understood this man was trained to be a killer—no remorse, no guilt. Yet, a glimpse of humanity shined through again and again, especially when it came to his sister.

"Rachel said you wished to speak to me." Erik tucked a hand in the front pocket of his dress pants.

"Sure, sit down." Clayton rose to pour a glass of water from the pitcher on the counter. "I'd offer you a sandwich, but this is the last pork chop."

"I'm fine." Pavel smoothed a hand down his collar. "Thank you."

Once Erik was settled beside him, Clayton dove right in. "Any new players in town?"

"If you're asking if Sheridan Bennett's father is in town, then the answer is yes. I've already been approached by another party asking for assistance."

"He's wanted by the FBI, and they know he's here, so I'd be careful about making any promises."

Erik tilted his head slightly. "I'm always careful."

"How's your case against Korzakov going?"

"I'm just an average business man." Erik sank back in his chair, waving one hand in the air. "I no longer work in such circles."

"Of course." Clayton shook his head before wiping his mouth.

Erik knocked his knuckles against the table then stood. "I came to offer some advice. If you are interested in this actress, stay close. Her father has brought a lot of garbage with him. They want payback, and they'll get it. Tell your woman to be safer than she's been."

"What's that mean?"

"Let's just say it's a good thing you were at Vera's restaurant the other night. It's being watched...by everyone."

Clayton shoved aside the last couple bites of his sandwich, and then raked his fingers through his hair. "She's in over her head."

"Yes, she is." Pavel met his gaze. "The fact that I'm here should express the severity of the situation."

Fury and raw fear shot through Clayton's system. Images of Sheridan and her sisters tortured and left for dead flashed through his mind. "No one touches her...or her sisters"

"I've done what I can." Erik hesitated for a moment, opened his mouth then closed it before shaking his head and leaving as quietly as he'd come.

Clayton would have to trust that Erik had spread the word to leave the Bennett sisters alone. Erik was not a man to be crossed.

But neither was he.

In his pocket, his phone chimed with Sheridan's ringtone.

"Sheridan?" He set the phone on speaker mode.

"No, sorry. This is Jenny. I'm using her phone, because I didn't have your number."

"What's wrong?" Clayton straightened and searched the countertop for his keys.

"Something very important has come up."

"All right." He stood and headed for the door.

"I'm part of a summer arts program, and I'm starring in a play this weekend. I'd like you to come."

"A play?" He halted with a hand on his front door knob.

"Yes. I have some extra tickets. You'll be sitting with Sheridan."

"Does your sister know you're inviting me?"

"No." Jenny scoffed. "But she's moping around the house, so I assume she did something stupid."

"Your sister isn't stupid." Clayton sank onto his couch, hoping his heart would stop pounding after the initial fear something bad had happened.

"You're good for her. I wasn't sure at first, but she was

different for a while. Happier. Then a few days ago grumpy Sheridan came back. I assume she did something...I-I don't know what...but Clayton, please don't give up on her. She's just scared."

"She's worried about you and Laney."

"I'm worried about us too...that's why I'd like you to give her another chance...or whatever."

"Jenny, I'm not abandoning your sister."

"Thank you." She sniffed then cleared her throat. "So, will you come to my play?"

"When is it?"

"Saturday night."

"I would love to attend."

Clayton listened as Jenny chattered on about how he'd pick up his ticket and a bit about what the play was about, but mostly he considered how different Jenny was from Sheridan. Jenny was vivacious and friendly. Sheridan was guarded and cynical. How was that possible? What had Sheridan endured that Jenny hadn't?

Through Sheridan's fame, she'd provided somewhat of an umbrella for her sisters to hide beneath, but she didn't fit. She remained under the dark clouds, getting pelted by the rain.

Wasn't it time someone sheltered her? He'd stand beside her and offer her comfort from the storm, if only she'd let him. He'd show her she could laugh, she could smile, and most importantly, she would see that storms passed much easier when you had someone to dance with in the rain.

CHAPTER 14

Saturday morning, Clayton pulled into his parking spot at the office, hoping to get some paperwork done before the big play tonight.

Rachel's car was in the lot next to a BMW SUV. The same BMW he'd had towed to a local repair shop in order to replace all four tires.

He glanced into the BMW's window and saw an Excel gym bag and a pair of pink boxing gloves. What the hell was Sheridan doing here?

Using the app on his phone, he turned off the security in the office so he could enter without the door chiming and alerting the women to his presence.

He took the back stairs and quietly opened the door to their offices.

Once inside, he tapped his phone a few times, reactivated the security system, and eavesdropped just outside Rachel's door.

"I'm sorry Sheridan, but I don't feel right about keeping this information from Clayton, and honestly, neither should you." Rachel's voice came across loud and clear.

"I'm only asking for advice on local security services, that's all. Maria's visit was a tipping point. I realize now that I do need additional security."

Clayton stormed into the room. "Maria Korzakov visited you? When?"

Sheridan covered her face with both hands, shaking her head. "You said he wasn't coming in today."

"I said he wasn't scheduled to come in, but I'm not his keeper." Rachel leaned back in her leather office chair.

"I thought we were friends of a sort, after the movie and everything."

"We *are* friends." Rachel nodded. "And as your friend, I wouldn't have kept this information from Clayton. Too much is at stake. Believe me, I've dealt with this mafia family before. I know how they operate."

"Did you call him? And not only that"—she turned and faced Clayton—"you just said, Maria. How do you know who she is? You said the Korzakov's wanted my father, but you never said why. Did you know?"

"Rachel, explain." Clayton leaned against the doorway, waiting to hear what trouble Sheridan was in now.

Sheridan huffed out a laugh. "Oh sure, disregard my questions like you disregard everything else."

He rounded the desk and stood beside Rachel. "Do not use the word disregard around me, Bennett. I have tried contacting you all week. Because, yes, I did have information to share, but apparently you didn't want to hear it."

"You never said anything about Maria."

"I said I wanted to talk."

Sheridan met his glare then looked away. "Fine. So, tell me now."

The thought of her around a Korzakov family member had him fuming. He couldn't talk to her right now. Not after she'd circumvented him and made a secret meeting with his boss. "Rachel, what's this meeting about?"

Rachel folded both hands across her stomach. "Sheridan asked to meet to discuss recommendations for a security team."

Sheridan gasped. "I thought we were in a private zone, but no, you just spill it all."

"I've been in your shoes, thinking I could handle everything on my own. I learned you can't, and I'm the better for it. I suggest you do the same."

"Well, for someone in the private eye business you're not very private."

"Enough!" Clayton slapped a hand against Rachel's desk. "I hate to break up your little cat fight, but Rachel, you can go. I got this now."

"Doesn't look like it." Rachel raised both brows.

"Out." He tugged her out of her chair.

"Let go of my arm, and calm down, Kincaid." Rachel jabbed a finger toward the vacant seat next to Sheridan. "Go sit down, because you're both going to listen. The only way forward is together. I'm sorry, Sheridan, but he needs to know."

Clayton plopped into the seat beside Sheridan. "I need to know what?"

"While at the pool the other day, she was visited by Maria Korzakov."

Sheridan groaned and rubbed her temple.

"She expects Sheridan to help her capture Jack Bennett. I know how the Korzakov's operate. They robbed my family of my brother and basically turned him into a psychopath."

Clayton winced. "A bit harsh, Rach."

She waved him off. "That being said, if either of you think you can handle that family alone, you're idiots. This isn't a business deal gone bad, this is Korzakov's sister getting fucked over by your father, Sheridan." Eyes raised to the ceiling, she shook her head. "It's personal and all about pride. Your father will die, and they might just take you and your sisters with him. So, I suggest you stop fighting Clayton's assistance and let him figure out a plan." Rachel shot out of her chair, and then paced behind it. "Clayton, Sheridan's leaving for California soon, so who do we know out there worth hiring?"

Clayton silently high-fived his boss. Maybe hearing the truth from Rachel would knock some sense into Sheridan's blonde head. "I've already compiled a list of worthy security men in that area."

Rachel flicked a hand at him. "Then go get it."

"Wait a minute." Sheridan held up her hand. "I don't want him involved. They'll kill him. I shouldn't have come here." She grabbed her purse and hefted it over her shoulder. "Maybe I should just pay them off. Save everyone a lot of trouble."

"No. They'll only want more." Rachel shook her head. "Sit back down. Clayton's involved, and now, so am I."

"I can go somewhere else. I don't need your recommendations."

"Oh sure, go ahead and hire someone who doesn't have a direct connection to the Korzakov family." Rachel rolled her eyes. "You're hiring us. We're putting GPS trackers on your phone, your vehicles, your purse. We're tapping in to your home security system. And Clayton and Scotty will work with you until we can hire more men. Period. End of story. Thanks for stopping by." Rachel sank back into her chair, or based on the way she'd just laid down the law—her throne.

"I spoke to Erik." Clayton crossed his feet at the ankles. "He says he's done what he can to ensure Sheridan's safety."

"I'm sure I don't want to know how he pulled that off."

"Probably." Clayton grunted.

Rachel met his gaze and shook her head. "Now that we've got that settled, I'll give you two a minute. I figure we're going to need lots of coffee."

Silence reigned in the room for a few seconds after Rachel left. Clayton focused on not shouting down the roof. On not shaking the woman beside him to come to her senses and realize that just because everyone else in her life had let her down didn't mean he would do the same.

Sheridan tapped her manicured nail against the metal chair's arm. "Did Rachel call you?"

"Rachel already answered that question." Clayton placed a hand over her tapping finger. "You may think ignoring my texts means you and I are done. But, Slim, it doesn't work that way."

Sheridan poked him in the chest. "Yes, actually it does."

"No." He wrapped a hand around the back of her neck. "It works like this."

He held her head in place as he kissed her. Drove deep into her mouth, tangling his tongue with hers as he showed her that passion came in many forms. Anger. Lust. And deep kisses that were meant to clarify his intent to stay in her life. To show her more. To make her feel.

For a moment, she returned his kiss but after biting his lower lip, she shoved him away. "Don't."

He licked his bottom lip. "I suggest you forget this fantasy where you and your father have some high-noon shoot out on an abandoned street. You've read too many movie scripts, sweetheart. This is real life. And if you stand alone, you'll die."

"That's inevitable." She sniffed and turned away.

"Fuck that." He gripped her shoulders, forcing her to meet his gaze. "Why the death wish? Why do you fight for everyone but yourself? What are you hiding?"

"Something you'll never see."

"Is that a dare?"

"It's a fact."

Clayton studied her face. "I'll say this again, and maybe this time it'll sink into that stubborn head, I'm not leaving you."

"You don't understand."

"So, explain." He released her.

"I-I need to be the one who stops my father."

"Why?"

"I can't tell you."

"You're still letting him control you. He's calling the shots. Is that how you want to live your life?"

Sheridan laughed. "As if I've ever had a choice."

"You do." He cupped her face with his hand. "You could choose me."

"And watch you die." She lowered her gaze. "I don't think so."

"I think you're more afraid of what will happen if we make it through all of this. If you end up feeling something for me after all."

"There is no 'we', so no, I'm not worried."

"You're sort of asking for another kiss, you realize this right?"

"No kissing." Rachel declared as she ambled through the door with a steaming coffee mug in her hand. "Let's call Scotty and see who else we can round up on short notice." Rachel squeezed by them and sank into her chair. "Coffee's in Clayton's office. He has the best machine. Mine's ancient."

"Thank you. I'll get a cup." Sheridan grabbed her purse again.

Clayton stood and pressed Sheridan back into her chair.

"If you don't stop pushing me, Kincaid...I swear I'll—"

"I don't trust you not to bolt. I'll get you a cup."

"Clayton, stop manhandling her and go get your file." Rachel flicked her fingers toward the door.

Assertive women. He was surrounded by them. But he wouldn't have it any other way. After Jenny's play, he'd take Sheridan aside and delve deeper into her assertion that she had to be the one to stop her father.

Right now they had to more pressing issues. Maria Korzakov had made her move now they would make theirs.

CHAPTER 15

Today had not gone at all as she'd planned. Clayton was not supposed to charge into Rachel's office, and Rachel wasn't supposed to turn into a bossy hen. The entire time Rachel and Clayton had been directing her life, she kept visualizing the news clipping that had been anonymously mailed to her years ago, *Local Private Detective Killed in Hit and Run.*

If Clayton or Rachel became another headline in her life, she'd never forgive herself. She lived with enough guilt already.

"All right, Laney. All zipped up." Sheridan patted her older sister's back. "You look very pretty." They'd curled her hair and added a little makeup to her face. She had a lot more of their mother's softer features. "Let's go downstairs and see if Jenny's ready."

Laney smiled. "She read her lines to me today. Just like you do sometimes."

"I'm sure you helped her a ton."

Laney beamed and headed down the stairs.

"Jenny." Sheridan hollered as she followed her sister, black heels in hand. "You ready?" Halfway to the kitchen, she heard a deep rumbling laugh—a man's laugh. She stomped into the kitchen. Ready to face off against the man who kept intruding into her personal space.

There Clayton sat, eyes twinkling with laughter. She'd never made him laugh like that. Never seen that glow about his face. She liked it. Wished she'd been the one to put it there. So of course, she went into annoyed mode, because she couldn't hope for happy moments. Not with her father still alive, holding mafia queen's jewels hostage. *The jerk!*

"What are you doing here, Clayton?"

"Good evening, Sheridan. You look real nice." He winked. "And who is this lovely lady beside you? Is that you Laney?"

"Yes, Clayton. It's me." Laney laughed. "Sheridan did my hair and she put on some makeup, but she hurt my eye so then she didn't do anymore."

"I've heard that eye makeup can be dangerous. At least that's what my Mom tells me."

"Your Mom?" Laney stared at him with wide eyes. "I have a mom too, but she's my foster mom."

"Jenny, can you and Laney go out to the car? I need to talk to Clayton for a minute."

"I want to sit by Clayton in the car, Sheridan," Laney said.

"If he rides with us, you can."

Laney frowned then took off toward the stairs, likely to hit the bathroom one more time before they left.

Jenny, however, didn't budge. "I invited Clayton, Sheridan, so leave him be. Besides I feel safer with him here."

Sheridan narrowed her eyes. Manipulation never sat well, but her sister used it to her advantage quite frequently. "That's fine. I only need to ask him a question, and we do need to get going. Don't want to be late."

Clayton's phone vibrated across the kitchen counter.

"Who keeps texting you?" Jenny arched a brow. "Your phone's been blowing up."

Clayton's cheeks actually turned a shade deeper than pink. "I'm required to have my phone on for work."

"Okay." Jenny picked up his phone and handed it to him. "Do you need to leave?"

"No. It's just a friend texting during her night out."

"Her?"

"Jenny." Sheridan glared at her sister even though she secretly wanted to know the answer too. "Clayton's friends are none of your business."

Clayton grinned. "Yes, the texts are from a girl who is a friend."

"Where are they?" Jenny kept digging.

"Chewy's in downtown Manchester."

Jenny nodded. "That's right. You're friends with all those football players."

"Yeah, my boss is dating Bronco Murray. He's the left guard on the Marauders' offensive line."

"I heard something in the news about the football player with the crazy girlfriend and how she went nuts at the Rec Center."

"She wasn't his girlfriend. But yeah, that was Jason. He's with Owen's sister, Maude."

"Who's Owen?"

Clayton laughed and shook his head. "Don't you follow your local football team?"

Jenny stuck out her tongue. "Sometimes."

His phone buzzed again.

Her sister jabbed his shoulder. "Is she going to text you all night?"

"Jenny, please. I need a minute with Clayton."

Laney came back down then, so Jenny took her out to the car. No arguments this time.

Clayton's phone buzzed again.

"If you're going to the play, you'll have to silence all that." Sheridan waved a hand at his phone. She braced a hand against the kitchen counter as she slipped on her shoes. "Didn't we decide not two hours ago that Scotty would be watching us at the play tonight?"

"As Jenny said, I was invited."

Sheridan sighed. "She likes you."

"She's smart." Clayton shrugged. "What's this mood tonight? I figured you'd come down and kick me out again."

"I'm feeling melancholy." Sheridan ran a finger across a picture of Jenny and Laney she'd posted on the fridge. "Yesterday, I went to Jenny's dress rehearsal. Saw her up on that stage, and I realized...she's not a baby anymore. Performing is what she was meant to do. She sings so beautifully." Sheridan tapped her nail against the photo. "Based on where we came from, I'm baffled at how she turned out so well."

"It doesn't baffle me, Slim." Clayton rose from his chair, crossed the room, and took her hand, caressing her knuckles with his thumb. "Her life and her singing gift has flourished because of you—your strength, your sacrifices, your hard work. She is up on that stage because you raised her to shine."

Sheridan enfolded his strong hand in her own, halting his light touch—a touch that had her on the edge of weeping. "Listen, about today—"

Clayton's phone buzzed.

"Seriously?"

"Sorry." Clayton glanced at his phone and, after opening the text, frowned.

"What is it?"

"Nothing."

"Work?"

"No."

"Constance?"

"Yes." Clayton shoved his phone in his pocket.

"I know this is ridiculous, but I find myself a bit irritated...or maybe...I don't know. Maybe I'm jealous." Sheridan laughed. "I've never drunk-texted a guy. I've only been to Chewy's maybe once. I don't go out much. Most people believe my personality is similar to my characters. As if I'm some femme fatale out every night hunting male prey."

"You go out to clubs when you're in California."

"My publicity staff sets those up." Sheridan shrugged and turned to grab a water bottle out of the fridge. "Everything in my life is carefully calculated."

"Not everything is calculated." Clayton turned her to face him, nudging her chin with his forefinger, his lips just above hers.

His phone buzzed in his pocket.

"Oh my gosh. What is her problem?" Irrationally irritated over her missed kiss, Sheridan eased back and dug into his pocket. "Give me your phone."

"I always knew you wanted in my pants." Clayton quirked a grin.

"I do *not* want in your pants." Sheridan rolled her eyes. "I want to send a text."

"I don't want a cat fight on my phone. I already broke one up earlier."

Sheridan bit back a smile. "I could totally take Rachel."

"I don't know. She's a scrapper."

"Maybe. But I could for sure take Constance, so you need to tell her to stop. I don't want anything interrupting my sister's moment."

"I've already asked her to stop."

"And what did she say?"

"She sent me a picture of her...um...chest."

"As if you haven't seen it already." Sheridan sipped from her water bottle, trying to stem the odd sensation coursing through her body. She'd claimed no rights, so why was her blood turning from red to pitch black? Or was the more accurate color—green? Portraying indifference took every ounce of her acting skills. Interesting. So, this was jealousy—thick and pulsing anger, firing through her like magma, calling on some until-now-undiscovered-warrior-instinct, that shouted, claim this man. A man looking very fine in his casual black pants, black jacket, and teal-blue shirt that made his eye-color pop. Of course, he'd dress to destroy any reservations a woman might have. Hers were dipping dangerously low at the moment. So low in fact that she stepped into his space and wrapped a hand around the back of his neck. "This is a big mistake, but right now I don't care." She angled her head and—

"Sheridan, will you come on!" Jenny shouted from the mudroom, which led into the garage.

"Give us a sec, Jenny." Clayton peered into Sheridan's eyes. "Are we finishing this?"

Sheridan blinked. "No. I'm sorry. I-I just…I don't know what came over me." She jerked back. "We need to go. Have you seen my phone?"

Clayton kept her in his arms. "Slim, kissing me is never a mistake. And you have no reason to be jealous of Constance. What she and I had ended years ago." Brushing her hair over her shoulder, he bent and kissed her cheek. "While you're in California, I want you to think about what we could be together. I know you've not had anyone you can rely on, but I won't let you down. I'll always be here for you." He kissed her other cheek and then held her tight for a moment before letting her go. "I'll meet you outside. We're taking my Expedition, and I believe Laney already called shot gun."

Sheridan watched him leave. Something he'd do again if he ever learned the truth. Once he knew who she really was. Like the painting of the literary figure Dorian Gray, so much lurked beneath the surface, so much she'd never allow him to see.

CHAPTER 16

Stages. Sheridan's life shifted from one stage to the next. Jenny's play which went exceptionally well, and her own movie, which didn't.

While on set, she'd allowed her mind and body to escape into another character, but in-between takes and at night, she balanced between holding strong to her convictions and bending to another's will. Should Clayton join her at this stage of her life? One surrounded by so much danger? Her mind said, no, but her heart said, yes. Maybe after her father was destroyed she could attempt a relationship with Clayton, but for now, she needed to keep him at a distance.

Not that her efforts had worked. The damn man checked in with her security guards every day. Called her every other day, and when she didn't answer, he had one of the men pin her down. No matter how hard she pushed, he hadn't budged. And that evoked so many unwelcome emotions.

Exhausted and grimy from the flight home, Sheridan couldn't wait to wash off the airplane germs. After that hose down, she planned on closing off from the world with a four-day slumber.

In the driver's seat, Scotty hummed a tune from a country song on the radio. They'd picked up a rental car, because Clayton hadn't been able to meet them due to being in court today.

"Glad to be home, Sheridan?" Scotty pulled into her garage.

"Yes, my own bed, my own pillows. I can't wait."

"I hear you. I'm just grateful for two garbage cans instead of having a mental breakdown when facing the fifty different recycling bins."

"I know. I was too scared to even attempt to throw away my stuff. I just had my assistant do it."

"I mean it's a good thing, but if you don't know the system…"

"True." She chuckled and got out of the car. She'd enjoyed Scotty's company. He was better than the other two very serious ex-military dudes she'd dealt with while in California. They took their jobs very seriously, which she appreciated when dealing with her sisters, but they'd rubbed her the wrong way more than once. "Thanks again for coming to California."

"Are you kidding? The whole movie set thing was cool. I enjoyed myself, so stop thanking me. Besides, I was getting paid." He tugged their suitcases from the trunk. "Crap."

His suitcase spilled open.

"Oh no. Your zipper must have broke. I told you not to stuff all those souvenirs in there."

Sheridan grabbed her bag and rolled it to the mudroom door.

An empty house awaited her, providing time to unpack her suitcase and lay out her sisters' gifts. A week ago, Jenny had returned early to start school and Laney had gone back to her job at Goodwill.

When Sheridan opened the door, she heard a clang that sounded a lot like kitchen pans banging together.

Someone was in her house.

With shaky hands, she stepped back into the garage and grabbed the .45 pistol stored in a tool cabinet. She glanced at Scotty, but he was on his knees picking up his clothes. Though, he'd probably ream her ass for it later, she crept past the running washing machine and peeked through the door.

A dark-haired man stood in front of the fridge, both sides wide open, perusing the contents as if he had every right to break into her home and steal her food.

How the hell had he got past her security?

Shoes were lined up on a rug by the door.

Tennis shoes and boots.

Men's shoes.

What?

Half her body remained shielded by the door's frame as she cocked back the gun's slide, which dropped a round in the chamber and interrupted the intruder's musings of her fridge. "I have a gun trained on your back. Turn around slowly. I've called the police." Sheridan leveled her weapon on the man while fishing her phone out of her front pocket.

Scotty barreled past her, gun raised. "Damn it, Sheridan. What the fuck are you doing?"

"It would be easier to rob you if you actually had something in this kitchen a man could eat." The intruder leaned against the open fridge but lifted his hands in the air. A cocky smile lit his face as his gaze travelled down her body.

She started to speak but a bolt of terror trickled down her spine as someone else plodded up the basement steps.

"Sheridan, get behind me," Scotty ordered.

The basement door shot open, banging against the wall.

She planted her feet, keeping both invaders in her sights.

"Sheridan, put the gun down." Exasperation traveled across the room with the familiar voice.

Lowering her weapon, Sheridan glared at the biggest intruder of all. "If you're going to crash here, tell your friends not to complain about the lack of edible fridge contents." Then she went straight for him, wrapping her arms and legs around him in a whole-body hug.

"Wait, Sher." Ryan LaSasso, her elusive cousin, steadied

them both, bracing his legs apart and squeezing her back. "Give me this weapon before you shoot yourself."

He took the gun, and after jostling her in his arms, unloaded it.

"Sheridan, who is this guy?" Scotty appeared at her side, tugging on her arm.

"Oh, I'm sorry. This is my cousin, Ryan." She met Scotty's annoyed gaze. "Ryan this is Scotty, my bodyguard."

"How in the hell did these guys get in here?"

Ryan lowered Sheridan to her feet. "It's what we do." He handed Scotty her gun. "Take this before she hurts someone."

"This is a serious breach." Scotty shoved her gun in his front pocket. "You almost got shot."

"Wouldn't be the first time." Ryan shrugged then bumped Sheridan's shoulder with his fist. "I find it interesting that in your texts, you never once mentioned a bodyguard. Tell me what's happening, Sher."

Sheridan ran a hand over his cheek. "You're awfully tan."

"That's what happens when you're deployed to deserts, and don't change the subject."

"Who's the gorilla by the fridge?" Sheridan avoided looking at Scotty again. His deep red hair was likely even redder due to the anger shooting out his skull.

"That's Joe." Ryan pointed at the fridge invader, who waved and began searching the cabinets. "Two others, Bob and Ed are crashing in the basement."

"As long as you're here, they can stay, too."

"We'll need more info on these guys before they can stay, Sheridan." Scotty braced both hands on his hips.

"He's right. Information would be nice." Brow furrowed, Ryan peered at her face. "Long summer, cuz?"

"Long summer." She nodded before resting her head against his shoulder.

#

Two hours and about six large pizzas later, Scotty and Joe were swapping insults over an Xbox game, so Sheridan decided to retreat to her room.

Ryan followed.

While organizing her laundry into piles, she chatted with Ryan. His presence severely out of place next to her rose-covered bedspread and pink pillows.

Danger exuded from his every pore. Massive, muscular frame—jet-black hair, light blue eyes. Eyes that had seen too much combat and bloodshed, but he'd never quit. Sometimes she wondered if he was staying in the military to atone for his father's sins.

"Sheridan, are you listening to me? The Korzakov family won't show any mercy. I'll stick around for as long as I can."

Her alarm panel chimed.

Ryan held up his phone. "It's Jenny." He showed a video feed of Jenny walking into the house.

"I don't know how you logged in without the security code, but I think you should teach me." She noted the time on his phone. "Is it that late already?" She carried a full basket to her door to take down later. "Jenny! I'm up here." Hoping to finish speaking before Jenny bounded up the stairs, she faced Ryan. "Thank you for agreeing to stay. With you here, Clayton and Scotty can take a break. Maybe you could pull some information from your mom about Jack's location. We give that to the Korzakov's and walk away." She huffed out a laugh. "I can hope for a speedy end to all this, but something tells me I haven't suffered enough."

"No more suffering." He shook his head. "Me and my guys got this. Your friends can step aside for now."

Her *friends* would do no such thing. Scotty had texted Clayton, but hadn't heard back yet. The trial must have run long.

"Ryan." Jenny softly spoke his name from the doorway before hustling in to give him a hug.

"Look at you, Peaches. You're almost as tall as Sheridan."

Growing up, Ryan and Sheridan were always off on adventures with little Jenny tagging along behind or trying to, anyway. As Jenny had grown, Sheridan noted that Ryan had gained hero status in her eyes. When he left to join the military, he'd broken Jenny's heart. They weren't true cousins since Jenny and Sheridan didn't share the same father. But Ryan had never seen Jenny as more than a sister, as far as she knew anyway. Good thing too, because he craved adventure while Jenny was a homebody.

"How long are you staying?" Jenny settled beside him on Sheridan's bed.

"We'll stay as long as you feed us." Ryan bumped her shoulder.

"Us?" Jenny shoved him back.

"My team's downstairs with Scotty." Ryan tugged on her long red hair. "Junior this year, right? How's school—" He tensed and shot off the bed.

Sheridan followed the direction of his narrow-eyed gaze.

Jenny's friend, Matt stood just outside the bedroom door.

"Hey, Jenny. I'm all done setting up in your room so—" Matt stopped once he saw Ryan's glare.

"Setting up in your room? What do you mean?" He looked at Jenny. "Room...as in bedroom?" Upon receiving no response, Ryan shook his head. "I don't think so."

"Ryan—" Sheridan reached for his arm.

"Ryan, this is Matt." Jenny jammed both hands on her hips. "We're working on a science project together."

"Work on your project in the kitchen. He doesn't need to study in your bedroom, unless he's studying your anatomy?"

"You're insane."

"I'm not." Jaw clenched, Ryan pointed at the door. "Set up

downstairs. Now."

Jenny faced off against him, cheeks bright red. "You think you can be gone for months, and then come back here and tell me what to do? I'm not a little girl anymore, and if I want a boy in my room, I'll have him."

Oh no. Sheridan caught the look in Ryan's eye as he stalked toward Matt, bumping the poor kid's shoulder before he turned in the direction of Jenny's room.

"Where are you going?" Jenny followed him out.

Matt shifted side-to-side in the doorway. "What was that about?"

Sheridan smiled before patting his shoulder. "Carry this downstairs for me, please." She hefted her laundry basket into his arms. "I'll come get you when it's safe."

Matt nodded and practically bolted toward the stairs.

Heading to Jenny's room, Sheridan's ears burned upon hearing a colorful assortment of words pouring from her sweet sister's mouth.

Ah, yes, home sweet home.

CHAPTER 17

At Excel gym the next morning, Sheridan dribbled down the basketball court. Side-stepping Ryan, she passed the ball to Ed. He went in then passed it back. She posted up for a three-pointer, but Ryan swatted her elbow.

Foul.

After scowling at her cousin, she lined up on the foul line and easily sank her two shots. "Eat that, cuz." She stuck out her tongue as she raced down the court.

On the other end, Sheridan maneuvered in front of Ryan, but he drove straight through her, knocked her on her ass, and made his shot.

Eyes narrowed, body covered in sweat, she raised her arms. "Help me up, jerk."

"Who's the star now, huh?" He grabbed her hands and pulled her up.

She used the momentum to keep going, knocking him onto the floor. Time to put her jujitsu to use.

"Sheridan, stop before you get hurt." Trying to prevent her from fully mounting him, Ryan wrapped his legs around her waist, keeping her in his guard.

She'd just executed a witch's elbow when strong arms grabbed around her middle and pulled her up and away.

Clayton shoved her behind him as he glowered at Ryan like an avenging angel in his white T-shirt and light blue gym shorts.

"No!" Sheridan jumped in front of Clayton and placed a hand against his chest. "Stop."

"Move Sheridan." Ryan spoke in a quiet undertone and rose to his feet.

Clayton clenched his hands into fists.

"He's my cousin," Sheridan blurted, wiping sweat from her brow. "Clayton listen, we practice martial arts on each other all the time. I'm all right."

"Ryan, hey buddy. Glad you're back." Elston popped up behind Clayton. Then he shifted in front of Ryan and began the introductions. "Ryan, this is Clayton Kincaid. I believe he thought you were being too rough with Sheridan." Elston turned to Clayton. "Kincaid, Ryan is her cousin. I'm sure she's mentioned him." When neither man shook hands, Elston continued. "They get in scrapes like this all the time. Sheridan can hold her own."

Clayton scowled at Ryan. "I know who he is. Scotty told me last night."

"Clayton, let's go." Sheridan tugged on his hand.

He glanced at her, and then his gaze went to their joined hands. With a final glare at Ryan, he walked away, towing her along.

"Sheridan," Ryan yelled. "I had you."

She didn't turn, but raised her free hand and gave him a middle finger salute.

Outside with Clayton, she tried breathing in the cool fall air, but the heat emanating off his body, stifled any hope of catching her breath. He hadn't said a word in greeting.

Rude.

They reached her SUV and she started to speak, but he grabbed her shoulders and pressed her against the passenger door. He fisted a hand in her hair, bent, and kissed her.

No quarter. Pure adrenaline.

Not one to back down, she returned his vigor. After the tense moment on the court, she needed to blow off steam. Although, this kiss only created more.

He slanted his mouth over hers.

The next day's headlines would read, *Sheridan Bennett found in a puddle outside an Ohio gym.*

She ran both hands up his arms, which were slick with sweat. Clutching his shoulders, she held on for all she was worth. Visions of sliding her slick skin all over his rushed through her mind and further heated her body.

He moved his hands up her sides to just under her breasts.

His touch was exactly what she needed after being away for months. Why not revel in the heat of their bodies for a moment? Enjoy the delicious tangle of tongues and the closeness of their bodies? All of Sheridan's reasons for physical distance were erased now that he kissed her as if he had every right to ravage her, own her, and destroy every barrier while standing in the middle of a public parking lot.

Clayton reared back, breathing heavily but keeping his hands on her body, resting his forehead against hers. "He was hurting you." He combed his fingers through her hair.

"No." She shivered and fought back the need to lean into his touch. This moment was so right and so wrong at the same time. Where was her willpower? All the resolutions she'd made while being gone had melted with his kisses.

He wrapped his arms around her and rocked back and forth. "I missed you, Slim."

At his words, something shifted deep inside her, an unfurling of her heart, maybe even her soul, but no, she had to shut down this moment. Pull out of the scene before it got too intimate. Lust was one thing, intimacy quite another. And love...love was a dream. But wasn't she already floating, dreaming of a life she could never have? None of this was fair to Clayton.

Clayton loosened his hold before kissing her again. Softer.

Light brushes, one right after another before nudging her mouth open. Using his hand to cradle her face, he ramped up the intensity most generally reserved for the bedroom.

Hopefully no "paps" lurked in the parking lot, hiding behind vehicles or carefully landscaped bushes. If they caught a snapshot of this kiss, it'd likely burn the lens—and any chance of Clayton having any privacy.

That thought had Sheridan pulling away—mentally and physically. The realities of her life scraped raw against her heart, and that pain helped her remember who she was and the danger she presented to this man. Placing a hand against his chest, she eased away. "I probably taste like basketball ass."

"Basketball ass?" Clayton laughed and ran his hand through his semi-sweaty hair.

"I have gum in my vehicle, but the bad news is, I have no keys." She upended the pockets of her shorts.

"I have my keys, but no gum." Clayton jingled his keys between them.

Jeers and shouts came from the front of the building. Ryan and his gorilla pals were leaving with Elston. He glanced over and gave them a friendly wave.

"Elston, hold up a sec." Sheridan waved him down, seeing her chance to escape.

Her trainer made a visor with his hand, peering at her then leaning against his hybrid Honda.

"I need to talk to Elston about our training schedule, Clayton. I'll chat with you later."

Clayton clutched her elbow. "We need to talk about your security schedule. Elston can wait."

Out of habit, she scanned the parking lot. Her gaze passed by a van then a spark of recognition brought her attention back. "Oh, no."

Definitely the same van and for sure the same blond creep behind the wheel. In her line of work, she dealt with obsessive fans, but this weirdo seemed different. Although, the more she studied his features in the daylight, the more she couldn't help but think she'd seen him before.

He smiled and nodded. His attempt at a hello came across as, I'll-eat-your-beating-heart-while-drinking-Mountain-Dew.

"Clayton." She tapped his arm. "Do you see—"

"Yes." Clayton shoved her behind him and started walking backwards. "Keep moving."

Quickly pulling his cell from his shorts' pocket, he snapped a picture of the van as it left the parking lot. "I got the plates." He pressed a few buttons on his phone then pressed it against his ear. "Lieutenant O'Malley, the blond of interest in Sheridan's case just left the parking lot of Excel gym. He turned right onto Westchester Street in a white, full-sized Chevy van with the plates, VHY 781. I'm taking Sheridan home…yes…yes…okay, that'll work, sir."

He hung up, skimmed the lot, and then practically dragged her to his Expedition.

"Clayton." She gazed at his very intense face. "My cousin and his friends are staying with me. I'm safe with them."

He opened his vehicle's passenger door and pressed on her head like she was some criminal being forced into the back of a police cruiser.

"Clayton, did you hear what I said?"

"Let me think for a second, please." He banged his fist against the top of the Expedition. "Damn it. I have to be in court again today. I'll take you home and send Scotty over."

"I told you my cousin is staying with me."

"I don't like him."

Sheridan blinked then huffed out a laugh. "That's a ridiculous thing to say. He's likely more trained than you."

"He may be more trained, but he isn't me. There's a difference."

"Did you get hit on the head or something?"

"Woman." His jaw clenched. "This is serious. You're home for five seconds and van guy already knew where to find you."

She folded her shaky hands in her lap. "I'll agree his appearance is troublesome."

Clayton rubbed his temples. "Troublesome? *You* are troublesome. That guy is something else."

"I know." Secured movie sets were over. Real danger existed on these streets. Every time she stepped out of the house, she needed to prepare for the worst.

Heaving a sigh, Clayton crouched beside her. "I'm sorry you have to deal with this the second you get home. I'd hoped that we…not hoped, we *will* come to terms. Very soon. But right now, I'm taking you home and you'll listen to how things will be until we have this blond guy and your father under wraps. You got me?" He tilted her chin his way.

"One, let go of my chin. Two, the whole 'we will come to terms' is so over the top, I don't even know how to address it. And three, what about me screams frightened maiden to you?" Sheridan faced the window. "My cousin is here. My family. So, as I said, Ryan has my safety covered."

Clayton blew out a long breath. "I get the family thing. And yeah, I'm coming on strong, but you need someone in your corner."

"What I need is for you to back off."

"I can't and won't." He leaned closer. "Did you ever stop to consider that maybe I feel the same way you do? Maybe I've seen people die for a fuck-all reasons. When I was a Ranger *and* when I was a cop. We both want the same thing. I'm just looking a little further ahead than you."

"You think I don't wish I could see freaking rainbows and kittens in the sky? That I don't wish I could have you in my life? I do, okay? Does that make you happy? I *do* want you in my life, but I've never gotten what I want. Not without a price. And sometimes that price is too steep. So, I'll wait, and yeah, maybe if we both survive we can do something, but my bet is on you walking away."

"I suggest you don't toss in your chips just yet." Clayton trailed a finger along her jawline. "How about we start over? I'll say I'm glad you're back, and you say, why thank you."

Sheridan looked into his aqua eyes. "You scare me in so many ways."

"You scare me, too."

"I have to do what I feel is right." Even though what felt right was dragging his butt on top of her and kissing him senseless.

"So, do I." He kissed her cheek.

"I guess my three months of living in a different world is over."

"Yeah, Slim, it is."

Shaking her head, she gasped as an unwelcome thought crashed through her mind. The blond man had seen her kissing Clayton.

If psycho stalker was working with her father and reported back to him, then he would use this information against her.

Suddenly nauseous, she closed her eyes and leaned against the cool leather seat. If anything happened to Clayton, she'd never forgive herself, because though she'd fought against it, she'd missed him, too.

CHAPTER 18

Clayton studied the rain pounding against his office window. A red leaf was plastered against the screen. On this chilly late-October afternoon, he felt for the leaf, as he couldn't move either. After dropping Sheridan at home, he'd headed downtown to give his testimony. Then he'd stopped by the office to discuss his schedule with Rachel now that Sheridan was back. *Wrong move.* He should've just driven straight past when he'd seen the dark sedan in the office parking lot.

With his sleeve, he wiped a smudge off his cell phone's screen before shifting his attention back to the man seated in front of his desk.

"That whole time Sheridan was in California, Jack didn't contact her once?" Agent Denver emptied a sugar packet into his coffee. "I find that hard to believe."

"He was injured at the police fundraiser. I assume he spent some time recuperating. Not to mention hiding from Maria Korzakov and her men."

"You've seen Sheridan since she's been back. Everything proceeding there?"

Clayton rested his elbows on his desk. Using the word, "proceeding" might be pushing the truth a bit. Denver didn't need to know about his personal relationship with Sheridan. He'd promised intel on the case, not his love life.

"An unknown blond man, likely the same one who assisted her father's escape from the fundraiser, watched her outside the health club's parking lot this morning. He was also outside her aunt's restaurant before Sheridan left to film her movie." Clayton pulled the file he'd prepared from his side drawer and slid it across his desk. "Here's the van's info. As you can see, the vehicle was stolen. Use that to bring him in for questioning."

Denver nodded. "We have information that Bennett is working with a younger man."

"Any idea who he is?"

"Not at this time." Denver cleared his throat. "We know two of Korzakov's men are in the area, asking questions. We've got eyes on their every move."

"And I assume you're keeping an eye on Sheridan too, right?"

"We do what we can."

"Not a reassuring answer."

"You're providing personal security, and her cousin's back in town." Denver sipped his coffee. "You know he's—"

"Army Delta Force. Yes, I know." A text popped up on his phone from his mother. He was due to attend his father's annual birthday party this weekend. How that would work was beyond him. Not when he was in the middle of this case. He flipped his phone over. "You say Korzakov's men are in town. I want photos. We need information in order to do our job. We agreed on sharing information. So get me what I need."

"I'll email what we have later." Denver stood and finished his coffee. At the door, he tossed his empty cup into the trash and glanced over his shoulder. "In the meantime, just keep doing what you're doing. Bennett will contact Sheridan again. I'll notify you of any information we find on this blond man." Agent Denver tapped the yellow folder against his palm, nodding at Clayton on his way out. "I'll be in touch."

Clayton rubbed both hands over his eyes. "That was an absolute waste of time."

Denver had an agenda that in no way matched his own. Likely the man hoped to bring down the Korzakov clan using Jack Bennett. And he certainly wasn't overly concerned with Sheridan's safety. In fact, Denver would happily use Sheridan as bait, tossing her into a pond full of starving piranhas.

Because of this, a trickle of unease slid down Clayton's spine. Working with the FBI without her knowledge might bring a real end to the trust they were building.

Why was she so opposed to working with the FBI? She seemed to trust O'Malley and he was in law enforcement. Had Denver done something to her? Maybe the agent had come on too strong. Clayton knew more than anyone how Sheridan reacted to that. He chuckled. She sure loved pushing him away, but this morning she'd kissed him as if she'd actually missed him.

Eventually she'd discover his dealings with the FBI, but she'd have to get over any feelings of betrayal, because her well being was paramount.

That being said, he would have to pool his resources with her cousin, Ryan. The stakes were too high not to bring all the players together, even if it happened without Ms. Bennett's knowledge.

"Daydreaming, Kincaid?" Leaning against his open doorway, Rachel arched a brow.

"I need you to speak to Sheridan."

"She's back?"

"Yeah, today." He proceeded to tell Rachel about the morning's events. "She won't listen to me, but for some reason, she listens to you and since she has a madman hovering, I think she needs to understand some things."

"Which are?"

"Too many to count."

"She's tougher than you think."

"No one's tough against a Russian mafia."

"True." Rachel tapped her index finger against her bottom lip. "Call her yourself. Work your charm and bring her around to understand she's only safe with a big bad man protecting her."

"Don't start that equality shit, Harris. She's in danger. That is a fact." He stood, and then jabbed a finger against his desk. "Do I think she can handle herself? Yes, but having backup never hurts. I would've thought you'd learned your lesson after all that went down with Bronco's family."

"Wow. A little oversensitive, aren't we?" Rachel narrowed her eyes. "We already had this discussion."

"What discussion?"

"Don't think I don't see that star struck gleam in your eye."

"If you're not going to be helpful, then leave." He waved a hand toward the door.

"Touchy." She tisked. "Clayton, she's a movie star. *You* are a private detective. What are you thinking?"

"I'm thinking I've got shit to do. So take the lecture elsewhere."

"Fine, I'll call her. And I'll support whatever it is you think you're doing with Ms. Hollywood. But dude, I said it before and I'll say it again, think about what this means for you."

Clayton met her gaze and nodded. "I have, and she's what I want." That said, he brushed past her out of his office.

Throughout his life, he'd followed orders, fell in line, and obeyed the law. For once, he wanted something forbidden. Something blonde, brave, and beautiful. Plus, regardless of Sheridan's occupation, she still needed love and a sense of security. He would gladly give her both.

CHAPTER 19

Shivering in her raincoat outside the shooting range, Sheridan dug through her purse for her phone. "Hold up a second. It's too dark, and I can't find my phone. I want to add chocolate milk to my grocery list."

"I'll pay for everything." Ryan stopped beside her.

"You will not." Sheridan glanced up from typing ingredients for tonight's dinner into her Notes app. "You're my guest."

"No arguments." He heaved a sigh. "Let's move. I'm not keen on standing in the middle of this parking lot like sitting ducks."

"We have an entire arsenal in this bag." She patted the range bag hanging off her shoulder. "Plus, I'm sure you have weapons stowed under your clothes." Sheridan flicked a hand in his direction. "Besides you're the one who looks like a creeper, wearing that black hat, the black jeans, and your...surprise, surprise long sleeve *black* shirt. Do you have any other colors in your wardrobe besides green, brown, and black? She nudged his shoulder, and then because Clayton had her all anxious, she searched the parking lot.

Down the row bright lights flicked on and an engine revved from a van—*the* van.

She lifted a hand against the glare of the headlights now

pointing directly at her. "This guy's really starting to irritate me." Sheridan dug her .45 out of the bag then grabbed Ryan's arm. "Keep walking."

Ryan's bicep tensed, and he removed his gun from his shoulder holster. "What is it?"

"Over there. No, don't look. I've seen that van three times now."

Ryan halted in the middle of the gravel lot. "Three times? And you're just telling me this now?" Ryan handed over his gun bag. "Hold this. I'll go see what they want."

"Ryan, wait!" Heart pounding, she tightened her grip on his arm. "Don't."

The engine revved again.

Rocks whipped out from under the back tires as blond guy hit the gas and made a beeline straight for them.

"Ryan, get out of the way." Sheridan tried yanking him behind a parked truck, but he didn't budge.

"Move." Using his free hand, her cousin shoved her shoulder.

Sheridan hit the ground but quickly rolled to her feet. "Ryan!"

Her cousin ducked out of the way just in time, landing on his hands and knees.

The van careened onto the road, barely missing an on-coming vehicle before turning onto a side road.

"Ryan." Sheridan shot forward and slid to his side. "Are you okay?"

"I'm fine. You good?" Sitting on his butt, Ryan brushed gravel from his knees.

"We need to talk to O'Malley." Sheridan winced as she pulled a small pebble from her hand. "Clayton was with me this morning when that creep appeared. He's looking into the van's owner."

Ryan grabbed her by her shoulders. "What do you mean

Kincaid's looking into it? Why didn't you tell me?"

"I'm sorry. I just thought van guy was a stalker or someone taking tabloid pictures."

"You just thought... " Ryan shook his head and got to his feet. "What's going on here, Sheridan? Why are you holding back information?"

"Weird stalkers do happen." Sheridan huffed. "They usually go away. Today was the...uh...first time he acted aggressively." Based on Ryan's frown she thought it best not to mention the kid had slashed her tires. Especially since the event occurred at his mother's restaurant.

"Next time...even if a guy is looking at you funny...tell me." After giving his directive, he picked up their gun cases, stormed over to her vehicle, and threw everything into the back seat.

Sheridan hopped to her feet and joined him. He did have every right to be irritated. They'd never had secrets from each other. Although, she did have one secret she'd never shared with anyone. A take-to-her-grave secret. But what if she told someone? What if she trusted someone enough to share that burden? Would they understand her choice or condemn her for it?

Only one person came to mind when she thought of sharing secrets. And that man would go ballistic once he discovered van guy had tried to make them road kill. Not only had they left Scotty at the house, but they'd also left with only each other. Clayton wanted two people guarding her at all times. Perhaps he'd give her a break since she'd been honing her shooting skills—ah, no, not likely.

"Earth to space cadet." Ryan stuck out his hand. "Keys."

Sheridan narrowed her eyes but handed over her keys and walked to the passenger side. Now was not the time to argue because her cousin's anger stemmed from worry about her safety and perhaps wounded feelings since she hadn't asked for help.

One thing she knew for sure though, was that van guy would require lots of help and very soon. Attempting to run down her family in parking lots deserved an extra load of payback. She should have blown out each of the van's tire then leveled her gun at the man who'd dared to hurt her cousin.

What kind of idiot tried to run people down outside of a shooting range? The desperate to scare her kind, most likely. His appearance twice in one day showed a level of bravado that frightened her a little. Why did this kid believe he wouldn't get caught? What lies was her father selling now? And why was this poor kid buying?

# # #

Clayton knocked on Lieutenant O'Malley's door after the man had called and asked him to join a discussion regarding the van guy. Events had apparently escalated at the shooting range this afternoon.

Mrs. O'Malley opened the door. A plump, cheery woman with a bundle of short, curly gray hair on her head. She wore jeans and a maroon sweatshirt with fall leaves embroidered on the front. "Clayton, come right in. So glad you could make it."

He followed her down the hall past the living room to the kitchen.

"The boys are in Patrick's office." She motioned toward a room off the kitchen.

The smell of fried chicken filled the air. Sheridan's blonde head was bent over a frying pan. Her hands were covered in a white sticky substance.

"Hello Clayton." She smiled and then wiggled her fingers. "If you're planning to lecture me, just remember I have chicken goo on my fingers."

Lecturing wasn't what he wanted to do. More like grab her and lock her away until all threats were vanquished. Seeing her hale and whole eased the twitchy feeling he'd had since O'Malley's call. He cupped her face in his hands, which forced her to meet his gaze.

She held her flour-covered hands at her sides.

"You all right?" He searched her blue eyes for distress.

"He almost ran over Ryan, not me."

Unable to stop himself, Clayton lightly kissed her.

Sheridan stiffened then glanced at Mrs. O'Malley.

He brushed his thumb across her bottom lip, regaining her attention. "Your stalker made a mistake today. He tried to hurt my girl." He bent and kissed her forehead.

She rolled her eyes. "I'm not your girl. And I just said Ryan was in danger, not me."

"You were there, so same thing. An issue we'll discuss tonight."

"I don't know what you mean." She lowered her gaze.

"Bravo, Ms. Bennett." Clayton clapped. "An actress performing the not-guilty face. I'm not convinced, so save that look for some court-room drama." He pinched her chin between his forefinger and thumb then faced Mrs. O'Malley who watched them with a beaming smile.

Sheridan sniffed, and then wrinkled her nose. "I expect to be filled in on your discussion."

"And I expect you to have two people with you at all times. I expect you to be a lot more careful." Clenching his jaw against a wish to continue his lecture, he sighed then raked his fingers through his hair. "Listen, I know you're strong, but you need someone to help carry the weight. You and your cousin need to stick to my plan. He's on my shit list too. What is it about your family that thinks you can handle everything alone? Frankly, you're both complete idiots and neither of you are taking these threats seriously."

"He didn't know about the van guy." Sheridan sighed and turned toward the sink. "So, take your anger out on me and leave him alone."

He studied her blonde head. Maybe she *was* starting to see

that her inability to share affected others. He'd discuss the issue with Ryan and leave her be—for now. Hoping to lighten the mood, he winked at Mrs. O'Malley, and then swatted Sheridan's behind. "Get busy fixing my dinner, woman. I'll be back in a bit."

"Watch yourself." Mrs. O'Malley shook her potato peeler at him. "That's my girl you're manhandling."

He responded by kissing her cheek. "I've got kisses for you, too."

Blushing, the older woman swatted at his chest. "You're awfully free with your sugar, handsome." She pointed down the hall. "Go on with the boys now."

# # #

Clayton gripped the top of the doorjamb, waiting while the Lieutenant spoke on the phone. The man's metal desk was likely a remnant from the police station, battle scarred with a large dent in the side. The scent of strong black coffee lingered in the air. Perhaps it emanated from that old desk, either way he could sure use a cup.

Ryan lounged in a metal-framed chair in front of the desk. The chair also seemed a police station remnant, probably from an interrogation room. Quite appropriate for its occupant.

Ryan turned and acknowledged his presence with a nod.

"You left her vulnerable today." Clayton crossed both arms over his chest.

"No, leaving me out of the loop is what put her in danger."

"Exactly. She *was* in danger. Two men at all times." Since any fight they had would likely result in a major home renovation for the O'Malley's, Clayton took a deep breath and tried to tone down the red haze in his vision. "If you're not going to protect her, then step aside."

O'Malley cleared his throat. "You two need to work together not be at each other's throats. Grow up." Running a hand through the short grey stubble that lingered on his head, O'Malley tapped a pen against his desk. "They're running the van's plates now."

"No need," Clayton said. "The plates were registered to a woman who recently died. The suspect must have stolen them from her home once he saw her obituary in the paper." Reaching into his back pocket for the rolled up report he'd prepared, he handed the papers to O'Malley. "This is his second set of plates. The first was from a sixteen-year old kid's new car. Our van guy is updating his plates to avoid being pulled over."

Clayton turned to Ryan while O'Malley perused the report. "Do you think you could describe him to a sketch artist?"

"Yes." Ryan remained facing forward.

"Head down to the station, Ryan." O'Malley sat back and rested his folded hands on his belly. "Sheridan thinks she can go after this kid herself, and I sure as hell can't trust her not to."

Nodding, Ryan straightened. "My men and I will sweep her home and the surrounding area for any surveillance. Though, her father or whoever could have found a way to tap into her system."

"I can keep her occupied." Clayton considered his next move. The big one—Sheridan meeting his family. "My father's seventieth birthday celebration is tomorrow night. I'll take her with me." Since he hadn't mentioned his association with a famous actress to his family yet, he knew they were in for quite a shock.

"Who will keep her safe from you?" Ryan stood and faced him.

"I'm not the one who almost got her killed today."

"You know nothing about her."

"I know not to jeopardize her safety, unlike you who—"

"Boys, that's enough." O'Malley rounded his desk and clapped Ryan on the shoulder. "Clayton's intentions toward Sheridan are honorable. Isn't that correct?"

"My intentions are my own business." Clayton kept his gaze locked on Ryan.

"Where is this family gathering?" Ryan's eyes narrowed.

"What family gathering?" Sheridan asked from behind Clayton.

He stepped aside before she thundered past him. This should be interesting. So far, dictating her movements hadn't gone over well.

"Clayton is sticking close to you for a couple days while we look into this…matter. You'll be attending a family event with him." O'Malley braced both hands on his hips. "After we eat, you and Ryan will go to the precinct to work with a sketch artist."

Sheridan's brow furrowed. "But I—"

"No arguments." O'Malley lifted a finger. "You asked for my help, and I'm giving it to you."

"What about his family's safety? I can't lead this psycho there."

O'Malley arched a bushy brow. "Sheridan, what about no arguments did you not understand?"

With a very loud growl, she left the room, but halfway down the hall she yelled, "Dinner's ready. Although, I should have poisoned everything."

"Well, that went better than I thought." Clayton chuckled and met O'Malley's gaze. "Maybe I should take some lessons before I leave."

"She's a brave one. Been to hell and back too many times already. Take care of my girl, or you'll answer to me." Emphasizing his point with a stern glare, he waited until Clayton nodded to continue. "Now, apparently the ladies have fixed us quite a nice dinner, so let's go enjoy it."

He trailed on down the hall, leaving Clayton with Ryan.

"Sheridan and I don't need you. But I never know when I'll have to leave on my next mission." Ryan clasped his hands behind his back. "My cousin has good reason to be leery of men. Plus, you're all about rules and regulations. Sheridan's an artist. She lives in different worlds. You'll stifle her."

"You don't know me, and I don't need your permission."

Ryan huffed out a laugh. "Yeah, you kinda do. And you sure as hell need hers. I'll be shocked as hell if she gives it to you. There's a lot to Sheridan you can't see, and until you see it all, you don't know her." He cracked his knuckles. "If she ever tells you the truth, I suggest you man-up because you walk away at that point...well, let's just say, I won't need anyone's *permission* to kick your ass." Walking past, he bumped Clayton's shoulder with his own. "She's all the family I got."

"What about Laney and Jenny?"

"Jenny's not blood."

"How's that?"

"Jenny has a different father. If you don't even know that, you're so far off course, I don't know why I'm worrying." Shaking his head, Ryan headed for the kitchen.

Hell yeah, Clayton was off course. Had been since the movie star had showed up unannounced at Rachel's book signing months ago. Not that he'd change anything. Still, a sense of unease lingered as he considered Ryan's words. What could possibly be so bad he'd walk away?

Even with every warning bell ringing to beware, for her sake and his own, he couldn't stop the inevitable. They'd likely crash and burn many times before they reached the end. But right now, he needed to make sure they stayed alive long enough to experience all those ups and downs.

Speaking of staying alive, he'd have to call his mother and notify her of an extra guest. How would his family react to a famous actress in their midst?

He chuckled and headed for the kitchen to a meal that may or may not be poisoned by now.

CHAPTER 20

"What is the point of my attending this party again?" Sheridan smoothed a hand over her sapphire blue cocktail dress, the sleeves were lace and the high neckline was ruffled. The pleated dress had an elastic waist and landed just above her knees. Swinging her legs onto the floor of the Expedition's passenger seat, she tucked her blue clutch at her side.

Clayton leaned over her, clicking her seatbelt into place.

"I'm not two. I can lock in my own belt."

He grinned. "The point of this party is to keep you occupied and out of trouble."

As if she could stay out of trouble, he had met her, right? She refrained from rolling her eyes and flicked a hand over his black dress pants, white shirt, and light blue tie. "It probably took you all of what, fifteen minutes to get ready and you come out here looking like that? Should be against the law or something."

"Complimenting my looks, Slim?" He traced a finger down the side of her neck.

She did roll her eyes this time. "You're gorgeous. Don't act like you don't know this."

"As you like to remind me, it's just a face." He patted her cheek. "Speaking of looking good, I like it when you wear your hair down."

His voice rumbled across her nerves, firing synapses in the wrong direction—straight down.

"All that light blonde hair framing that beautiful face." He pulled her close for a long, slow kiss.

She pressed a hand against his chest. "Clayton, what are you doing?"

"Kissing you." He gave her a quick peck. "We were due."

"Due for what?" She grinned despite the fact her smile would only encourage the man.

"You look very nice, too. I like that dress. It enhances your...figure."

He turned on his heel and rounded the front of the Expedition before hopping into the driver's seat.

Sheridan frowned. "This dress is tame compared to the ones I've squeezed into for red carpet events. It doesn't enhance anything. Besides, I thought I was too skinny?"

"Why would you say that?"

"Because you always call me Slim."

Clayton faced her. "You are very slim and yet, in some areas, you're filled out quite nicely." He ran a finger along her side, brushing against her breast.

Gasping, she squirmed and slapped away his hand. "Both hands on the wheel."

"Sorry."

"No, you're not." She crossed both arms over her chest before she begged him to touch her again. His constant presence was starting to affect her in naughty ways, which made this little "date" a big mistake and an even bigger mistake was meeting his family. They were probably nice people, and here she was leading a band of psycho's to the birthday party. "Me attending your father's shin-dig is completely stupid."

"A point you've made clear all day." Clayton turned on the truck and headed down her drive.

"And did you listen?" Sheridan jabbed his shoulder. "No,

135

you did not. I honestly think you wanted me to meet your parents, and you're using this excuse to get what you want."

"You'll like my parents." Clayton stopped and waited for the wrought-iron security gate to open. "Is there any music you would like to listen to?"

"No, I don't want to listen to music. No, I don't want to meet your parents. I'd rather be at home where I'm safe."

"Safe from what? Meeting people who are important to me? Standing by my side for the evening? Facing what you and I could have together if you weren't so stubborn?"

"I'm sorry if I don't equate my being stubborn with keeping you safe." She stared out the window, tired of arguing her point. This whole idea was insane, but as she'd prepared for the evening, she considered how Clayton would feel attending a family event without his brother. That thought was the only reason she was sitting beside him now.

Clayton was quiet for a while, driving to the country club on the Northwest corner of Manchester. His family had rented out the main room for the evening. This birthday celebration was an annual event that the Kincaid's used to gather family and friends.

"It's okay to be nervous about meeting my parents, Sheridan."

"Word will get out about us after tonight. News stories will pop up everywhere. Plus, your family will wonder what we're doing. Questions always arise when I spend an evening with a male friend."

"But I'm more than a friend." Winking, he squeezed her knee.

How could he be so adorable and she wanted to choke him at the same time? "Meeting your parents means something to you, and I'm not sure I like the direction of your thoughts. I told you I'm not the right girl for you. I'm headed to a country club for fuck's sake. What am I supposed to say when your Mom asks about my family? About where I grew up?" Sheridan shook her head. "We lived in a run-down brick building with cracked concrete sidewalks. The only green in my neighborhood was wrapped up in a one-hitter."

Clayton turned his Expedition into the country club's parking lot. "Sheridan you've been to parties a lot more glamorous than this one."

"But this is different."

"Why?" He navigated into a spot close to the building.

"Because this is where I'm from. I don't have to be the real me at those parties, but here, I can't escape who I am."

"Then why stay here? Why not move away?"

"Because I don't run." Sheridan clenched her hands into fists. "And I didn't want to move away from Laney or raise Jenny someplace else."

"That says it all." Clayton brought her hand to his lips and kissed it. "Don't you see how beautiful you are on the inside? How far you've come from your past? You did it all by yourself. You're an amazing woman, Sheridan Bennett. I'm proud to introduce you to my parents. So, tonight, for one night only, how about you step out of your world and step into mine."

Sheridan swallowed the lump in her throat. "Have I mentioned how much you scare me?"

"Yeah, you have." He answered in a soft voice. "But you're fearless, remember? And for as long as you'll let me, I'll make sure you stay that way."

"How about you ease those fears by leaving me alone? You go. Poof. Fear gone."

"Is that what you really want?"

Sheridan stared at the white building that looked like it belonged on a plantation in the south rather than northern Ohio. Pillars lined the front porch. Vibrant mums planted along the landscaping added a splash of color. Long windows made visible the people milling about inside.

"What I really want? Good question, Clayton." Sheridan

blinked back the tears forming in her eyes. "I used to know. My whole life was focused on keeping my family safe…and now with you…with you, I want time to stop spinning. I want that country club to be empty. I want to close my eyes and slow dance with you. I want to feel your heartbeat as you hold me tight. I want to tell you so many things. *Those* are the things I really want. But regardless of how far you think I've come, I'm still stuck in that red brick apartment, cold and lonely, the walls closing in, death imminent, because I'm cursed. Jack Bennett is my father, and until he's gone, I can't want anything."

Clayton cupped her cheek in his hand. "Even for one night?"

Sheridan met his gaze. "You don't know when to stop pushing, do you? I rip open my chest, reveal my heart, and still you want more. So fine, tonight, I'll try. For you."

"I'm trying for you, too. Every day, not just tonight."

"Don't do that. Don't hope for more." She cursed the tears trickling down her cheeks. "I can only give you one night."

"All right, Sheridan." Clayton brushed a tear off her cheek then kissed her forehead. He pulled back and smiled, but she knew the grin was forced, as it didn't reach his eyes.

She'd hurt him. But didn't he understand that she hurt, too? He was whole. And she simply wasn't. After tonight, she'd have more memories she'd have to bury in her heart right beside all the nightmares that kept her chained, broken, and alone.

# # #

"Clayton, I see you made good time." A tall dark-haired man approached seconds after she and Clayton entered the building. The man, likely his father, greeted his son with a slap on the back.

Sheridan's heart went from slight trot to full gallop as if trying to jump through her ribs and escape the situation. *Sorry, pal. You and I are stuck, so calm down.* She plastered on a smile and decided she'd pretend this was another part. A meet-the-parents-slapstick-comedy that didn't end with bad reviews—or death. She could fake it. She was a professional, after all.

"Dad, I want you to meet someone." Clayton placed a hand at the small of her back. "Sheridan, this is my father, Campbell Kincaid. Dad this is Sheridan Bennett."

"Nice to meet you." Mr. Kincaid held out his hand. "Glad you could join us."

"Happy Birthday." Sheridan shook his hand. He had a firm grip and a familiar smile.

"Katie, dear." He waved at someone behind her. "Come and meet Clayton's new girl."

New girl? Fantastic.

Clayton didn't disagree with his father's words either. *Great.*

And now, the Mom. Weren't they supposed to be the worst? Evil mother-in-law's and all that? But as Clayton's mom joined her husband, Sheridan only saw a woman with kind eyes—the same beautiful shade as her sons, and a welcoming smile. Her dress was a soft mauve topped with a set of pearls. Her hair was a bit lighter than Clayton's but nicely styled in a short, curly bob.

"Sheridan, it's so nice to meet you." Katie grasped both of Sheridan's hands, lifting them out to the side, while looking her over. "Clayton has told me so much about you."

"Hey, what's going on out here?" A young man bumped into Clayton's side.

"Introductions." Clayton settled an arm around Sheridan's shoulders. "Sheridan. This is Tate, my cousin."

"Nice to meet you, Tate." Sheridan bit back a grin as Tate stared at her with dropped jaw and wide eyes.

"I-I don't believe it." He swallowed visibly. "I thought he was bullshitting me."

"Tate!" Katie swatted his arm. "Language."

"Sorry, it's just she is…Do you know? I mean, you realize who she is, right?"

"Yes, I know who she is." Mrs. Kincaid made a shooing

motion with her hands. "Go back inside now that you've embarrassed our guest."

Sheridan shrugged. "It's okay."

"I'm looking forward to speaking with you more, Sheridan. Please step inside. We'll join you as soon as we've greeted all the guests." Clayton's mom lightly squeezed her hand. "If Tate gives you any trouble, you come see me." She winked. "Oh, my! Camille just arrived." Katie ran her pearls through her fingers. "Well...I should probably say hello." She cleared her throat. "Clayton..." His mom sent him a look that Sheridan couldn't read. "You'll say hello, won't you."

"I will, Mom."

Sheridan turned to see why Camille's arrival had caused such a change in Clayton's tone.

Ah...Constance. The blonde stood next to an older woman who must be Camille as Clayton's mother greeted her with a hug.

"Sorry about that." Clayton clasped Sheridan's shoulder, turning her to face him.

"About what?" She furrowed her brow. Was he speaking of Tate's shock or Constance's appearance? Her head was still spinning from the introductions, and her heart had yet to break its hopes at winning the marathon.

"I should have told you Constance would be here with her family."

"Oh. No problem. You said your families are close.

"Yes. They are friends."

"I'm fine with her being here as long as she doesn't text you all night." Sheridan snorted out a laugh and punched his shoulder.

"Let's hope." Clayton agreed.

"Wait a sec." She grabbed his arm. "You really think she'll text you?"

"I'm more worried about what she'll attempt with you." Clayton brushed a lock of hair over her shoulder.

Ignoring the sensations brought about by his simple touch,

Sheridan frowned. "Aquaman, in case you've forgotten, actual criminals are after me, so ex-girlfriends ain't nothing."

"True, however a few years ago, Constance approached a girl I was dating and threatened her."

"Really?" Sheridan's outlook on the evening began to look a lot brighter. Brawls she could do, happy-family stuff—not so much. "Oh, yes, please. Let her threaten me. I need an outlet for my pent up aggression."

"Play nice." Clayton tipped her chin with his index finger.

"I will if she will."

"Dear God, what have I gotten myself into?"

"Exactly what you asked for." Sheridan grinned up at him.

Grinning back, he wrapped an arm around her waist and pulled her close. "I wouldn't change a thing." He kissed her a few seconds too long for such a public place. "Come on, let's go shock some more people."

"Mr. Kincaid, how ungentlemanly of you." She wrapped her arm around the crook of his elbow. A moved she'd learned while walking the red carpet with co-stars.

He bent and whispered in her ear. "Shall I show you just how ungentlemanly I can be?"

Sheridan shivered. "I think I'm good. Thanks."

Seeing Clayton interact with his parents created this odd feeling of envy. She couldn't do the family gig with Clayton and that stung. Her insides were scarred and hollow places he'd never see. Places she'd never shared with anyone. O'Malley had suggested she stay by Clayton's side to keep her safe without ever considering that being here…she wasn't safe at all, because she'd rather face down her father than face down her heart.

CHAPTER 21

Clayton's comfort and confidence with others and himself shined throughout their entire evening. He kept her by his side, dodging questions about their relationship like a pro. He'd even turned down Tate's request for a photo, a decision she'd quickly vetoed. Plenty of people were taking shots without permission—at least Tate had asked. Hopefully word wouldn't spread so quickly that news vans would be waiting outside the country club.

After two glasses of water, she excused herself from Clayton's side and hit the restroom. Washing up, she wasn't at all surprised when Constance entered and locked the door behind her.

Clayton was all concerned about keeping her safe, and yet, he never stopped to consider the nastiness that happened between girls in bathrooms. Why was that? What about bathrooms screamed boxing ring?

Constance had probably never been in a fistfight in her life. Girls like her fought with petty slights and veiled insults. In a true battle against her, Constance would lose horribly.

"Good evening, Constance. Locking people out when they need to pee is rude." Sheridan finished drying her hands with the embossed hand towel.

"And you'd know all about rude wouldn't you, Sheridan."

"I don't have any idea what you're trying to say." She clutched both hands together at her waist to keep them from swinging.

Constance flashed her bright white teeth. Her black cocktail dress dipped low over breasts that looked a little too perky and full to be one hundred percent real. "Are you having fun acting the part of Clayton's girlfriend, because that's all it is." Her words were rushed together, as if she was hyped up on something "I put up with so much from him, you know. He's always messing around with these *women*. I told him, you're supposed to be arresting filth, not dating it."

Do not consider how she'll look with a slightly crooked nose.

Smiling at that visual, Sheridan stepped past her. "Excuse me." She unlocked the door and stepped out of the ring. Hitting Clayton's ex-girlfriend in a country club bathroom didn't go along with the image she was trying to portray tonight. *Pity.*

Just outside the door, she stopped when a couple of girls she'd seen talking to Tate earlier asked to take her picture. She blew out a long breath, brought herself down from the adrenaline rush, and agreed. They did a couple serious shots before she suggested they do some silly ones, too. She needed a little fun. Plus she loved her fans.

She smiled as she walked away from the two girls who promised to love her forever. Those girls didn't think she was filth. But sometimes, just sometimes, she wondered if she was. Growing up in squalor, barely graduating high school, no college education, surviving by her looks, selling herself on the big screen. Living in her skin seemed impossible sometimes. She lied to everyone about who and what she was, which was why acting made such a great escape. On screen, she wasn't the daughter of Ellen Mae Bennett, the drug addicted whore. She wasn't a helpless girl who'd been bloodied and abused. She wasn't filthy.

She'd risen from the ashes of her childhood, dusted herself off, and had become someone else. So, why let Constance's words get under her skin? Maybe because deep down she agreed. Constance *was* the better woman for Clayton. Constance could give her body as well as her heart—and she could not. The stark reminder shot an arrow of pain through her chest.

Just outside the entrance to the party, she collapsed into a comfy cloth chair.

"Hey."

Tate startled her out of her blues.

"Hey, Tate."

"Are you all right?"

"Yeah, why?"

"You look sad."

She gave him a lop-sided grin. "Studying psychology?"

"No. Law. Body language is very important to us."

"Tricksters."

"Not me." He placed a hand against his heart.

"Hmmm…"

"I saw Constance come back in a few minutes ago. She had your same face, only angrier."

"Would you put that as an answer on your test? The defendant looked angrier."

He chuckled. "I might. Don't worry about Constance."

Sheridan tilted her head back and forth, considering. "I understand her position. I'm okay, but thanks for your concern." She smiled at him before bumping his shoe with the tip of her heel.

"He's in love with you, you know."

"Uh…" Sheridan blinked then averted her gaze. What the hell? How did one process such a statement? In love. With her.

"Why so shocked?" Tate bumped her shoe back. "Though, given how visible you are…eh…might not be so smart with his job." He leaned over and clasped her shoulder. "Clayton is the best guy I know. Whatever's holding you back won't matter to him." He shrugged. "Give the guy a chance."

"I'm not sure what to say. I'm still back at 'he's in love with you.'"

Tate nodded. "You're watchful, observing everything around you. You take it all in while at the same time not letting it touch you. He'll barrel over those walls, so watch out." He smiled then clapped his hands together. "That's this evening's one and only sales pitch."

Sheridan rose to her feet and kissed his cheek. "He's lucky to have a cousin like you."

# # #

Clayton stood at an angle and watched Sheridan talking to Tate. She'd been gone for a bit too long so he'd decided to investigate. He'd hired a couple off-duty cops to keep an eye on her tonight. One was standing by the door, watching her. *Good.* He hadn't wanted Sheridan to know he'd taken any extra precautions, so he was paying these guys out of his own pocket.

"Sheridan's even more beautiful in person." His mom took his arm.

He pulled his gaze away from Sheridan and smiled into eyes as blue as his own.

"Talk with me for a minute." She led him to a quiet corner.

"I wondered when I'd get the twenty questions." He settled her into a seat at a round table, currently vacant. Only crumbs from tonight's dinner and the centerpiece remained.

"Twenty questions? I'm your mother. I'm allowed at least thirty questions." She chuckled. "Sit. She's fine out there under the eye of the men watching her."

Clayton faced his mother and raised a brow.

"You wouldn't let her out of your sight if someone else wasn't watching her. I know you."

"You do." He leaned down and kissed her cheek then sat beside her.

"I never thought Sheridan Bennett would be so genuine and kind." She sniffed, and then rolled her pearls between her fingers. "This will teach me to skim those magazine articles at the store. She's quiet, maybe a bit reserved."

"Yes, she is. She has a lot on her mind. Plus, she finds it hard to trust people."

"That's understandable." His mom nodded. "How did you meet her?"

"I met her at Rachel's book signing. Plus, she's a member of Excel gym...the one I switched to after..." He wouldn't say after Michael's death but his mother knew. He couldn't belong to the same gym as the men who'd attacked his brother so he'd switched. "She swims."

"Ahh, of course." His mother leaned back in her chair. "Are the two of you really dating?"

"Yes, she just doesn't fully understand what that means."

"And what does it mean?"

"It means I've found the woman I want to spend the rest of my life with. I'm done." Discomfited due to discussing his feelings, he ran his foot across the carpet. A carpet that had weathered many a celebration. But at the moment, even when considering a future with Sheridan, he couldn't celebrate. Not when so much was at stake.

"Hmm..." His mother puckered her lips. "I'm happy for you...but her life is so public and with your job...I just don't know, dear. Plus her movies, they are a little...sexual, don't you think?"

"It's only a part, plus she mentioned something once about body doubles. Believe me, she is nothing like her risqué characters." As a matter of fact, he was quite clear intimacy was something new to Sheridan. Something she feared. She always seemed a little surprised to find herself kissing him.

"Clayton." His mom squeezed his arm. "Are you listening?"

"I'm sorry. What did you say?" He met her gaze. She'd

weathered a lot in her life, and he loved her not only as his mother, but also as one of his truest friends.

"I *said*, be careful. You value your privacy, and if you pursue this relationship, you won't have any. I read once that Sheridan grew up in foster homes, is that right? Then she's raised her younger sister, plus helping her older sister. Her life hasn't been easy. However, I think you need a strong woman at your side. I like her. Don't mess it up. I need grandchildren."

"Wow." Clayton's eyes went wide. "Grandchildren. That's...I think... I'll just say, I love you, Mom." He wrapped her in his arms. "Thanks for being nice to Sheridan."

"Well..." She sniffled. "I love you, too." She squeezed him tighter then after a moment, she sighed. "I missed him today."

Clayton could only nod. What would his brother think of Sheridan? He'd never know, because Michael was gone when so many memories were yet to be made. Clayton clenched his jaw, fighting back tears. "Just imagine all the shit he'd be giving me over dating a movie star. Kid would've never shut up about it."

His mom chuckled, but the sound was more of a half-sob.

"What's going on over here?" His father interjected as he walked over to join them. "I want a hug, too."

"Come on over." Clayton grabbed his Dad and then engulfed both parents in his arms.

"Thanks for making Sheridan feel welcome." Clayton squeezed them both. "I'm incredibly lucky to have you as my parents."

"Oh, my goodness." His mom glanced at him with watery eyes. "I will make Sheridan feel welcome any time if this is the result."

"She doesn't have anyone, and I guess...I'm sorry I don't say how I feel more often...especially after Michael's...after..."

His dad patted his shoulder. "It's all right, son. We know."

Clayton nodded and watched them walk away, arms around each other.

Did they really know how fantastic they were? He'd been avoiding his family since Michael died. Out of guilt mostly, but that wasn't fair, because out of anyone, his parents understood. They'd lost their son, and they shouldn't be closed off from their remaining one. He'd be better. He'd change. He couldn't ask Sheridan to walk away from her pain if he couldn't do the same. Time to start looking to the future again.

A future filled with one shining star—a star currently kissing his cousin.

CHAPTER 22

"I leave you alone for a few minutes and you're kissing my cousin?"

"I saw Constance kiss you earlier. Full mouth on mouth." Sheridan raised a brow as Clayton stepped between her and Tate. "I had to make it even. Although, I would've had to lick his tonsils to accomplish that."

"You're over exaggerating, and I didn't kiss her back."

"Full mouth on mouth is what I saw. Just sayin'"

"Sheridan, *my* mouth is entirely at your disposal," Tate piped in.

"Your mouth is more like a *garbage* disposal." Clayton placed his hand flat against Tate's face and pushed him away.

"I can take a hint. Sheridan, my mouth and I will see you later." After flashing a cheeky wink, Tate walked away.

Clayton swirled the drink in his hand. "What was that about? I can't get you to voluntarily kiss me, and yet here you are kissing my cousin."

"Oh yeah," Sheridan huffed. "We were really going at it. Good thing you interrupted us or we'd be on the floor."

"You seem so relaxed with him. I don't like it."

"He's a good guy, and the reason I kissed his *cheek* is because he was being a good friend *to you* at the moment, so there, satisfied?"

"Not really."

"Would you like me to kiss you then?"

"I want you to *want* to kiss me."

"Geez-a-loo, I do. I thought I explained that earlier."

They were becoming far too serious, so she cracked a grin. "It's just…well, you have Constance chum in your mouth"

"Chum? Really?"

"Yes, I am afraid that is the case."

"Whiskey is a disinfectant." Clayton emptied the contents of his glass into his mouth before swishing it around and visibly swallowing. "All clean." Opening his mouth wide, he stuck out his tongue.

"Gross, like I want to kiss the inside of a whiskey barrel." Laughing, she punched his chest.

"Now that we've had our first fight, we should kiss and make up."

She stared down at her shoes. "I do want to kiss you."

"What?" Clayton bent closer, his question drifting like a warm breeze across her cheek.

She lifted her chin and lightly brushed her lips across his.

Apparently overwhelmed by her invitation, Clayton took over, grasping the back of her neck before sliding his tongue deep.

He did taste like a whiskey barrel, and the flavor burned all the way down to her toes as his mouth slanted over hers again and again. She became drunk on his taste alone.

Flexing his hand in the hair at her nape, he deepened the kiss, pulling her closer. Making her forget everything. Wiping the slate clean.

Seeking more, she slid a hand up his arm, touching his warm skin.

Then…nothing but air.

Sheridan blinked. "Clayton?"

"What do you think you're doing?" Constance hissed at

Clayton, grasping the back of his shirt.

"Let him go." She shoved at the blonde's arm.

"What are you going to do about it?" Constance jabbed a finger against Sheridan's chest. "You think he gives a shit about you? You're just another girl he'll fuck then dump. Only you're famous, so he thinks he's hot shit this time. He doesn't care who he hurts, and you're another in a long line." Constance nudged her again with that manicured fingernail. "I don't care if you are famous. As far as I can tell you've played nothing but whores, and it doesn't look like it took much acting."

"Constance." Clayton stood between them. "That's enough. When you sober up, we'll discuss this."

"What? You don't want to discuss it now? Don't want Ms. Hollywood hearing the truth?"

"What truth is that?" Clayton's face had turned a little red, and his tone was soft yet clipped.

Sheridan considered intervening, but figured this tiff had been a long time coming.

"I know what you want from me. What everyone wants from me. But what I want is for you to leave." He pointed toward the exit. "Now."

Constance glared at him then faced Sheridan. "You think people don't know what kind of girl you are?"

Sheridan bumped her fists together. "The kind of girl that is about to forget all the reasons I have for not knocking you out? Yeah, that's me."

"Are you threatening me?" Constance shoved Sheridan's shoulder.

"Enough!" Clayton practically shouted down the roof. "Calm down. You're drunk and causing a scene. Sheridan's with me regardless of what you may believe, so leave it."

Studying the entrance to the main room, Sheridan saw that all eyes were indeed on them with no Director to call cut. Everything suddenly seemed just a little too real.

"Hope you enjoyed the show." After executing a bow, Sheridan headed straight for the exit sign.

# # #

"Sheridan, please stop."

Instead of heading outside, she took the stairs up. On the second floor, she leaned against the outer railing and stared out at the golf course's green grass lit by the moonlight.

Ignoring Clayton bounding up behind her, she breathed in a lungful of the cool air.

"I'm sorry—"

"Don't!" Sheridan spun around and lifted a hand between them. "Don't you dare apologize for her behavior."

"Sheridan...Let me—"

"Stop, just stop and let me breathe for a minute." Turning away, she wrapped both arms around her body. Constance had said those things to drive a wedge between them, but Sheridan's insecure side whispered the words were true. "I won't let you use me. I'm not a doll or a dim-witted beauty or a character on a screen. I'm real. I hurt. I feel. I ache sometimes. My job and my looks do *not* define who I am. Everyone thinks they can get inside me, maybe figuratively and sure as hell, literally, but you can't." She blinked away a tear. "You can't."

"Don't tell me what I think, Slim." Clayton grasped her shoulder and turned her to face him. "As far as Constance is concerned, she needs real help at this point. She won't let go of this notion of a happily-ever-after between us. Frankly, her insistence is starting to worry me." He ran a hand through his hair. "I *am* sorry Constance spoke to you the way she did. And yeah, I have dated my fair share of women. I won't apologize for that, because I've just been waiting for you."

This whole night had gone from fun to fucked. And now they were talking about two different things, which wasn't his fault, because he didn't really know what she meant when she said, people couldn't get inside her. And based on something Constance had said maybe she didn't really know him either. "What did you mean?"

Clayton frowned. "I've maybe had two serious relationships, but every other time, I—"

"No, not that." Sheridan waved a hand between them. "What did you mean when you said you know what Constance and everyone else wants from you? What is it they want?"

Clayton took a deep breath and ran a hand over his face.

"Just tell me." Her stomach churned. And here she thought she was the one with secrets. What was he hiding?

"When I was eighteen, I inherited my great-aunt's estate. My father had always been her favorite, which caused her affections to transfer to me. During her lifetime, I became like a grandson to her, probably because she lost a son early in her marriage. Upon her death, I received an inheritance, but I put the money away until I could decide what to do with my life."

"Why's that so horrible?"

"She left me a lot of money. And that's not all."

"Okay." Sheridan drew out the word, unsure of the problem.

"On my thirtieth birthday, I'll inherit a trust from my grandfather. That along with what I received from my aunt leaves me set financially."

"What about your brother? Did he get anything?"

"No."

"So, that's it?" Sheridan narrowed her brow. "You have money?"

"Well, Hollywood, it is quite a bit of money for an average guy."

"Average guy?" She shook her head. "Seriously, I mean look at you. All disgustingly handsome, successful in business, great family and friends, and since you were in the military, you're all like a hero protector guy. Women love that kind of stuff."

Hands stuffed in his front pockets, he rocked back on his heels. "I probably have more money than you."

"Oh, well aren't you just king of the fucking world." She pitched her head back and forth with each word. "I could give two shits about your money."

"You've got a dirty mouth on you sometimes." He wrapped both arms around her, squeezing the breath from her lungs. "You are entirely more than I know what to do with, but I love you anyway." He kissed the top of her head then stilled. "Ah, hell...I didn't mean it to come out like that."

"Then how did you mean it?" Heart thundering, Sheridan eased back and met his gaze. "*Did* you mean it?"

He opened his mouth, but then shut it again. "Let's go inside. We'll sit at the bar, okay?"

"No, it's absolutely not okay. Did you mean it?" Her voice hit a shrill level that would likely damage any birds flying overhead.

"Yeah." He lightly kissed her. "I meant it because you're brave. Because you're loyal. Because you fight for your family. Because you're beautiful. And because you think you don't deserve love when you do. All those reasons are why I love you, Sheridan Bennett. And why, I'll never leave, which if I'm not mistaken I'll need to prove over and over again."

"You love me?"

"Of course, doesn't everyone?"

"No."

He grinned.

She didn't.

"Let's get you a drink."

"Okay."

Her legs moved of their own accord, following Clayton down the stairs.

Love—that word wormed around like an alien probe trying to enter her brain. She hated aliens. Green little assholes invading shit and doing weirdo experiments. And why the hell was she thinking about aliens? Clayton had just declared his love, and she'd stood there like she had an actual probe up her ass.

Should she say it back? Was that how this went? She *did* care for him as a friend. But love...what did that word even mean? She'd said I love you to other actors in movies before, forced herself to feel the emotion, but this was real life.

Maybe if she went back on the roof and hummed the *Close Encounters of the Third Kind* theme song, she'd really get abducted. Seemed the best course for now because she'd really misled him.

Time to tell the truth. If Clayton had these feelings then he deserved to know that the person he loved didn't truly exist. She'd falsely represented everything. Her own fault. Hadn't she always played a part in her own downfall? And each time she'd taken someone with her. Why should her life be any different this time?

Clayton would hear the truth and he would leave, but at least this time, he'd be the one person she left alive.

CHAPTER 23

Sheridan kicked off her heels and flexed her feet. "I enjoyed meeting your parents tonight." While certain portions of the evening's events still had her tied in knots, she'd had a nice time watching Clayton interact with his family.

"Are you tired?" He took her hand and tugged her toward the basement door.

"Yeah, but my mind won't shut down." She followed him like a woman taking her last steps on death row.

"I received an email earlier. No trace of van guy in the area, and Korzakov's men have suddenly left town. Maybe they were summoned home for some nefarious reason or another. Your father hasn't been sighted either."

"Maybe Maria has already taken care of him. What else did O'Malley say?" Sheridan grabbed a water bottle from the fridge in the basement's small kitchen area. "Want one?"

"The message wasn't from O'Malley." He cleared his throat. "Got anything stronger?"

"Sure." She grabbed a beer. If she was brave enough to go through with her decision, she figured Clayton might need the whole case. Stomach churning, she settled beside him on the couch. "I hope O'Malley isn't working with a blabber mouth. All I need is to end up in the news with a story about my father and the mafia. The media storm would be insane."

"Yep." Clayton took a big draw from his beer then took her hand. "Listen, Sheridan, there's something—"

"Wait." She squeezed his hand. "I need to tell you something. This will be a super busy week with my trip to New York. Ryan and his crew are leaving Tuesday. So, I feel…after what you said tonight, I feel I should tell you the truth about my past. I've misled you, and I need to fix that."

Clayton pulled her onto his lap. "Stop worrying. Everything will work out fine." He rubbed her back, a soothing up and down motion.

"I wish that were true."

"It is." He tilted her chin, bringing her mouth to his. Kissing her softly while repositioning them so that they lay side by side. "Do you have any idea what it does to me to see you like this? Moist lips. Hair mussed. You are beyond beautiful both inside and out."

Shaking her head, Sheridan closed her eyes and inhaled deeply, trying to catch her breath for all the things she knew she would have to say. "I can't do this."

"I understand why you're scared. I know something happened to you that frightened you away from men." He brushed her hair over her ear. "I've been taking it slow, but I think we're ready for more. I won't hurt you, and if it's too much, you only have to say stop."

"Clayton, it's just…you don't…" Tears streamed down her face.

"I won't allow your past to come between us. Look at me, please." He eased her hands away from her face. "I love who you are now. I want to show you what that means to me. I want to make you mine completely."

"No, Clayton, it can't be." Wiping her cheeks, she shook her head again.

He kissed the top of her head. "Yes, it can. You just need to trust what's building between us."

"You don't know what you're saying, because you don't know…it's…I've never spoken to anyone about my past, and the reason for that is because it's disturbing and repulsive." Sheridan straightened on the couch, pulling her knees up by her chest. "Could you get me a tissue or a paper towel, please?"

"Sure." Clayton stood and grabbed a paper towel off the roll on the kitchen counter.

Sheridan blew her nose while waiting for Clayton to sit. "Earlier you said you love me, but the thing is, you don't know me. Not really."

Clayton started to speak but she held up a hand.

"No. Just listen…my life up until I turned fifteen was complete hell. I didn't grow up with a nice family. My criminal father came in and out of my life, leaving a chaotic mess behind. My mother was a drug addict who didn't care about anything but her next hit." She crumbled the paper towel in her hand. "My mother is the one who hurt me, Clayton."

Clayton braced a hand around the back of her neck. "Sheridan, let me hold you."

"Please don't touch me." She leaned away from his touch. "I need to be strong if I'm going to tell you this." She stood and paced in front of the couch, shoving away the wood-framed coffee table. "As I said, I'm leaving for New York, and I would prefer it if you didn't contact me until I get back."

He shook his head. "You can't go alone."

"I understand that, and I'm fine with you picking someone to go with me. But it can't be you, because I want you to think about what I'm about to tell you. If you decide you don't want any kind of relationship after tonight, I will understand. One more thing before I begin…Jenny doesn't know any of this. No one does. *That* is how much faith I am giving you."

"Sheridan, I know about Jenny's dad, and what he did to you. I know about your time in the hospital. I read the police reports.

It's all right." He grabbed her hand, pulling her toward him.

Sheridan squeezed his hand but pulled away. "Those reports you read are full of lies. No one knows what really happened that day, except the other two people who were there, and one of them is dead." How that person had died was another story all together. One she wouldn't reveal today or hopefully ever.

"All right. I'll listen but know this, I love you." Clayton drew her between his legs, placing his hands on her hips. "I won't betray your confidence, and I won't abandon you. Is that clear?"

Sincerity shone from his eyes, but they'd soon turn to a pitying gaze. Or one filled with disgust. Either way the time had come. "Clayton, don't make declarations until you've heard the truth." She stepped back and chewed on her thumbnail, unsure of where to start, scared to death of the outcome. She had no choice but to give the whole unvarnished truth. Nothing left but to begin.

# # #

"When I turned five, my mother, Ellen Mae met Jenny's dad, Ted McCord. They were both serious addicts. He played in a bar band where Ellen worked as a waitress. Shortly after they met, Ellen got pregnant with Jenny. Eight months after Jenny was born, McCord was arrested for selling drugs. It wasn't his first offence, so he got put away for a couple of years. He came back when Jenny was four and I was ten."

"He helped my mom pay bills, bought groceries, and even took the time to cook meals. Since he worked a late shift, he would always be there when Jenny and I came home from school. Always very affectionate and interested in our day. Not something we were familiar with at all. Jenny was really excited to have her father back, and I liked someone actually taking care of us for once."

Sheridan took a deep breath, she'd practically worn out the carpet with her pacing and she hadn't dared to look in Clayton's direction.

Oh God! Don't puke. Just get through this.

"Then the parties started…so, I barricaded Jenny and me in our room. And even though I was sure I'd locked the door, I would wake up sometimes and see McCord sitting by Jenny's bed stroking her hair and face. I was jealous at first, but then I got this creepy chill because something wasn't right. I may have been young, but I'd already seen a lot."

"That's how most sexual abuse begins. The person is nice, making you feel indebted…then bam, the evil slips out. McCord would try to get Jenny alone, but I stuck by her side."

Taking another deep breath, Sheridan bit her lip before continuing, because next came the hard part. She ripped more paper towels off the holder. "Clayton, please don't say anything during this next part. Just let me finish then I need to go upstairs alone."

"Sheridan, I told you I won't leave you." He'd remained on the couch, hands folded and hanging between his knees.

"I need you to leave tonight and give me some time. I've never said any of this out loud before."

With a grim smile, he met her gaze. "You told me not to make declarations I couldn't keep."

She knelt between his legs and grasped his hands. "Please, promise me you'll leave when I'm done. I'm not sure how I'll react. I have some pills I can take, so let me go."

"I would rather stay." He caressed her cheek.

"No, or I won't tell you the rest."

"I can guess the rest."

"No…you can't." She grabbed his hand and kissed his palm before pressing it against her cheek a moment then she stood once more. If she was to finish her story, she had to stand alone. "Clayton?" She ran her fingers through his soft dark hair.

"Yeah."

"Will you please leave after this next part?"

"You aren't safe here alone."

"Okay, but will you just not follow me upstairs then."

"I won't follow you. Sit, please."

She sat beside him on the couch. Head down, she studied her nails for a moment. "I think I'm due for a manicure."

"Sheridan." He tipped her chin. "You stopped at McCord trying to get Jenny alone, so keep going."

She nodded then ran both hands through her own hair, scrubbing back and forth. "Okay...so...one afternoon, McCord and I were alone because my mother took Jenny to a doctor's appointment. I'll not go into all the sordid details, but he threatened me, told me he would do things to Jenny if I didn't...ah...service him. He said he would take her away and I'd never see her again. He played on my biggest fear—losing Jenny. I had no choice and so...I tried to stay away from him, but..." Sheridan breathed through the bile creeping up her throat. His hands, his mouth, his touch, so dirty and disgusting. She bit her bottom lip and drew in a deep breath.

"It wasn't your fault." Clayton brushed away her tears.

Sheridan shrugged. "You know people say that, but this *was* my fault. I let him touch me so he'd leave my sister alone. I was complicit. I still remember the sick knot in my stomach. I remember...too much." She stood and, keeping her back to Clayton, clutched a hand to her chest. A wave of dizziness struck but she closed her eyes and breathed. Bracing her hand on the kitchen counter, she continued. "One day, he caught me alone in the kitchen, but my mom came home...when she saw me without my shirt, she went crazy, but her anger wasn't directed at him." Sheridan's entire body shook so she clenched her hands into fists at her sides. "In my mother's mind, I had drawn him in. S-so she...so she...um...s-she grabbed a knife from the block and plunged it into his back, knocking him over and then...and then..."

Sheridan crumpled to the floor, clutching her head in her

hands. "She screamed and screamed…saying, 'Is this what you want, you little slut? I'll give it to you. I'll cut you up and no man will ever want to fuck you again.' My mother took…she took the knife and stabbed my thighs and my belly. The pain was like fire shooting from my center out to my limbs. Non-stop and searing, and I could feel the blood trickling down my sides. Finally, McCord pulled her off."

"Blood covered the cracked linoleum, my stomach, my hands. I could hear my mom screaming while McCord beat her." Sheridan stared at a point on the wall right above Clayton's head and concentrated on that until her stomach stopped trying to remove its contents. "The pain was unbearable. I tried to let go, to lose consciousness, to die. But then…I turned my head…and there stood Jenny in the doorway. Her face … I'll never forget the look. I saw her open her mouth to scream but I couldn't hear it. I think I started to die, but I fought it. I had to stay and take care of Jenny. I couldn't leave her behind with those people, couldn't let them do to her what they'd done to me. I was destroyed. Done. Broken. But not her, never her. I screamed at Jenny to call 911 with the only breath I had left and she did. She saved me."

"My mother lay unconscious and McCord ran away, but Jenny stayed with me. Thankfully, she doesn't remember what happened that day. Maybe she's blocked it somehow. I remember waking up in the hospital and she asked if I wanted a SpongeBob bandage." Sheridan laughed which came out more like a sob.

"O'Malley was the lead detective, and he came to the hospital to question my mother. She blamed the whole thing on McCord. The lies slipping easily from her tongue. I agreed with her story. So, they tracked him down, and he went to jail." Sheridan got to her feet and began pacing again. "Should I feel guilty about sending a man to jail for something he didn't really do? Well, I don't, because he *was* killing me. Slowly. Day after day. I have no doubt he'll come after me someday, seeking revenge. I hope he does because this time I'm not a child. This time I'm ready. This time he won't touch me." She shivered and turned to see the judgment in Clayton's eyes.

He stared down at the carpet, shuffling his foot back and forth in the threads.

A tear fell and landed on his shoe. *Oh God!* What had she done to this man? And she wasn't even done.

Though she wanted to comfort him, to tell him she really was all right, she just moved closer to the stairs.

"That's why I cannot be physically intimate with you, Clayton. I've been sliced open."

Her heart and stomach were fighting for the lead role in who-can hurt-the-most. Wrapping an arm around her stomach, she leaned a shoulder against the wall. "You say I'm beautiful and yet you haven't seen the ugly scars that cover my body." Oh hell, why had she eaten anything today? She'd see it all again soon based on the way her stomach was churning. After that pleasant experience, she would literally take her blanket and pillow and hide in her closet until she could breathe without this restriction caused by whatever clogged her throat—fear, pain, despair—likely all of the above.

Heading for the basement steps, Sheridan glanced over her shoulder at Clayton and mentally said goodbye, which almost sent her to her knees again. "I cannot love you as you deserve. I am, and always will be, broken."

CHAPTER 24

Unsure how he'd made the drive home, Clayton sat on his couch, his body shaking and his mind so full of fury, he could barely breathe. He'd called Scotty and asked if he could stay with Sheridan, because she was right—they both needed time. Her cousin and his team might not have left yet, but he still felt better with one of his men in her house.

As a cop and as a Ranger he'd seen just how dark this world could be. Knowing everything she'd suffered tore his heart to shreds. He couldn't comprehend her sheer terror at facing down a man and then having her own mother turn on her. However, he found it interesting she hadn't mentioned her father during her horror-filled tale. Where was Jack during this time? What else had Sheridan endured?

For now, he'd be grateful Sheridan trusted him. This wasn't a step back, but a huge leap forward, and he sure as hell would never turn away from her. Never.

Restless, he slowly got to his feet and headed to the kitchen for a drink. Grabbing a cold beer, he ran the bottle across his heated forehead. In one long swallow, he finished, and then tossed the empty bottle into the recycling bin. The loud clang reverberated through the silence and seemed to indicate an end to his thoughts.

"I love her and that's the end of it." Nodding his acceptance, he headed down the hall to his bathroom in order to prepare for the next day.

Once in the shower, he heaved a sigh as the hot spray hit his body. Scrubbing his hands though his hair and over his face, he considered how they could overcome Sheridan's reticence toward a physical relationship. Perhaps they could visit a psychologist or a couples' counselor. Maybe he could go on his own to help garner his own understanding of how to be a true friend to Sheridan. Had she ever consulted a professional? Knowing her, the answer was a big fat *no*. Plus, she hadn't shared her story until now.

Her tears and world-weary eyes had broken his heart. So many times, he'd wanted to leap up and hold her in his arms. But, she'd needed to stand strong, not be coddled by him.

He'd give her time then he'd have a discussion of his own. They would move forward. Whether as friends or lovers, he'd stick by her side. She may be broken, but he would pick up each piece and make her whole again.

# # #

After an hour of watching YouTube videos featuring psychologists discussing how to deal with survivors of abuse, Clayton jerked to attention when someone pounded on his door.

Grabbing his gun off the coffee table, he crept forward and shouted, "Who is it?"

"It's Constance."

What was she doing here at midnight?

He unlocked the door, opened it, and instantly saw red.

Literally.

Her entire body was splattered with red.

"Holy shit, are you hurt?" Heart pounding, he yanked Constance inside, shoving his gun in the back of his jeans. "Let me call an ambulance."

"Clayton." She shook him off and, with a shaky hand, held out a gift bag. "I-I'm s-supposed to give this t-to…to you."

"What the hell happened?" He led her in to his kitchen. "Is this blood yours?"

"P-paint. It's paint." She held her arms out at her sides. "He threw it on me."

The smell finally penetrated. Not copper, but paint.

"Let's get you out of these clothes." Clayton set the gift bag on the floor. He'd deal with the contents after he got Constance secured. "I'll send your clothes to our private lab. Perhaps they can garner some details from the type of paint used."

"I-I think you should call the police." Teeth chattering, Constance lifted her arms as he removed her paint-soaked shirt. Her pants were splattered, as were her shoes.

"Let's get you out of your pants and shoes, okay?"

She nodded and then sniffled. "I'm so scared, Clayton."

After he tossed her clothes aside, he wrapped her in his arms. "It's okay. I will call the police, but first let's both calm down a little. You scared me, and I'm still trying to recover." He took her hand and led her to the bathroom. "Come on."

"He told me to come here."

"Who?"

"The guy in the black van."

"Black?" Clayton halted in the hallway.

"Yeah."

"Okay." Clayton led her to the bathroom, slid open the glass door, and then turned on the spray. "Most paints are water-based, so if you scrub you should be able to clean your face and most of it out of your hair." Jaw clenched, he fingered her red strands. "Although, only your left side got hit."

Shivering in her underwear, she took his hand. "Stay in here, please."

"Constance, I'll wait just outside the door."

"I'm really scared."

"All right. I'll get a washcloth from the kitchen since they have scrubbers on the back, and I'll be right back." With one hand, he tested the water temperature. "It's good now. Go on in."

"You'll be right back."

"Yes. I'm so sorry, Constance, but I'll fix this."

"I didn't know what else to do." She wrapped both hands around her body.

"You did the right thing."

"Okay." She bit her wobbling lower lip.

"Give me a minute." Storming down the hall, Clayton pounded a fist against the wall. "So this is how you want to play it? Fine." Van man once again made this fight personal, attacking people he cared about. Issuing warnings. He couldn't wait to get his hands on the man for putting that look of fear in Constance's eyes. Not to mention his terrorizing of Sheridan.

Once he hit the living room, he grabbed his phone and dialed O'Malley. The Lieutenant answered after the second ring.

"Sir, this is Clayton Kincaid. I need you at my place. Van guy made a reappearance."

O'Malley said he was on his way then hung up.

Clayton grabbed a washcloth from the kitchen drawer then jogged back to the bathroom. Entering the room, he shook off a trickle of unease at seeing her nude. Ridiculous. His long-time friend, and yes, ex-girlfriend was scared, which was his fault. *Get over yourself, dumbass.*

Keeping his gaze down, he handed her the dishcloth then lowered the toilet lid and sat. "Can you tell me what happened?"

Steam filled the room along with a string of curses as Constance scrubbed at the paint in her hair. "I know you're around stuff like this all the time, Clayton, but I can't handle it."

"I still get scared. The day I don't is the day I need to hang up my hat. Hell, I'm scared now. But I'm even more pissed. I'm trying to think like a cop and not as your friend. Isn't working too well."

"I'm glad to know you still care."

"Of course I do." Clayton heaved a sigh. "Let's talk about what happened."

"Fine." She rubbed the washcloth over her hand. "I was driving home after going to dinner with some friends. I was at a stoplight and this van bumps me. I got out and all of a sudden, he comes running up and throws this small can of paint on me. Then he hands me this bag and says, 'give this to Clayton.'"

"Did you get a look at him?"

"Blond. Bulky. Maybe early twenties."

"Was he much taller than you?"

"I don't know, Clayton." Constance slammed her washcloth onto the shower's marble ledge. "The guy was kind of bent as he threw paint all over my face. I couldn't really gauge his height while I was frightened for my life."

"Okay, okay...sorry." He raised both hands.

She wrenched off the tap and grabbed the towel off the shower hook. "What are you into now, Clayton? And why are they following me around, handing me stuff, and scaring me to death?"

"I won't lie to you Constance, they're sending a message."

"And what message is that?" After drying off her long limbs, still splattered with bits of paint, she tucked the towel around her body.

"They want me to know they'll hurt people I care about if I don't back off."

"Who's they?"

"Well, now that's the question." Was blond guy acting alone or under the direction of Bennett?

"I'm staying here." Constance jabbed a finger against the sink's countertop. "I don't care what you say. This is your fault, and I'm not leaving until I know why some guy hunted me down and threw paint all over me."

"I'm sorry. I promise I'll take care of this." Sheridan was right, he really should consider his declarations before he spoke, but he *would* handle this. He had too. These were the moments he'd trained for, lived for. Protecting others was his calling, one he'd heed now.

Constance nodded then rubbed her nose before she burst into tears. "Why did he do this to me?"

Clayton stood and wrapped her in his arms, soothing her while he considered his next step and his resources. He'd hire more personal security guards and pay their salaries himself. Van man wanted to play dirty. He could do dirty. The kid might have a devious mentor, but Clayton had the Manchester police department and an abundance of funds. If he had to pay off Sheridan's father himself, he would. Might be the best course of action for now anyway. The Korzakov family would eventually track down Jack Bennett, and then Sheridan's father would be a danger to no one.

"Constance." He tugged a couple tissues from the box on the bathroom counter. "I'll grab you some clothes and we'll talk to the cops."

"We're going downtown?"

Her voice wobbled, and her eyes were red-rimmed. He'd done that to her by underestimating his opponent.

"No, they're coming here. They'll want to talk to you and see what's in the package."

"Probably has a hand or someone's finger."

"Let's hope not. I've seen enough red tonight to last a lifetime, both literally and figuratively."

# # #

Dressed in his sweats and an overly large T-shirt, Constance was sitting in the corner of his couch wrapped in a blanket and clutching a steaming mug of coffee.

The doorbell rang, and almost like a hard clang to his head, that sound shifted Clayton's focus from caregiver to detective.

"Who's here?" Constance's eyes went wide.

"O'Malley." Clayton opened the door, scanning the perimeter as the Lieutenant stepped inside.

"What's going on, Kincaid?"

Clayton locked his door then tilted his head toward the kitchen. "Coffee's fresh. You might need a cup."

"Always the best way to begin." The grizzly old man clapped him on the back. He sported jeans and a sweatshirt topped with a heavy jacket featuring patches along his sleeve, revealing his rank and years of service.

Clayton led O'Malley to the kitchen. Constance waved hello but didn't speak.

Once in the kitchen, Clayton grabbed two mugs. "That's Constance Grey, an ex-girlfriend and the reason I called." Clayton proceeded to tell the story and explained he was willing to fund all precautionary measures. "She's frightened, and with good reason. Sheridan's father likely learned about scare tactics during his time with the Russian mafia, but we both know how quickly things can turn deadly."

"Yeah, we do." O'Malley nodded before topping off his coffee. "Let me talk to the young lady and see if we can gather more info now that she's had time to settle."

O'Malley sat next to Constance and asked her questions similar to his own. The only additional information he gained was that the attacker wore dark clothes and laughed the whole time. She also added that he'd taken a picture of her after throwing the paint.

O'Malley patted her knee then met Clayton's gaze. "Where's the bag he gave her?"

"Kitchen."

"Have you looked inside?"

"No."

"I'm bringing in my whole team now. We've tried on our own, but we need more men." O'Malley stood and headed for the kitchen. "You understand what will happen when I make this official?"

"News vans."

"Yep, I swear the paparazzi have a team specifically tuned into Manchester happenings."

"Great. Luckily, Sheridan's headed to New York for a couple magazine interviews. Should be interesting to see how she avoids answering questions."

O'Malley chuckled. "She should've been a politician the way she can evade a question. She's certainly a pro, but then she's had lots of practice." He plucked a wooden spoon out of a canister on the kitchen counter and eased open the edges of the black gift bag decorated with a thick spattering of red paint. "It's that kid's game. Operation. Did you save Constance's clothes?"

"Yes." Clayton peered over O'Malley's shoulder at the kid's game in the bag.

"Lab'll be able to determine the paint's brand, most likely."

"Should we open the box or do you want to wait for forensics?"

"Let's see what we're dealing with. Here's some gloves." He pulled a couple pairs from his back pocket.

"Nice." Clayton grinned. "Quite the boy scout."

"I'm always prepared, son." He slowly tugged the game free and placed it on the counter. "Let's hope there's no bomb. Although, I don't know what her attackers would hope to gain by sending her here only to blow you both up. Seems more like a warning."

"I agree." Clayton straightened and glanced toward the living room. "Are you sure this is safe?"

"The game isn't vibrating." O'Malley poked the box with the end of the wooden spoon. "Some bombs vibrate, but the newer versions don't. At least that's what they told us at one of the last conferences I attended. I'm going with my instinct here though. I think we're good to proceed."

"Let's do this." Clayton carefully eased the game board out of the box, but stalled when it got stuck on a couple protruding papers. Sweat dribbled down his spine as he pressed the papers down and tugged the game free. "What's all this?"

A photo of Constance was cut out and taped over the top of the red-nosed man. Clayton always thought the guy on the Operation table looked like one of the *Three Stooges*.

O'Malley pulled the picture off the game and underneath was a picture of Clayton's mom then one of his dad.

"Damn him." Clayton's blood pressure shot to stroke levels. "He thinks this is a game."

Photos of Jenny and Sheridan followed.

O'Malley rubbed at the scruff on his chin. "We're dealing with an unhinged individual."

The last was a picture of Clayton. At least the head was…the bottom portion was of a nude man, but his balls were cut out. In its place was a note.

This is how we oparate.
Back off or the next splash of red will be real.
And remember, don't sit off the alarm.

"Great. We're dealing with a psychopath who can't spell." Clayton flicked the note and his "photo" onto the counter.

"What's that?" Constance entered the room, the blanket still wrapped around her body.

"It's nothing." Clayton eased between her and the pictures.

"I deserve to know what's happening. What are all those photos? Is that your Mom?"

"Yeah. It's a warning."

Constance studied the picture of him. "This is really bad Photoshop. I could do better in Google Nik." She shook her head then furrowed her brow. "What's with the game?"

"It's another message."

Constance spent way too much time on social media cataloging every moment of her life. He didn't want this news spreading too fast. And he knew the minute she calmed down, she'd be posting about her experience.

"Am I in danger?" Constance faced O'Malley.

"I'd say, yes. I'm sorry, but you might want to think about personal protection. I believe Clayton can speak to that. I've got some calls to make." He stepped out of the room.

Constance glared at Clayton. "Personal protection? From who?"

"It's complicated—"

"Do *not* take that placating tone with me. I just got rear ended and attacked. I deserve the truth."

"Sheridan's got a stalker."

"Yeah, so?"

Her hair still had streaks of red paint. And she had one small spec on her neck. Clayton sighed. "This isn't something you can share with the world."

"Oh, like I can be quiet about a wrecked car and paint all over everything."

He led her back into the living room. "I'll put some men on you for a while, and we'll track down this guy."

"Seems like paint guy is the one doing the tracking."

"Believe me. I know." Clayton sat beside her on the couch and pulled up his contact list on his phone. Time to bring in reinforcements, and he'd have to warn Scotty to be prepared for a shit storm of press.

CHAPTER 25

Early the next morning, Sheridan finished her ginger pear white tea and rubbed her tired eyes.

"Did you get my medicine?"

Sheridan turned and faced Laney who stood just inside her bedroom door.

"Oh no, Laney. I forgot."

"But I need my medicine, Sheridan."

"I know, honey. We've just been overwhelmed with all the people in the house."

"I need my medicine, and I miss my mom." Laney's lower lip began to wobble.

Taking her sister from her foster parents and her home and throwing her into this chaos perhaps wasn't the smartest move. But the Masers home had a limited security system, and her sister's safety was paramount. "I know all these adjustments are hard." Sheridan crossed the room and hugged her sister. "I'm sorry, but you should be able to go home soon."

"I want my mom." Laney sobbed against her shoulder.

"I'll head out right now and get your medicine. Okay?" She couldn't take her sister's despair. Plus after her reveal to Clayton last night, she needed to get out of the house—without her security detail. "Laney, I need you to do me a favor. Go to your room and watch TV for a little while. I will get your medicine and be back right away. If anyone asks, tell them I'm in the basement cleaning stuff, all right?" She gave her sister a final squeeze then handed her the box of Kleenex she had on her nightstand. "Take these."

Sheridan's heart raced. Clayton would kill her if he knew what she was doing, but she had to go. Her sister needed her.

After seeing Laney to her room, Sheridan grabbed her purse, gun, and phone then crept to the basement. Walking through the furnished portion, she came to the door of the storage area. "Oh God, what am I doing?" No one but her and the builder knew of her secret escape hatch in the basement—and the one in the floor of her garage. They both led to an old barn that held her Ford F-150 King Cab truck and enough supplies to survive an Apocalypse. "I'll be in and out of the store super fast. Clayton will never even know I left. Besides it's early. If he slept like I did last night, he probably isn't even up yet. Okay, Bennett, let's do this."

She opened the storage room's door then headed toward the back. Moving a box of Christmas decorations off the escape hatch, she lifted the lid then climbed down the metal steps. Every couple of months, she completed practice runs through the tunnels. This one served not only as an escape tunnel but also as a survival shelter. The round bunker was made of steel and had a first class air filtration system. She could live down here for a year without ever having to return to the surface.

Passing box after box of supplies, she walked through the tunnel. Reaching the end, she climbed up the metal stairs, unscrewed the lid, and shoved it open.

Out of the hatch, she took a moment to appreciate the crisp November air and essentially her first taste of true freedom in months. Her favorite holiday was Thanksgiving and if she had to celebrate with a table full of bodyguards, she'd go mad.

Tugging her purse over her shoulder, she checked the area before heading for her truck. The keys were in a lock box hidden under the wheel well. She retrieved them then hopped into the driver's seat. "Should I do this?"

Clayton had put so much effort into her safety and here she was running off to get her sister's meds. "I've got my gun. My father isn't going to shoot me in the middle of the store." She bit her bottom lip. "At least I hope. But maybe if he does show up, I can shoot him and be done with this whole mess." Rubbing her damp hands along her jeans, she turned the key in the ignition and headed down the bumpy dirt lane to the main road. At the end of the dirt path, she turned away from her house so her cameras wouldn't catch her truck. Flipping on the radio, she drove down a familiar escape route through country roads, passing fields full of cows and old farm houses, before working her way to a main road that led to the store.

She parked as close to the entrance as she could, hopped down, and scanned the area. *Good. No vans.*

On her way to the back of the store to pick up Laney's prescription, she halted by a display of Honeycrisp apples. Laney's favorite. She ripped off a plastic bag and inspected a few of the huge fruits.

"Quite the scam they have going here."

A familiar voice speared through the produce section—and her heart.

"This organic, no-fertilizer-on-my-food scam is completely ridiculous. Although, I do wish I'd come up with it myself. I'd be quite well off and wouldn't have to waste my time coming back to this shithole town."

Across the apple display, Sheridan stared at her father. She hadn't gotten a good look at him during their foray at the fundraiser, but under the produce lighting he created quite the picture. His blond hair was slicked back. He was well dressed in a pair of black dress pants paired with a white button down long-sleeved shirt. Fancy attire for grocery shopping, but then he'd always been meticulous about his appearance, letting his children walk around in rags while he wore designer labels.

Sheridan tossed an apple from one hand to the next. "I do believe you're right. This whole section isn't natural at all, but disgusting and very, very foul." Hand shaking, Sheridan dug her phone out of her back pocket and swiped across the screen. "I'm calling the police. This find-Sheridan-and-scare-her game is over."

"Not so hasty, my girl." Her father flashed a grin, wrinkles appearing beside his blue eyes. "Children are meandering around the store with their mothers. Such a shame if one of them went missing, especially when I never come without back up. You know taking a child and selling it to the highest bidder is my favorite past time." He winked and cracked his knuckles. "I'm surprised to see you alone. What will Clayton say? Oh, but he's distracted with his ex, isn't he? You do know she spent the night at his apartment, right?"

"Nice try." Sheridan wouldn't focus on his lies. Not now. "Your 'back up' wouldn't happen to be a pasty blond with a creepy van now would he?"

"You'll meet him soon enough. Now, as you may be aware I ran into a little trouble, and I need money to disappear. You see, dear it's a win-win. You pay, I go." He clapped his hands together. "Problem solved."

Sheridan's phone rang. Looking down at the screen, she saw Clayton's number but let the call go to voice mail. He would keep calling or have her tracked with his private-eye spy gadgets. *Oh, hell.* Her phone. The GPS. *Shit snacks.* He'd have her tracked in no time.

She shoved Clayton from her mind and focused on her father. "If I pay you, you'll ask for more. And even if you don't, your mafia friends will think I'm willing to give them funds. So, no, I don't have a dime for you or for them." She pulled her gun from her purse and held it just under her arm. "Now, I suggest you leave before I decide to use your face for target practice. Plus Clayton has a tendency to worry when I don't respond. He's likely on his way now."

"Ah, yes, your Mr. Kincaid." Her father held a ripe tomato in his hand before slamming it against the metal display. "You think you're safe living in your little bubble with your wittle private eye...think again. If I don't get paid then...pop." He kicked over a stand of avocados. "I want ten million cash this time next week. I'll text you the drop location."

"Go ahead and text whatever you'd like. I'll just send the information to Maria." Sheridan pulled the woman's card from her purse. "Oh, what's this? A card with Maria's number. Let's give her a call, shall we? Anything you want me to say? Maybe the location of the jewels you stole."

Her father's eyes widened then quickly narrowed before he barked out a laugh. "Ah...little girl, you think you have everything worked out." He shook his head. "I'm sure you remember what happened the last time you went up against me."

Sheridan struggled not to flinch.

"That's what I thought. Now, have a nice trip to New York. Once you return, I'll expect my money."

Sheridan widened her stance then punched in Maria's number. A man answered. "This is Sheridan Bennett. My father is at the grocery store on 83rd street. He's wearing black pants and a white shirt."

The man thanked her and hung up.

"I'd run if I were you." Sheridan smiled at her father.

He took a step toward her. "You'll pay for that."

"Not if Maria finds you first." She tossed an apple in the air before taking a big bite. "Run along now, Daddy. Because my next call is to the police."

He glared at her for a moment before taking off toward the back of the store.

Still on alert, she kept her hand on her gun, but moved it back inside her purse. Backing against the wall of lettuce bags, she crouched down and sucked in air. Calm down. Breathe. Focus.

Tiny tennis shoes with neon green laces appeared in her line of vision. A pint sized boy stood before her. A stocky little bruiser with the Hulk featured on his long-sleeved shirt.

"Why are you sitting like that?" He bent his entire body to look into her face. His mouth was outlined with some sort of brown substance.

Sheridan had to admit his question was legit. Why was she sitting here instead of calling O'Malley or Clayton? She'd just let her father go rather than beating his ass in the middle of the fruit section.

This kid was why.

She couldn't let her father hurt another child. He would. He'd proven that quite clearly once before. She shivered against the horrific memory and tried smiling at the little boy. "The pineapple fairy told me to sit here and wait for a special boy to come along."

"Miss, are you all right?" Hulk-boy's mother interceded. "Would you like me to call someone?"

"No." Sheridan waved a hand. "I just had a dizzy spell. My stomach."

After nodding the lady walked off, nudging her little boy along then she glanced back and tilted her head. "Are you—"

Sheridan's phone rang again. "Excuse me." She lifted her phone to her ear. "Hello."

"Sheridan?" Clayton growled across the line. "Damn it. I've been calling. Why does your GPS say you're inside the supermarket?"

"Um…because I am." She held the phone away from her ear as he yelled every curse word he knew.

"I'm coming in. Where are you?"

"By the salad."

"Stay there."

A few moments later, his tall, lanky form appeared around the corner. Spotting her, he practically stomped over before kneeling beside her. "Damn it, Bennett. What are you doing on the floor?"

# # #

Willing his heart to stop hammering, Clayton grabbed Sheridan by the arm and tugged her out of the store. He'd called her this morning, ready to explain the events of the evening concerning Constance and when she didn't answer, he'd checked her location. Then he'd called Scotty to see when they'd be done shopping, but the man had informed him Sheridan was in the basement of her home. While his friend searched to see if Sheridan was in the house, Clayton had set off to track her down. The level of fury raging through his body was off the charts.

"Why in the hell are you alone?" Ending their less than leisurely stroll to his Expedition, he shook her shoulder. "Are you insane?"

She opened her mouth to reply but then her body suddenly went rigid.

"What?" He glanced around the parking lot.

"It's him." Sheridan pointed to a blond kid standing beside the cart return.

The kid lifted his index finger and thumb, mimicking a gun.

"Bang. Bang." His eerie voice reverberated across the partially empty lot. He smiled before sprinting away.

Sheridan glared then took off running.

Damn it!

Clayton raced after her. She wouldn't be able to sit for a week once he caught her. What kind of fool ran after their own stalker?

A Cadillac sat idling on a side street.

"Sheridan stop!"

The blond guy hopped into the open side door.

Sheridan made a grab for him as the driver tore off. She fell forward onto the pavement, her momentum knocking her off balance.

Halting beside her, Clayton bent to help her stand. "Sheridan, are you all right?"

She rubbed her palms where she had a nasty case of road rash. "Stupid asshole."

The car careened around a corner at the end of the street.

Dusting herself off, she glared at Clayton. "Stupid pasty blond freak thinks he can threaten me." Mumbling to herself, she started walking back toward the store.

"Wait just a damn minute." Clayton yanked her to a stop, rage still flowing. "Are you out of your mind? What would have stopped him from grabbing you and throwing you into the car with him? Why would you do something so stupid?" He grabbed both her shoulders and shook. "Have you no concern for your safety?"

"Let me go." She snapped back.

"Tell me what's going on. Now."

"How did he know where I was?"

"They've got someone on you. Or it was dumb luck…emphasis on dumb." He took her hand and led her toward his SUV. He would get her cleaned up and then take her back home to spank her ass before she answered every one of his questions. "No more evasions, Sheridan. Why are you here?"

She sniffed. "My sister needed her medicine."

"What?" He shouted. "You left your house to get medicine? You have people who can do that for you. What the fuck, Sheridan?" He paced away from her. "Why would you do something that could jeopardize your safety?"

"I was extra careful."

"Wait a minute." He stopped about ten feet from his vehicle. "How did you get here? We've got your place locked down. How did you get by all the security?"

"I took my truck." Biting her bottom lip, she sighed then

walked the rest of the way to his Expedition.

"What truck?" She had a BMW and a Mustang. No truck. Not one he'd seen anyway. He followed her to his vehicle. The only one he had. How many more vehicles did she have stored around her property? "Where is this truck?"

She pointed to a heavy duty F-150 parked close to the store.

"And where is this truck kept? It's not in your garage."

She leaned against the back of his Expedition. "I have it parked behind my house in an old barn. I'm sorry, Clayton. I know I shouldn't have—"

"Don't." He shook his head. Not ready to hear her apology. He'd experienced fear before but knowing she was out on the streets alone had torn him up inside. "Your actions today show a complete lack of trust in me, in Scotty, and in every bit of effort we've put into keeping you safe...but we'll discuss this later. Right now, I want to know how you were able to leave the house undetected."

Sheridan crossed her arms over her chest and met his gaze. "There's a dirt road that leads to the main road, I took that to the store."

"That's not what I asked. I want to know—"

"My father was in the store."

"He what? Well, that's fantastic...and it proves my point that you should not leave the house alone. When will you get that through your head? You are not alone in this. Damn it, Sheridan." Clayton paced away before he said or did something he'd regret. He tugged his phone from his front jean pocket and plugged in O'Malley's number.

The man answered on the first ring.

"Sir, this is Clayton Kincaid, Sheridan was accosted by her father at the store this morning. She's all right, but I wanted you to know his last location."

After speaking to O'Malley for a few more minutes, he hung up and pointed his phone at Sheridan. "What did your father say?"

"Why would you call him?" Sheridan glared with both hands planted on her hips.

"Call who?" Clayton frowned. She had no right to use that tone with him. Not this morning. Not when he'd only called the police like she should have the moment her father arrived.

"O'Malley. He's an old man and now you've got him all worked up."

"No." He held up a finger. "No, it's not me who has him worked up, it's you. *You* are the one gallivanting around town in your truck. *You* are the one who left the safety of your home. *You* are the one who hasn't listened to a goddamn word anyone has said. So, you know what, fuck it." He threw up his hands. "Go ahead and chase after dangerous men in parking lots. Go ahead and believe you're strong enough alone. I'm done trying." He rubbed his pounding temples and met her gaze. "You say you only want a professional relationship. I can do that. I *will* do that."

"No, Clayton." She reached for him. "That's not what I want. I said, I'm sorry. I knew I shouldn't have gone."

He stepped out of her reach. "But that fact is, you did go. So, get your ass in my truck and wait there until I can get someone to take you home. I can't be around you right now."

"I know I was in the wrong, but there's no need for you to speak to me like that."

"Oh, there's every fucking need." He grabbed her wrist, hauled her against him, and kissed her hard, punishing and deep before shoving away. "You say you're sorry, but how can I trust you not to run off again? I'm angry, but most of all, I'm hurt. Apparently, I'm alone in hoping we could be more to each other." Heart aching, he huffed out sigh. "You're tearing me up inside. And I can't do this alone anymore. I can't." He gazed out over the parking lot. She'd always claimed they couldn't be more, but he hadn't believed her words until today. And yet, he couldn't abandon her, because *he* didn't break promises. "I'll maintain our professional relationship, but that will be all. When and if you're ready to escape your past and look to a future with me, come find me. But be prepared, because if you do, I'll take that as a sign you're all in and act accordingly. Until then, get in the truck Sheridan. O'Malley can take you home."

She blinked then opened her mouth to speak, but then shook her head and did as he'd asked.

CHAPTER 26

Two days later Sheridan stared up at her bedroom ceiling, desperately trying to sleep. She'd cancelled her trip to New York, which had her agent fuming, but she couldn't leave with her father roaming the streets.

She tossed off her blankets and headed downstairs for a cup of tea. Perhaps the hot brew would erase the feelings of regret and loneliness coursing through her body, not that herbal teas had worked so far. She had Clayton-withdrawal. Nothing else made sense. She couldn't eat, couldn't sleep, couldn't listen to music—which was really beyond the pale.

Why couldn't he understand she only wanted to keep him safe? His ex-girlfriend had been targeted because of her, for God's sake. O'Malley had driven her home after the grocery store debacle and reamed her a new one for leaving. He'd also explained what had happened to Constance. Her father had been right, after all. Clayton's ex *had* spent the night with him.

Even thinking about Clayton hurt her heart. He'd frozen her out. Only replying to her via text or through Scotty.

Going to the store alone *was* a stupid move.

Sitting on a barstool at the kitchen counter, she sipped her tea and considered what she could say to Clayton to make amends, or if nothing else, figure out a way to become friends again.

Jenny shuffled down the stairs in her scruffy green slippers and light pink pajamas. "What's in the tea pot?"

"It's lavender tea with honey. I needed a stress reliever."

"Still haven't heard from Clayton then?" Jenny pulled her favorite cup out of the dishwasher.

"I tried calling him, but he doesn't answer. One minute I think it's for the best, the next I want to hunt him down."

"He's right, you know." Jenny poured tea into her mug.

"About what?"

"That you're being a big baby scaredy cat." She braced a hand on one hip. "And an idiot."

"Excuse me?" Sheridan sputtered, almost choking on a mouthful of hot liquid.

"Give him a chance. You always say we need to move forward, well apparently that's only words, because you aren't following your own advice. I know your father hurt you, but Clayton isn't your father. He's become important to me too, you know." Jenny shifted her weight. "I believe he's sincere in his feelings, and I don't blame him for being fed up with you. *I'm* fed up myself. You're basically dating him now anyway, so what's the problem? Your whole 'I'm tough and I don't need anyone' attitude is super stupid."

"Well geez, Jenny." Sheridan picked her jaw up off the floor. "Just say what you think next time."

Jenny didn't remember that *her* father had done real damage. Irreparable damage. Plus, getting a lecture from a younger sister seemed all kinds of wrong.

"Whatever, Sheridan." Jenny rolled her eyes before heading back upstairs.

So much for sisterly solidarity.

Sheridan stared at a lone tealeaf circling the inside of her cup. Jenny didn't know the whole truth. Her sister was unaware of the nasty scarring that marred her skin, making a physical relationship impossible. That wasn't what her doctor said, but what did she know? Yeah, right, Sheridan, a doctor didn't go to college, didn't study, didn't know anything.

"Great, now you're arguing with yourself." She tossed the leftover tea into the sink and headed upstairs.

Clayton wanted someone who would trust in him. Rely on him. Fine. They both knew the risks, now maybe they should reap the rewards. The whole idea of a relationship in the middle of this mess was ludicrous...but she missed him. Even wanted him at her side, because she *did* need him. She'd believed she was strong on her own, but he made her stronger. He'd crashed through all her barriers and instead of falling apart she'd finally come together. Plus, if her father killed her within the next couple weeks, shouldn't she die with a satisfied smile on her face?

So what now? How would she tell Clayton she was ready to make the leap when he wouldn't speak to her?

Sheridan grabbed her phone and pulled up Rachel Harris's number. His boss would know where to find him.

Sheridan would get all up in his business and tell him, that yeah, they were doing this.

Choice made.

CHAPTER 27

After begging Scotty not to tell Clayton her plans, Sheridan thanked him as he dropped her off at the party being held at Owen Killion's house. Owen played on the offensive line for the Manchester Marauders. Rachel had explained that Clayton would be here tonight. The team was celebrating Thanksgiving early due to their game falling on the actual holiday.

Luxury cars, trucks, and SUV's lined the driveway. The house was lit up inside. Music thumping loudly.

She tucked the bottle of red wine at her side and knocked on the door. Scotty would follow her inside once he'd parked. He wasn't about to leave her alone after he'd gotten an earful from Clayton after misplacing her the other day. Plus, he'd been all excited about partying with football players from his favorite team.

Hopefully, Rachel had told Owen her plans. She didn't want to be known as a party-crasher. Smoothing the front of her black cocktail dress, she took in a deep breath and released it slowly.

Stay strong, Bennett.

A tall, curvy redhead answered the door. "Oh…" She stepped back. "Rachel said you were coming…and here you are." The woman remained in the doorway, openly staring. "Oh my gosh, I'm so sorry. Come in. I had a moment of shock, but it passed. Plus, it's so crazy in here. Boys and bourbon don't always mix." The pretty redhead cleared her throat and stuck out her hand. "I'm Ember. I'm so glad you came."

"Ember. You're dating Owen, right?" Sheridan stepped inside and bopped her head to the hip-hop music pounding through the room. She loved to dance. Some nights when just her sisters were in the house, they'd crank up the Pointer Sisters and lip synch to all their songs. The thought made her smile and eased her mind a little.

Groups of people stood in circles, laughing, talking, and eating. Most wore Marauder green and white, while others had dressed similar to her, in cocktail party attire.

"Yes. In answer to your question, I'm with Owen." Ember smiled and glanced around the room. "I think he's out in the garage. Can't get him out of there."

"I'm sorry for crashing the party."

"Oh, don't be sorry." Ember patted Sheridan's arm. "Having a movie star here will be a highlight. The boys will talk about this forever. Is that wine for me? That's so kind. Thank you. I'm babbling, aren't I? I'm sorry. Do people normally act this way around you?"

"Yes, but it's okay. Although, I wish you could see me as…well, as Rachel does…she doesn't care who I am. She treats me the same as everyone else."

"Rachel isn't intimidated by anyone, is she?" Ember laughed.

"No, but then I think you must be pretty brave yourself. I heard about your horrible experience. I'm sorry for what you went through." The poor woman had almost died a year or so ago. Based on what Sheridan understood from the story, she and Ember had a lot in common.

"Rachel said you're here to see Clayton. Last I saw, he was in the kitchen." Ember took her elbow and led her through the house.

As Sheridan followed, she heard her name being whispered.

Stopping for fan photos wasn't on her agenda. She wouldn't stop until she found Clayton and voiced all these thoughts spinning through her mind. Although, she would like to find a private room. *Oh no!* Perhaps, a party packed with people wasn't the best place for an intimate conversation.

Walking behind Ember, she experienced a shiver of that awareness that only one man could create. She froze, and then rose up on her tiptoes, peering through the wall of bodies.

There he stood in the kitchen doorway, watching her.

Her heart slammed against her chest as he pushed off the wall and prowled to her side.

"Oh my." Ember brought a hand to her mouth. "I'll let you guys…well…I'll talk to you later." She chuckled, and then skittered off with the wine bottle.

Without saying a word, Clayton grasped Sheridan by the back of the neck and kissed her, parting her lips with his tongue, unashamedly slanting his mouth to deepen the kiss.

Tasting alcohol, she pushed away. "Are you drunk?"

Raising a brow, he lifted his mouth into a sexy half smile. "I *have* been drinking."

"We can talk another time then." She turned on her heel and stuttered to a stop. Everyone was looking their way, and some were even taking pictures. *Great.*

"You're not leaving." Clayton picked her up, lifted her onto his shoulder, and headed down a quiet hallway.

"Put me down! What are you thinking?"

"I'm done thinking."

"Excuse me? You must be drunk if you think you can carry me around like some kind of barbarian."

In a room, with a queen-sized bed topped with a plain white comforter, he slid her down his body then hauled her against him again, crushing her mouth with his. Moments later, he released her, his mouth glistening from their wild kiss. "Sit down." He pushed her onto the bed.

Then the crazy man turned and locked the door.

"What are you doing?" Was he thinking they would use this bed? Now? Sure, she'd made a choice to be with him, but sex was way down the road. Wasn't it?

With an arched brow, Clayton studied her, leaning against the bedroom door. So sexy in his dress pants, white shirt, and his blue tie undone. He hadn't shaved so he was all scruffy.

Why did women have to do gymnastic contortions to shave yet men walked around with prickly faces and it was a major turn on? If she had hair on her face...*What? Why was she thinking about facial hair right now? Good lord.*

That sexy mouth spoke, a deep vibration that melted her resistance even further.

"I believe I made it very clear what I expected if you came to me. You are here now, that means you've accepted you are mine."

"I came by to talk, Clayton. Not to be your drunken play toy."

"No more talking, and I like playing with toys." He grinned wickedly as he walked toward her.

"Wait, I have something I want to say." Sheridan lifted up onto her elbows. "I am willing to—"

"No more talking," he growled before yanking off his tie, unbuttoning his shirt, and kicking off his shoes. Then he braced himself above her.

She ran both hands up and down his back. Every inch of him was perfectly formed. And all hers if she was brave enough to take him.

He leaned down, his mouth drifting over hers.

"Clayton, wait..."

"No more waiting"

"Stop. Please." She shoved against his chest.

He sat back on his heels. "I did warn you."

"Yes, you did, but first, I want you to understand that...you were right about me. I do have trust issues, but I'll try to consider you as a partner from now on. I'm willing to give whatever this is between us a chance. I don't want to lose you even though I'm worried my father will hurt you." She cupped his face in her hands. "If you want to be with me physically, even though, I'm *so* not ready for that, maybe...maybe it would be best...I can't believe I'm going to say this, but could you look at me first? Then if my scars are too much...I-I can go."

"You're not going anywhere, and I will love every piece of you." He dropped a quick kiss on her lips.

"Are you sure you're not drunk? My stomach is hurting, so how about we agree we're doing this whole relationship thing, and we go back to the party. Maybe Ember has some ginger ale."

"No."

"We are at a party. In some person's bed."

"Owen won't mind."

Sheridan groaned and covered her eyes with both hands.

He kissed her fingers then pulled them away from her face. "I told you I love you. Every inch. Nothing will ever change that, all right?"

She nodded, although in a dark portion of her mind, she sensed a wiggle of resistance trying to rear its ugly head.

"I like the idea of looking you over. But since you're nervous, I'll start." He removed his dress shirt then pulled off his white T-shirt. He reached for her, but pulled back. "Wait a minute. Are you here alone?"

"No, Scotty is out there somewhere." Sheridan flicked a hand toward the door.

"Good."

With brevity she didn't know she had, Sheridan ran a hand down Clayton's bare chest. His light dusting of dark hair narrowed to a V before disappearing beneath his pants—where an interesting bulge had formed.

"That feels real nice, Slim." He took her hand and kissed it. "I'm glad you're here and that you've made a positive decision. I hate that your past was holding you back from me and from us. I really want to stay in this moment, but if you don't want to show me now, you don't have to."

"No. It means a lot that you're willing to let me wait, but you're right, we're in the moment, and I can do this. I need to do this." She sat up and undid the side zipper of her dress then slowly worked the fabric off her shoulders.

Clayton's gaze raked down her body. The heat from that look fired along every inch of her skin.

She held her arms over her heaving chest before rising to her knees and scooting her dress down to her hips.

With an index finger, he traced the scars along her abdomen, her upper and inner thighs, and above her panty line.

She shivered and swallowed the lump in her throat.

Some scars were a faded pink on the outside. Others were a shiny white, almost silver. A few were small slits. Others were longer.

"How have you hidden these? In the movies, I mean."

"Body doubles. I have a no nudity clause written into all my contracts."

"So, I'm the only one then?"

Smiling, she nodded. "You're the only one."

Leaning forward, Clayton kissed her stomach just above the scrap of lace covering her core. "I'm going to touch you. If it's too much, or you get frightened, just tell me, and we'll slow down. All right?"

"Yes, if you're sure that's what you want." She looked into his true-blue eyes. He had to be thinking about how she'd received these scars. The thought disgusted her, and almost had her running for the door. But she was taking this chance, allowing Clayton an opportunity to make new memories. Better ones.

"Don't." Clayton pulled her onto his lap, settling her thighs on each side of his. "When we're together like this, it's just you and me, no one else. We'll be so close nothing will ever come between us. Leave the past behind, Slim. These marks on your skin show that your body has healed." He placed soft kisses upon her chest. "Now, let me heal your heart."

Sheridan nodded, biting her lip as she fought back tears. "I will try to see myself as you do."

"Just you and me."

"Yes."

His lips quirked before he wrapped his arm around her waist and pulled her against his warm skin. A faint scent of woodsy-citrus filled her senses.

"How about we try this." He brushed her hair over her shoulder. "Scene one, the heroine leans in to kiss the extremely handsome aquatic super hero."

Sheridan smothered a laugh then kissed him. For the first time, she led, drawing him in, tangling her tongue with his, and allowing herself to feel.

Throughout her kiss, he brushed his fingers along her back, her arms, and down over her legs.

"Scene two, he removes her bra." After unhooking her lacy black undergarment, Clayton tossed it to the side of the bed. "You doing okay, Sheridan?"

"Yes, don't make me think. Just do it."

Nodding, he bent his head, taking her taut nipple into his mouth.

A shot of lust traveled straight to her middle. Her hips arched as if they had a mind of their own and were ready to get as close as possible.

He kissed across her chest before licking the tip of her nipple while continuing to gently caress the other.

"Oh, that feels amazing." She ran her fingers through his hair, encouraging him.

Easing away, he smiled before covering her lips with his. Passionately slanting his mouth over hers, making her crazed.

This was what she'd fought against? *So stupid!* Dragging her nails down his back, she again lifted her hips in invitation. Her mind and heart might not be ready, but her core screamed, "Hello! Get this party started!"

Clayton cupped her breast, shaping it in his palm. He moved his hips with her own motion, imitating the sexual act.

She was a loaded gun, just waiting for him to pull the trigger. She moaned into his mouth and followed when he pulled away.

He tugged at her thin panty string. "Shall we remove these?"

"I'm not…I don't know." She bit her bottom lip. How much farther could she go? Her entire body started shaking and tears escaped and trickled down her cheeks. Sensations had overloaded her circuits. She'd never been with a man without direction or a film crew hovering. How was this done?

"Hey." He lifted his head and met her gaze. "Why the tears? Should we stop?"

"I didn't think we would get this far today." Taking a deep breath, Sheridan scooted off his lap and sat on the edge of the bed. "I only came here to talk, and now I'm basically naked and feeling things I've never felt before. I'm afraid, and I hate it. I want to be brave." She wiped away her stupid tears. "I'm trying, but now that I'm in the moment. I just don't know what to do, or how to feel. I've never been with a man before…well, other than movies, but they don't count and then…well, my childhood situation…I don't know…I've got all these thoughts crisscrossing in my head. I'm overwhelmed."

"Then we'll stop. Come here." He wrapped an arm around her shoulders. "Lie down and let me hold you."

She fell back and let him situate her on the bed beside him. He kissed her hand before placing it above his beating heart.

His willingness to stop meant everything.

Even when his body was on fire. Even when his erection was pressed against her hip. He'd stopped.

His love was real, thriving and thumping deep within his chest. He'd always been patient, dealt with her wishy-washy feelings, and her stubborn refusal to accept his help, and through everything he'd remained by her side. Steadfast and true.

She twisted onto her side. "I'm grateful for your patience."

"Every time we're together we take another step forward. And that's a good thing."

Sheridan squirmed and nudged him with her hips. "I feel all ooey-gooey inside."

Clayton groaned and placed a hand upon her thigh. "That's a good thing."

"Yeah." She lifted up onto an elbow. "I think it is. I want to finish."

"No. I think we've gone far enough tonight."

"But what about the ooey-gooey?" She bit her lip and stared up at him from beneath lowered lashes. "I never said I wanted to stop, only that I was overwhelmed." She took his hand and pressed it against her breast. "Touch me again. Kiss me. Show me how it feels to be with someone who loves me. I want to know."

Clayton brushed his thumb across her nipple. "I do, too. But only if you're sure."

"I'm a mass of goo. I need to come so bad I can't stand it." She squeezed her thighs together.

"What?" He eased back, eyes wide.

"I *have* had an orgasm before."

"How?" Wearing a cocky grin, and looking absolutely adorable with his ruffled hair, he slipped a finger under her panties thin string along her hip.

"I'm not so sure someone who uses the term ooey-gooey is qualified to continue with dirty talk." She chuckled, sure her face was bright red.

"I like it." He brushed a quick kiss against her lips. "Thank you for trusting me. For letting me see you. Understand this, Slim, when I look at you all I see is a woman who dares me to be just as strong as she is."

"You like it when I dare you?" She arched a brow.

He nodded and then trailed a finger along her lower lip.

"Would you like me to dare you now?"

"I'd love for you to dare me now."

"Well then, I dare you to show me pleasure." She ran a hand along the back of his neck. "I've dreamed about how I'd feel beneath you, now I dare you to show me."

CHAPTER 28

Hearing Sheridan say those words and seeing the need in her eyes, unleashed something inside, giving Clayton the confidence to take the dare.

She wasn't the only one needing, wanting, and hoping for bliss.

At first he'd been a little unsure. Worried how he would react when he saw the marks another had put on her body. But nothing detracted from all her lush curves. The dip of her stomach, the heavy weight of her breasts, the soft glow on her cheeks. He loved every inch of her, and now that she had revealed her scars, he would show her how much he appreciated her trust.

Moving over her body, he kissed her deeply, sliding his hand along her smooth skin until he landed between her legs. Through the thin slip of silk, he circled her wet nub with his thumb. "Oh, Sher, you're so ready." Keeping a steady rhythm, he kissed her languidly, fluid, as if her lips were clouds he couldn't catch. Biting and nipping, seeking more.

Brushing aside her panties, he eased his finger across her wet folds then into her core, entering with a slow slide.

She whimpered. "You are so acing this dare. That feels amazing."

Her long blonde strands framed her face in loose curls. He'd never expected tonight to end like this, but once he'd seen her, he'd wanted to take her. Show every man in the room she was his. And he would, with the music thumping in the background and his friends partying away the night, he'd stay here with this woman and take the moment that only belonged to them.

With a long moan, she arched against his hand.

He bent and sucked her nipple, tugging and licking as he worked his finger within her slick channel.

Her mouth parted, and her body turned an enticing shade of pink.

"Feel good?"

"Mmm...hmm." Moving her hips in time with the movement of his hand, she tightened her grip on his wrist. "Please, don't stop."

He slid his tongue across her breast before kissing his way up to her neck and landing on her mouth.

She eagerly returned his kiss. Sloppy and wet, she sucked on his tongue. Then she tore away and dug her nails into his back. "Clayton... I think...please...if you just...yes, right there..."

He maintained his deep dip into her body, kissing her again, until she twisted away and shouted his name.

Her hips rose and fell with each of his thrusts, her entire body shuddering as she hit her peak. Her chest heaved, and she panted out in short bursts.

After a few final spasms, he withdrew from her core and blew out a long breath. Her scent. Her warm breath upon his skin. Her soft sighs were more than he could handle.

Her arms flopped to her sides and she opened her eyes, met his gaze and drew him down for a kiss. A long drawn out kiss that started soft but quickly raged out of control. He worried he'd rip off his pants and take her right then and there.

His dick was like an iron rod between them, begging for its own release after she'd sung to him with her sweet cries. "Sher...we need to cool it down a little. I'm hanging by a thread here."

She blinked, but released her grip on his neck. "Clayton, that was the most beautiful experience of my life. Everything in me rose up then shattered. I think my heart exploded." She placed one hand upon her heart then took his other hand and brought it up to her plumped lips for a kiss.

"I'm honored you came to me tonight."

"I'm honored I came to." She giggled. "Ah, funny. Now, what about you? Can I touch you?"

His dick said, Hell, yes, but his heart said, Slow down, Mushroom-head.

"*Can* you touch me? Sure, but I can wait."

"Are you in pain?"

"It's a good pain." He winced and shifted onto his side.

"I've missed you the past couple days. I don't like it when you're mad at me." Sheridan wrapped an arm around his waist.

"Then don't do things that put your life at risk."

"I don't want to. I feel like if I'd had you by my side all those years ago, I would've been all right." She shook her head. "Not that you would have saved me, but at least I wouldn't have been fighting alone. I don't know what I'm saying. All this emotional and physical release has made me sleepy. But, I guess we should go back to the party. I can hear it now that I'm not screaming your name."

"I'd rather hear you then whatever this music is." Clayton ran a finger down her nose.

"So no dance music for Clayton Kincaid, is that what I'm hearing?"

"Yes."

"Hmm…maybe I'll have to dare you to get on the dance floor sometime. You certainly handled your last dare well."

He slapped her bottom. "Don't remind me. I'm trying to be good."

She kissed his chest then yawned. "I haven't been sleeping

well."

"I've got you." He drew her head against his shoulder. "Get some rest."

As he watched Sheridan's eyes droop closed, he smiled knowing that he did indeed have her, just as she had him.

#

Clayton awoke to a flash of blonde hair and white legs bustling around the room. "Slim, what are you doing?"

"I'm getting dressed."

Her bra was hanging open in the back and she had on his briefs.

"First off, interesting combo. Second, why the rush?" Clayton gripped his pillow tighter, watching as she put on his socks.

"We're in someone else's house." She whispered but it came across as more of a whisper-shriek.

Her nipple peeked at him from over the bra's cup.

"That settles it." He surged forward, tossed her back on the bed, and kissed her senseless. Once he'd achieved that dazed look in her eyes, he plucked the socks from her feet and carried her to the bathroom.

Waiting for her to make the right choice these past couple days had been complete hell, but having her in his arms now was worth it. She'd become his world. His reason to smile. His friend. And last night, she'd taught him what it meant to have someone completely trust you. And yet, he still kept a secret from her. He needed to tell her he'd met with the FBI agents, but not now. Now he had other plans.

"Let's get cleaned up." Stripping off the rest of her clothes, and then his own, he stepped into the shower and tugged her inside.

Once he finished giving her a very thorough washing, he

rinsed her off then pressed her against the shower wall. He devoured her mouth with a deep kiss, his hands moving up and down her body. "I can't get enough of you. I know we'll need to leave Owen's someday, but honestly I'd be happy just living here for a few weeks, maybe months."

"I like touching you, too." Sheridan glanced at his dick. "You're very…firm this morning."

"Don't mind him. He's a selfish prick." Laughing, Clayton kissed her neck then sank to his knees on the shower floor. Focused on her needs, he placed his hands upon her thighs and parted her legs.

"Wait." Sheridan covered herself with both hands.

"It's all right. Just another step." He caressed her inner thighs, soothing her. "Relax."

"Its just. I-I it's not pretty."

"Oh, Slim, it's about to get real ugly." Moving her hands back to her sides, he plunged his tongue between her folds, licking and sucking until her knees wobbled.

She jerked when he sank one finger inside her core. Moving within her, he slid against her silken wetness until she tightened around him. "Clayton, it's happening again, but I-I…" She bit the pad of her thumb and moaned his name.

He licked her clit again, once, twice then her entire body stiffened. She tightened her hand in his hair as she shivered then came.

"That's it. Feel how good we are together." He slowed his deep caress then kissed her thigh before removing his finger and straightening.

Gasping for breath, she met his gaze. "You are a master. No wonder the girls chase after you."

"Oh, I imagine there will be much weeping and gnashing of teeth upon hearing I'm off the market."

"Yeah, off the market." Blinking, she glanced down at his dick again then ran a finger along a thick vein. "Do you dare me to touch you?"

He gripped her wandering hand. "We've done enough steps today…and last night." His dick literally wept at his words, seeping pre-cum from the slit. "We'll try that some other time."

"I want to try now." She ran a finger along the tip of his dick. "I may not be any good, but I would like to try."

He heaved a sigh. "Let's get dried off, Aquagirl."

After retrieving two very fluffy brown towels, Clayton stood outside the shower with the worst case of blue balls he'd ever had in his life. His lower body wrapped in a towel, he combed his fingers through his hair. "We'll have to sneak out. I'll call Scotty and have him bring up the car."

"No." Naked as the day she was born, Sheridan grabbed him by the waist and dropped to her knees. "Let me do this."

"If you're sure, I don't know that I can argue with you in that position. It'd take the will of a much stronger man." He loosened the towel, but stopped to wipe off the leaking tip so she wouldn't receive too much of his essence at the beginning.

Sheridan pushed him against the sink's edge. With her finger, she traced a vein along his length before licking the tip. Holding him at the root while drawing him into her mouth, she squeezed his twin sacs in her free hand.

Holy fuck. Where did she learn that move?

Peeping up at him, she unreservedly took him deep before laving her tongue around his thick head.

He placed a hand on her cheek. "That's so good."

She tightened her hand around his base and drew him deep, her cheeks hollowing with the suction. Over and over she repeated the move until his balls tightened, preparing for release.

"Fuck, yes…pull back, baby…" Groaning, he cursed again as his orgasm slammed through his body, his hips jerked, and his hot warmth hit the back of her throat.

He hissed as she continued to knead his balls and work him with her mouth until he went limp. Loosening his grip on her hair, he pulled free of her mouth, emitting a satisfied hum before dropping to his knees in front of her.

Sheridan wiped her mouth with the back of her hand.

"I always knew you'd bring me to my knees." Wrapping his arms around her, he rested his head on top of hers. "I think maybe now we're not so broken. Now we have hope."

"I'm still broken, but you're helping me find the pieces." She leaned back, cupping his face in both her hands. "But I'll take hope if that's what you're offering. Lord knows we're going to need it."

CHAPTER 29

Two days later, Clayton rubbed his eyes, trying to erase erotic visions of Sheridan from his mind. Memories of her sighs of pleasure, her soft skin, her sweet pleas delivered in her husky voice had him contemplating jumping over his desk and hunting her down.

He loved her in a way he couldn't even begin to describe. And because they were a team now he needed to come clean about his FBI dealings. He also wanted to speak to Erik Pavel again.

This morning, lying next to Sheridan on rose-covered sheets, he'd touched her silky skin to verify he wasn't dreaming. She opened those blue eyes, and smiled. Then she'd said something suggestive. He might've said something back, and they'd ended up wrestling on the floor by her bed. After that…well, it'd been a very fine morning.

Groaning, he shifted his semi-hard dick in his jeans. They still hadn't made love, but they would. Right now, Sheridan seemed to be gorging herself on a feast of kisses and caresses. Introducing her to intimacy was no trouble at all. "Patience man. You can do this." He plopped his head in both hands, and then rubbed his temples with his palms.

"You doing all right in here, Kincaid?"

"Damn it, Harris." Frowning at the intruder, Clayton straightened. "Don't sneak up on a man who's only had one cup of coffee."

Rachel leaned against his doorway, her own cup in hand. She wore jeans and a bulky, purple sweater. "What's all the moaning about?"

"I may think about sex at work, but I'm not actually shutting the door and thinking everyone else in the office can't hear what's happening. You need to get your desk disinfected."

"Thinking about sex with who?" Rachel arched a brow.

Trust her to zero in on the one thing he'd never discuss.

"Men think about sex every seven seconds." He shrugged. "Scientific fact."

"I'm sure." Rachel crossed her feet at the ankles, tapping her nail against the top of her mug. "So the paparazzi should be arriving at our door any day now, is this what I'm hearing?"

"If they find out about us, Sheridan will send out a statement that she's hired Harris Investigations for a little security work."

"Right, like anyone will believe that."

"Don't care what they believe." Clayton shrugged again. "Although, she did mention she might take a break for a year or two. If she's not constantly in the spotlight, she'd have a little more freedom."

"And what's she going to do during all that time?"

"She's talked to the director of the local playhouse. She thought maybe she'd organize plays for charity. Fundraisers, that sort of thing."

"Huh…I guess that's a good plan." Rachel sipped from her mug.

"Yep." Clayton stood and tapped a handful of papers against this desk, lining them up so he could file them. "Thanks again for inviting her to Owen's the other night."

"I was tired of your mopey-face."

"I'm not sure that was the case, and anyway, how about we

talk about work?" He had been a complete jerk during the time he'd given Sheridan her ultimatum. And now that he thought about it, she still hadn't explained how she'd been able to bypass all the security at her house. He'd been so wrapped up in her that he was missing important details. *Not good.*

Rachel cleared her throat. "Clayton?"

"Sorry, what did you say?" He snapped back to attention.

"I asked if you were able to track Sheridan's father using the number from her phone?"

"O'Malley tracked it to a dumpster outside of Vera LaSasso's restaurant." Clayton sighed and sank back into his chair. "This morning I visited some of our underground contacts and promised hefty rewards in exchange for information on the Korzakov family and on Bennett. Yesterday, I got a lead at that hardware store just up the road. This pretty brunette cashier said a young blond kid paid in cash and flirted her up a bit. Said his name was Sheldon Bennett."

"Sheldon Bennett?" Rachel met his gaze.

"I know." Frowning, Clayton tapped a pen against his desk. "Odd, right? Blond, same last name, which suggests he's Sheridan's brother."

"Will you tell her?"

Clayton rubbed his chin. "No. She might feel sympathy for the kid and that's the last thing we need. She needs to remain alert and consider everyone on her father's side an enemy."

"I see your point, but you're walking a fine line."

"Things are coming to a head. I can feel it."

"Have you shared these thoughts with her?"

"Ms. Bennett and everyone else I know is under guard twenty-four-seven."

"That's not an answer, Kincaid." Rachel pressed her lips together, shaking her head.

"For me it is."

"I don't know that Sheridan would agree."

"She knows things are reaching a tipping point. Probably even more than I do. I'm scared to death she'll slip off and face her father by herself."

"Would she do something like that?"

"Hell yes, if she thought she was saving someone."

"You need to get that shit in check."

"Oh, that's fantastic advice coming from you." Clayton glared at his boss.

"What?" Rachel bit her bottom lip, likely holding back a grin.

"You have a history of charging forward and apologizing later, so don't dictate to me. I still don't know why Bronco puts up with you."

"Because I'm awesome."

Clayton shook his head and tossed a pen at her head.

She caught it and tossed it back. "Bronco's coming by for lunch. Let me know if I can borrow your can of Lysol." After flashing a wicked grin, she turned on her heel and headed for her office.

"Didn't need the visual, Harris." He picked up his phone to check his messages.

Rachel popped her head back in and waggled her brows. "You'd need a *very* wide screen."

Clayton groaned. "Why do I work for you again?"

Her heard her chuckle and couldn't help his own.

Then the outer door buzzed, alerting him to his appointment.

Clayton buzzed up Agent Denver.

Once all the polite chitchat was out of the way, they settled in his office.

"Agent Denver, thanks for coming in today." Clayton handed the agent a cup of coffee.

"If you hadn't called, I'd likely have come by anyway." Denver blew across the top of his steaming coffee. "Maria Korzakov is back in town and this time she brought a much larger entourage. Two of her fine fellows have been patrolling Sheridan's neighborhood. We had a local cop pull them over yesterday so they'd know we're aware of their presence. On top of all that, Vera LaSasso has gone missing. She hasn't been seen in three days."

Clayton leaned back, stomach churning as this news hit. "Damn it. I hadn't thought to put anyone on her aunt." He'd have to tell Sheridan about Vera, and she'd have to notify her cousin.

"Has Sheridan been contacted by her father?" Denver continued.

The man seemed awful calm.

Clayton wasn't. Especially knowing dangerous men were cruising his woman's neighborhood. "Other than the morning at the store. No, I'm not aware of Jack contacting her."

"Well, get aware, Kincaid." Denver shot out of his seat. "Maria is seeking revenge for Bennett's betrayal. Her presence means they know he's still here. Bennett is smart, though. Skilled at evasion. Plus, he's familiar with this area."

"Sheridan and her sisters need your assistance, even more so now that her aunt's gone missing."

Agent Denver stopped pacing and met his gaze. "She'll never agree to that."

Clayton tapped a pen against his desk. "Don't give her a choice."

"We've tried to work with her in the past."

"Was it working with her or interrogating her?" Clayton had never understood why she wouldn't accept help from the FBI. At first he'd thought her stubborn, but as he studied the man in his office, he realized something else—or someone else, must have warranted her disdain for the agency. "Why is she so reticent to work with you Denver? What did you do to her?"

"I may have come on a little too strong at first." He winced.

"Yeah, she's not a fan of that." A fact he knew all too well. She'd fought against his assistance every step of the way. He could only imagine if he'd cornered her and demanded she cooperate. She would've clawed and scratched like a feral cat.

"Maria wants Jack Bennett, but she'll go after Sheridan if this lasts much longer." Denver braced both hands against the back of the chair he'd vacated.

Clayton cracked his knuckles. "She can try."

"We've got eyes on Sheridan and her sisters."

"Somehow that doesn't seem like enough." Keeping his gaze on Denver, Clayton tested the waters a little more. "Any word on the identity of the blond man?"

"No." He answered just a little too quickly

"I see." Clayton understood why Sheridan didn't share information with Denver—it wasn't reciprocated. "Cut the bullshit. If you have any knowledge on who the van guy could be, I suggest you tell me now. I can't protect Sheridan if I don't know who we're dealing with."

Denver heaved a long sigh. "We believe he is her brother."

Well, well a little honesty. *Good.*

"Thank you. The kid's loyalty makes sense if Bennett is his father." Plans and worries churning in his mind, Clayton stood and glanced out the horizontal window behind his desk. Not much of a view, but he could still see the gray skies and the coming storm.

CHAPTER 30

That night, dressed only in a pair of gym shorts, Clayton sat on the edge of Sheridan's bed, tossing her gift back and forth between his hands. He'd prepped for this moment, thought he was ready, but damn if he wasn't nervous. This woman was it for him, and he'd make this experience something special and memorable, something that expressed everything in his heart. He could do this—make them both feel good.

Upon hearing the master bath's door open, he turned and barely kept a gasp from escaping. Smooth pink skin and nothing else.

Without a word, he strode across the room then stopped before her and trailed a finger between her breasts.

She shivered.

And so did he. "This is for you." He held out the tiny blue box that signified a world of hope.

"What?" She gasped, covering her mouth with a hand. "Oh my."

He eased her trembling hand from her face and placed the box in it. "Open this, please."

She lifted the lid, revealing a sapphire ring, surrounded by four diamonds. "Clayton, what is this?" Eyes wide, she met his gaze.

"I'd like you to wear this as a sign of our commitment."

She paused for a moment before nodding. "I'll wear it because it's beautiful, because it's a gift from you...I-I haven't received many gifts in my life." Pulling the ring from the box, she held it out to him. "Why don't you slide it on my finger?"

He kissed her hand before sliding his gift onto her left ring finger.

She wiggled her finger then a sly smile lit her lips. "Good thing I know you're a wealthy man or I'd feel bad about accepting such a gift."

"That so?"

"Yep." She laughed before launching herself into his arms and kissing him.

The stone scraped against his neck and he lost all control. He braced an arm under her sweet ass and backed her against the wall. With an animalistic groan, he dove for her neck, dropping kisses on his way to her chest. Her skin emitted some flower and lemon mixture, and he knew he'd die with that scent floating through his senses. Hell, he might die now.

She arched against him, inviting him to taste.

So he did, he bit and licked her peaked nipples. Then he journeyed up to her mouth for light teasing kisses before devouring her mouth, slanting his head, and delving for more.

Gasping, she rotated her hips against him.

After recapturing his breath, he wrapped her hair in his hand and pulled back, offering up the side of her neck for his pleasure. He kissed his way down, lifting her higher in his arms. Hungry for more, he circled her taut nipple with his tongue.

Sheridan moaned and grasped his head with both hands.

The sound reverberated through him, making him aware of where they were. He couldn't take her against the wall—not at first.

Locking her mouth against his, he gripped her tighter then

walked to the bed before dropping her to her feet.

"It's time, isn't it?" Sheridan glanced at him, biting her lower lip.

"We talked about this." He brushed her slightly-damp hair over her shoulder. "If you want to wait, we will."

She licked her lips. "You won't need these." Working her hand under his waistband, she scored her fingernails over his butt as she pushed his shorts over his hips. She rubbed her thumb against his cock's leaking tip. "So this is what you'll use to bring me pleasure?"

Hissing out a breath, he gripped her hand. "Slim, I want you to touch me. All of me. But right now, how about we take this slow and easy?"

"I think I'll like slow and easy."

"We both will." He laced his fingers through her hair, meeting her gaze before he kissed her. After she was pliant in his arms, he nudged her down onto the bed.

Kneeling before her, he caressed the insides of her thighs. "Spread your legs for me, Sheridan."

Once she obeyed his command, he circled her silky folds with his fingers.

"Use your left hand to touch your nipple."

"Clayton...no..." Her hair rustled against the pillow as she shook her head.

"I want to see the ring on your finger while I'm pleasuring you." As an incentive, he eased two fingers into her wet heat. "Show me."

She shuddered, her head falling back as he continued the rhythmic plunge into her core.

He lifted her hand from the side of the bed. "Touch yourself."

"You're so bossy."

When she tentatively plucked her nipple, she sent his on-the-verge-of exploding-cock into a whole new dimension. The ring on her finger, the moans coming from her lips, the heat between them was everything this moment should be.

"I want to finish with you inside me." Sheridan tugged at his hand. "Please…let me finish with you."

"All right, Slim, but let me taste you first." He settled between her legs and licked her taut bud before driving his tongue deep within her body. Once, twice, three times until she scooted away.

"Clayton, please." She touched his cheek. "I-I'm too close." She shifted further back on the bed, beckoning him with an index finger as she let her knees fall open.

"This is it, love." He settled between her legs, holding himself above her. "You're all mine now." After grabbing the condom off the side table, he slipped it on and stroked his cock. "I'm going to come so quick."

She smiled and ran her fingers down his arms. "I'm trying not to be scared. You've been so patient with me, and I don't think I can wait any longer. No matter what happens, this is the best moment of my life."

Heart full of emotion, he took her hand and kissed her ring finger. "Mine, too."

"Bet you say that to all the girls." She tapped his bottom lip.

"Not anymore." He gripped her hips before working his tip into her yielding passage. Torture was too small a word for the gentle easing into her body.

"Wait." She tensed beneath him.

Jaw clenched, Clayton met her gaze. "Everything's okay. Just you and me."

"I know. I know." Eyes wide, she swallowed hard. "Just maybe go slow."

"We can stop." The hardest three words of his life, but he'd give her time.

"No." She covered her face with both hands. "I'm so sorry. I've ruined the moment. I just never thought—"

"Sheridan, look at me." He placed her hands at her sides. "I'll love you no matter what. We can wait." He leaned down and kissed her long and deep until she squirmed and clutched his sides.

"I can do this. Go ahead now." She blew out a slow breath.

He slowly eased back then forward again. "This okay?"

"Yes, please."

His entire body shuddered. "That's it. Oh, Sheridan. Fucking hell." He plunged to the hilt, pulled back, and then did it again. Gaining his rhythm, he rocked in and out of her body, building to that final bliss.

Her hair was like a halo around her face. Her skin flushed and her slightly open mouth was wet and burnished red from his hungry kisses.

On the edge of coming, he ground out, "It's right there, Slim. Let go."

She tumbled over, screaming his name and clenching him tight.

No longer able to hold back, he joined her, rumbling out incoherent words as pleasure pulsed through him. On a final groan, his arms wobbled and his entire body went slack.

Though his breathing was labored, he lifted to kiss her. Each cross of his tongue against hers turned hotter and hotter as he toyed with her lips

Still within her body, he slowly rolled his hips, drawing out the feeling as he teased her mouth. The intensity wasn't fading. He lost himself in the kiss, pouring out all his pleasure, showing her his appreciation.

His cock thickened, so he pulled back.

"Why are you still hard? I thought you were supposed to soften." Sheridan wiggled beneath him.

He shrugged. "Simple. Want you." He'd lost the ability to use complete sentences. Easing from her body, he shifted to lie back on the bed and brought her head against his chest, reveling in the glory and beauty of this woman in his arms.

She'd trusted him with her body. Trusted him with her life.

At dinner, he'd told her about her missing aunt, but hadn't explained where he'd come by the information. He hadn't wanted to ruin their evening together, but now, with her plaint in his arms, he couldn't help but consider how honest she'd been, while he continued to lie.

CHAPTER 31

Waking the next morning, Sheridan lay on her side, her head tucked under Clayton's arm. His woodsy-citrus scent filled her senses as she ran a hand across his bare chest and noted his upper body was cold to the touch.

He rustled, turning to wrap an arm around her before pulling her close. He rubbed his cheek against her hair, humming contentedly. "You feeling all right this morning?"

"I'm so relaxed. I feel boneless." She ran a finger down his chest until she bumped into her new friend. An ugly, capped fellow, but one she'd enjoyed getting to know twice last night.

After her horrific first experience with a man, and because of her ugly scars, she hadn't believed she could truly enjoy sex. Not without fear or flashbacks. Yet, Clayton had eased his way into her life, sneaking past her barriers with his touchy-feely ways and convincing kisses. So that now she just wanted to take. To soak up as much affection as possible, because life was short and she'd been alone for far too long. Clayton was right, she'd let her past dictate her future. She smiled as she considered all the pleasure to come—or right now, which she preferred. "Someone is up and ready for the day." She trailed a finger along his thick cock.

"He's always ready around you."

On impulse, she sat up and straddled him. "I want to try it this way."

Running his hands up her thighs, Clayton smiled lazily. "Be my guest."

He grabbed a condom off the side table and handed it over.

"I don't know how to put that on."

"So learn."

Narrowing her eyes, she plucked the package from his hand and opened it. "This part goes down right." She snapped the rubber around the tip of his cock then slid it down.

He tugged on the tipped end. "Good job."

"Thank you." She reached down and placed him at her core. Lifting slightly, she pressed him inside and wiggled until she'd stretched enough to accommodate his girth. Once he was fully embedded inside her, she met Clayton's gaze and licked her lips. "You like that?"

Clayton responded with a low growl, gripping her hips while keeping his eyes locked on hers.

Emotions overwhelmed her. Being in this position, holding him deep inside, seeing the love in his eyes was an amazing experience.

She'd never believed anyone would accept her.

But he had.

He closed his eyes and arched up. "Ride me."

"Maybe you need to slap my ass."

His eyes popped open. "You sure?"

"Yes, please."

He slapped her twice, which had her so hot she rocked her hips faster and harder. Next time, she'd turn on a dance mix and make love to him to the beat of the music. For now, he slapped her again, egging her on. "Come on baby, work that ass."

"Oh, yes. Make me work for it. Spank me."

"Not yet." He rose up each time she came down, sweat trickling along the side of his face. "Now, Sher. Come for me now."

A hard slap was the final push to completion. She reached for it, continuing to move upon him as sensations shot to her core. Crying out, she clenched around him. Her orgasm pulsed through her and tears of pleasure poured down her face.

He moaned and joined her, jutting his hips as he came. Then he grabbed the back of her neck and kissed her hard, invading her mouth as he'd invaded her body. Offering no quarter.

He flipped her onto her back and nudged her legs apart before he lowered his head and worked her throbbing bud with his tongue.

That familiar stirring began again. "No, no...too much." She tugged on his head.

Shrugging her off, he sucked and licked her wet folds, hitting the center spot over and over until she found bliss once more, screaming out his name.

Rising above her, he kissed her, tangling her tongue with his, the taste of their mixed pleasure a glorious blend in her mouth. That thought almost had her coming again. Reveling in that thought, she trailed her hands down over his ass and squeezed. "You have a really nice ass."

"Is this a fetish I need to be aware of Ms. Bennett?" He grinned.

"Possibly." She shook her head and drew him down against her body. "All this sex just makes the way I feel for you worse, because I don't want to need you. Plus your life in danger, but none of that seems to matter because I'm addicted to you now. All your practice with other women apparently paid off." She smacked his ass this time.

"Hey!" He lifted up on his elbows. "Enough with spanking."

She sighed and brushed her hair away from her sweaty neck. "The way you make me feel it's...so intense. I've buried everything so deep, and when I'm with you, I feel raw and exposed. It's unsettling. Maybe that's why I like to be spanked. Maybe I can't have pleasure without a little punishment. I don't feel worthy of happiness. I don't know." She shook her head. "I'm a disaster."

He grinned. "A disaster who knows how to ride."

Lips twisted to stop her grin, she shoved a hand against his face. "Shut. Up."

He grabbed her hand and braced it by her head. "I didn't hurt you, did I?"

Hurt her, no, he'd destroyed her and built her back up again. "No, Clayton. I'm fine." Clutching his face in both her hands, she poured every emotion she had into her kiss. Time to let go. Time to drop the emotional barriers. She now understood what "more" meant, what love was, nothing else could describe the feelings coursing through her body.

Easing back, she met his gaze. "It seems impossible to be here like this. I've always felt so ugly and ashamed. I didn't think anyone would want me or that I could handle anyone touching me. I want to let go, allow myself to feel safe with you, but it's hard. I still have a lot I need to work through, but I'll get there."

"*We'll* get there." Clayton kissed her before rolling onto his side and placing an arm over her waist.

If only she could stay trapped in this moment, but she couldn't. She still had a tale to tell. Catching the glint from his beautiful gift on her finger, she sighed before getting out of bed. So relaxed she could barely stand, she wobbled to her dresser and dug out a T-shirt and fresh panties. She sat on the bed cross-legged, grabbed a throw pillow, and placed it in her lap. Pulling at the pillow's lacy fringe, she stalled a little, not sure where to begin. "I need to tell you some…things."

She had to tell Clayton about her father—and her mother. He deserved to know the kind of man they were up against. And more importantly, he needed to truly understand the woman at his side.

# # #

Hearing the seriousness in her tone, Clayton lifted one lid. "I thought we were in a bubble." He folded his arms under his head and closed his eyes again. "Sheridan, we just had mind blowing sex. My brain is shut down. And not only that, no matter what you say, I'll still love you."

"Clayton, you can't really love me, know me, until I tell you everything about my past." She nudged his shoulder. "This confession defines who I am more than anything. It explains why my focus is to protect myself and my sisters. I find it is easy to forget who I am when I am with you, but that isn't reality. Who I really am is something you need to know before we can go any further."

"You're serious about doing this now?"

"Yes, I'm very serious about telling you now."

"All right, give me a minute." He tugged the condom from his flaccid cock and tied it into a knot. He shuffled into the bathroom, grabbed his jeans from the floor, and then pulled his cell phone out of his back pocket. "Where is your cell phone?"

"Why?"

"Ears are everywhere. Rachel and I use FlySpy all the time. Once the software's installed into your target's phone, you simply make a call whenever you want to secretly listen through the microphone. The phone doesn't ring or show any signs of an incoming call, but it will answer and turn on the mic. Discreet, remote, and available online." Glancing over his shoulder, he heaved a sigh. Rumpled hair. Rumpled bed. Plump pink lips. Long legs. Thoughts of taking Sheridan again flashed through his mind, but she was willing to trust him with more information from her past, so making good on those images would have to wait.

"Why are you looking at me like that, Mr. Kincaid?"

"I'm considering whether or not I should make love to you again so you'll know I mean what I say."

"I think I got the picture." Lips quirked, Sheridan pointed at her chaise. "Anyway…I have two phones in my purse. A pre-pay cell might be in there, too."

"Why do you have a burner cell?"

Sheridan shrugged. "I'm always prepared."

Clayton shook his head. "I need coffee. Do you want anything?"

"I'll have a sip of yours."

Handing over her purse, he waited as she dug out, not three but four phones. Two were pre-pays. He wouldn't go into twenty-questions regarding their purpose like he wanted to. Not when she was so willing to share other more important information.

"Let's go downstairs." Once he was in the living room, he placed their phones next to the TV's speakers. Sheridan had a high-end surround sound system, so he found a rock music channel and cranked up the volume.

She'd followed him down, and now wore baggy pink sweats along with her T-shirt. After discovering his love of coffee, she'd bought a pod-machine. He hadn't had the heart to tell her those weren't as good as dripping steaming water over freshly ground beans.

Sitting at the kitchen table, he sipped from the cup she'd placed in front of him then took her hand. "All right, Slim. I'll listen to what you have to say, but as I said, my love for you is unconditional. Whatever you tell me will not change that."

"Oh Clayton, you really have no idea if that will be true." Sheridan walked to the sink, opened the red and white-checkered curtains, and stared out the window. "Sometimes when I'm standing here looking into my backyard, I feel like time stops. The only thing I see is what is contained within this square. No future, no past, only this boxed representation." With her index finger, she drew a square in the air then she heaved a deep sigh. "I can only hope when I explain my world as it was, you'll see me more clearly. Right now, you see the false cover I've created, but today, we're going past all those false, boxed-in impressions. I'm breaking the glass and when I pull back my torn, jagged hand, you'll see just how dark my blood is."

CHAPTER 32

Sheridan fingered the misshapen rose-colored vase set on the edge of the kitchen window. The vase was a project from Jenny's grade-school days. A memento from a happy day, one of very few.

"I don't know where to begin, so I guess I'll start where I left off before. After my attack by McCord, Jenny and I were put in a foster home until my mother got her act together. She really did try. I think the extreme damage she caused changed her or perhaps she actually felt guilty."

"Jenny's father was convicted of attempted murder with a dangerous instrument, which is a class 2 felony, and he got fifteen years. I never spoke to my mother about what she did. I wouldn't have accepted any of her excuses or apologies anyway. I was done with her, and we both had to live with the knowledge we put a man in jail for a crime he didn't commit."

"Didn't he?" Clayton grumbled from behind her.

"I could spend days debating the level of Ted McCord's guilt but that isn't my focus right now." She gripped the sink's edge and continued. "Once we were back with Mom, we were fine for a few years. She got a job, paid bills on time, actually cooked meals. She quit the heavier drugs, and there were no men. Jenny was about to turn eight, and I was almost fourteen. My mother had even gone to see Laney a couple times, which was kind. I kept waiting for the ball to drop, and it did the night Jack Bennett came back."

Sheridan heard Clayton rustle in his seat but didn't turn around.

"My mom brought him home expecting me to be happy. I didn't know him. He had left so many years before and all I could remember was that he had been abusive to Laney. *He* was the reason she had been put in foster care prior to her adoption by the Maser's. He seemed nice though, very handsome, well groomed. And Mom was sure he would fix us up with the money he kept waving around."

"He took her shopping for dresses and shoes. They went to bars and casinos, leaving Jenny and me behind. They would be gone for days and when they did come back, it was obvious my mom was back on the heavy stuff. He started getting chummy with Jenny and me. As well as buying us clothes, pajamas, food, he even took us to the movies. He insinuated himself into our lives while simultaneously destroying my mother. I didn't trust him. I knew nothing was given freely in life. I'd already had any naiveté ripped out of me. I watched him like a hawk around Jenny, knowing that if he put one finger on her, I would kill him."

"And did he? Touch her?" Clayton growled out his questions.

Sheridan swallowed the lump in her throat. "Please, just let me finish."

His chair scraped across the floor. "Slim, let me—"

"No! Don't come near me. Sit back down, or I won't finish." She tightened her grip on the sink.

He grumbled out a curse. "Fine. I'm sitting."

"Good. As I was saying, my mother was completely hooked on heroin again. Her arms were covered in track marks. She spent days in the bathroom or just gone. I called O'Malley one night after she started puking blood. He tried taking her to rehab, but she wouldn't go."

"My father talked about moving Jenny and I someplace else.

He seemed very worried about leaving us in our mother's care. He also knew the truth about what my mother had done to me. She'd told him in her intoxicated state. He offered to take me to some fancy resort where I could have everything I wanted. I didn't believe him."

Sheridan took a deep breath. Memories of her fear and uncertainty during those days remained vivid as if tattooed onto her soul.

"Ryan and I followed my father one night as he left Aunt Vera's restaurant. Ryan is four years older than me, so he had his license. We ended up at this rundown hotel. Ryan snuck in behind dear old Dad as he went into the building. About a half hour later, Ryan came back out—pale, his eyes red, and he wouldn't speak of what he had seen. All he said was, my father was in there, too."

"I didn't understand what he'd seen, and I told him if he didn't explain I would go back the next day. Ryan grabbed me and shook me so hard my teeth rattled. He said I was never to go there. That we would go away and he would get a job in another town. I asked him what my father was doing but he wouldn't answer. To this day, I don't know what he saw."

"Did you ever find out?" Clayton spoke in a deep, scratchy voice as if he too was overcome by the emotional tale.

"Yes. I'll get to that." Sheridan concentrated on the trees outside her window. The next part was the hardest to tell. "After that night, Ryan was on a mission. He started making plans, preparing Jenny and me to leave in three days. I stashed clothes, hid any spare change I could find, and slipped cash from my mother's wallet. I looked old enough to pass for sixteen, so Ryan figured I could get a job somewhere once we left. He'd even said he would tell O'Malley the hotel's location once we'd gone."

"I came home from school on the day we were supposed to leave and waited for Jenny to get off her bus. At eight that evening, we were to meet Ryan three blocks from our building. He already had all of our things, so I just needed Jenny. I waited at the bus stop, but she never got off."

Sheridan closed her eyes as crystal-clear memories of her absolute terror during that moment raced through her mind.

"Slim, let me hold you. I can't take watching you go through this alone. Let me come to you."

"No." She sniffed and opened her eyes. "I need to pretend you're not even here. This next part...I-I can't look at you when I speak it."

"You're killing me."

Sheridan huffed out a half-laugh. "Yeah, I'm good at that."

"What's that supposed to mean?"

"Listen, please." She rubbed her temples. "So, again, Jenny wasn't at the bus stop, so I raced back home thinking someone else had picked her up. Mom was there—dressed in a fancy black dress, store tags still dangling from the fabric. She was high as hell, and for some inexplicable reason, washing dishes. I asked if she knew where Jenny was and she said not to worry, everything had worked out, and then she asked if I liked her new dress. I remember her modeling her shoes as she held onto the side of the sink so she didn't fall over. I was frantic, asking her again and again about Jenny. My mind started clicking everything together when she said we were going out to dinner to celebrate."

"Time stopped, sound erased. Even my blood stilled as I went ice cold. Yet at the same time, I had sweat on my upper lip, on my brow, and trickling down my back. We didn't go to dinner because we didn't have money. We never celebrated anything, because what would we have to celebrate? How could she pay for all the drugs she'd obviously just taken, not to mention her black dress and her sky-high heels, and still have enough for a celebratory dinner? With a sick feeling in my gut, I asked once more, where is Jenny?"

Throat dry, Sheridan grabbed a coffee cup out of the cabinet and filled it with water. Once she'd finished the whole thing, she continued. "My mom sat me down and told me she'd sold Jenny to my father. That she'd never meant to have Jenny in the first place, and she was glad to be rid of that red-haired burden."

"I remember seeing flashes before my eyes, red, white, black. I barely kept from passing out as all the air left my body in a single whoosh. The disgust I had for my mother escaped and covered me in a haze." Sheridan clenched her fists at her sides. "In that moment, I was no longer human but a personification of vengeance. I left all consciousness behind as darkness swallowed me whole. I cannot explain it. I lost my mind in that moment, while at the same time everything around me sharpened. I knew exactly what I had to do."

Heart racing, Sheridan paused for a moment and took a deep breath. "I said, you know Mom, you're right. Let's celebrate. We'll start right now. I went to the drawer where she kept her heroin, and said I wanted to try it, but she needed to show me how it worked first. This excited her. She would finally have me as her party partner. She went on and on about how much fun we would have. She told me not to be afraid to use my body to get what I wanted from a man, because I wouldn't be young forever."

"Sheridan, please. Let me hold you." Clayton was behind her now, his hands on her shoulders.

She tensed. "Please, just let me finish."

He pressed a kiss to the back of her head.

She bit her bottom lip and closed her eyes, holding back a shit storm of tears threatening to rain down at any moment. "I can't do soft right now. Back off, or I won't be able to finish."

Clayton squeezed her shoulders. "All right. I'll sit, but I don't like you standing here alone."

"I'm not alone. You're with me, but I can't have you so close right now, or I'll lean on your strength and fall apart."

"Okay. I hear you."

Sheridan heard the rustle of him settling back into his chair. She hadn't turned to look at him, because one glimpse into his eyes would reveal everything he felt and she couldn't deal with his feelings while shifting through memories of her own.

"I remember my anger and my absolute hatred of my mother. The intensity of that moment is something I haven't forgotten. I was nothing but rage. I watched as she injected the heroin. Then I went to the kitchen, got out a bottle of Jack Daniels, poured her a drink, picked up the needle, loaded it with more, and stuck it in her arm. I had no idea how much heroin it took to kill a person, but I knew if you mixed it with alcohol, the chances of an overdose were higher. I turned up some music and drank with her. After our third shot, she looked at me and said I was nothing, just like her. She said that men would fuck me and use me. That I would never be anything but a worthless whore. She laughed then, stating that at least she'd received money for Jenny."

Sheridan shook her head and released another long breath, wiping the tears from her eyes. "If she hadn't said that, I might have let the fury lift. I might have stopped. But by bragging, she nailed her coffin shut."

"I sat there, drinking until the bottle was empty and loading her needle until her breathing slowed. She kept drinking because she said her mouth was dry. Then she just stared off into space perhaps dreaming of her life before she fucked it all up, who knows. She had taken a knife to me, and I ended her with a needle and alcohol."

Sheridan closed her eyes against the vision of her mother's lifeless body. Her open glassy eyes, slack jaw, and her head tilted as if asking, "Why would you do this to me, Sher?"

No! Don't go there right now. Finish.

"Afterwards, I...uh...I called Ryan and told him we wouldn't be able to make it that night. I told him my Mom was sick, and I had to stay with her. He didn't believe me and said he would be by as soon as he got off work at seven."

"That gave me an hour to find Jenny. I didn't want Ryan involved, because I knew if he went back into that building, he would do something that would ruin his life forever. Better to let me take the fall."

"I found the remainder of the cash my Mom had received for Jenny, and I called a cab. I had the guy drop me off about a block from the hotel we'd trailed my father to only days before. I asked the driver to call O'Malley. I told him to ask the Lieutenant to come to this building right away. I had no plan or any idea of what I was going to do, the red haze had yet to leave me. I only knew I would get Jenny out of there, even if it meant I'd take her place."

"The old hotel was only two stories, small balconies stuck out from each room on the second floor. I walked around the back just as Ryan had done."

"The pool behind the hotel was full of stagnant water, the smell at any other point in my life might have knocked me flat but my vision had taken over all my other senses. It led me forward. I had to see anything that might come at me. Who knew what watchdogs my father had about."

"I came to a door at the back of the building, I remember looking up to see only the flashing X remained on the EXIT sign. That alone should have been enough for me to turn back and wait until I had back up. But no, I opened the door, half expecting an alarm to sound. Nothing happened."

"I walked down the corridor to the first room. Opening it, I found nothing but an empty bed. I heard voices ahead and the muted sounds of TV so I moved on to the next room. A huge number four was written in permanent marker on the door. The door directly across said thirteen. I didn't know what the number represented until I opened the door and saw her—that number was her age."

"Oh, fuck, Sheridan. You don't have to go on." Clayton spoke from behind her. "It's okay."

"No, it's not okay! You don't know what I saw. What I felt." Sheridan wrenched a paper towel off the hook hanging on the sink's lower cabinet and wiped her wet face. "You didn't see *her*—the tiny girl with the vacant stare, lying listless the bed. So dirty and wearing a pair of faded pink pajamas. As I got closer, I noted she wasn't tied to the bed, so I nudged her. She turned her head, and then shuffled a little before lifting her PJ's over her bruised thighs. Horrified, I fell to my knees."

"I had entered hell. It was staring back at me through a pair of blue eyes on the face of a little girl with stringy black hair. I didn't think it was possible to become any more horrified, that the black haze surrounding me could get any darker, but I was wrong. I reached across the bed, took her hand and said, We are leaving this place, come with me. She remained still, unmoving so I yelled, Get up now! Luckily, she complied."

"I had to get Jenny. Was I already too late? Was there some disgusting pig with her now? If there was, he was a dead man. Someway, somehow I would kill him. I had reached a point of no return so by the hand of Fate or God, I don't know which, I found Jenny in the next room. Room number 8. She was balled up on the bed, crying. Upon seeing me, she ran over and wrapped her arms around my waist. I told her we had to go, we didn't have time to cry. I told both girls to move, and we started to make our way to the exit. We were at the end of the hallway, two steps away from freedom when I heard my father's voice. *'Where do you think you're going with my property?'*"

"Property? I was still in the blackest regions of the red zone and that word made every dark emotion bubble over the surface—fear, hate, anger, disgust, betrayal. I let that focus me before I turned and faced him."

"Oh, Clayton, he held a very small girl against his body. She couldn't have been more than five and tears streaked down her dirty cheeks. She was wearing Dora the Explorer pajamas. They hung on her body, sliding to reveal one little shoulder." Sheridan choked back tears, biting down hard on her lower lip.

"Eyes wide, the little girl looked at me, her hand held tight against her mouth. Her blonde hair stuck to her cheeks. Her little body shaking, but she made no sound. How was that possible? Her face was so hollow. More ghost than girl. A horrendous sight made worse because my father had a gun pointed to her head."

"You will not leave." Jack shouted down the hall.

"I will."

"If you walk out with my property, then I will kill this girl. You want her death on your hands?"

"My hands? Wasn't there blood on them already? Hadn't I helped my mother shoot up enough heroin to end her life? Plus, I doubted he would kill the girl. It would cause too much of a mess, and he was very fastidious."

"Right then, I made a choice. Keeping my eyes on him the whole time, I backed Jenny and the other girl toward the stairwell. When I heard the gunshot, I screamed, the sound reverberating through my body. I didn't want to, but I glanced back."

"Keeping his gaze on mine, my father threw the girl to the ground—blood spatter covered the walls and a deep, dark pool had formed around her head. A tiny spiral of smoke rose from the wound on the little girl's forehead. I wanted to escape with that tiny wisp, just float up and away, but I was frozen in place."

"I fought to breathe and managed to keep Jenny behind me, shielding her from the macabre scene before us."

"My father wiped his hand against his pant leg."

"You just cost me a seasoned worker, and you will repay this debt on your back."

"Sirens erupted nearby, though I wasn't sure the sound wasn't my own screams. Men and a few women scrambled out of the rooms between my father and I. Each person desperate to escape before they were found in the one place they never should have been."

"Once outside the building, I remember every sound seemed muffled, tires screeching to a halt, voices shouting, car doors being slammed. Taking advantage of the chaos, I grabbed Jenny and girl number 4 and dashed down the stairs. O'Malley was in front of the building, and I ran straight for him. After handing Jenny over, I collapsed at his feet and didn't wake up for two days."

"When I woke, I was in a strange bed, and I had no idea where I was. I shot up and ran for an exit. On my way out of the foreign house, I glimpsed Jenny sitting at a kitchen table eating cereal like a normal little girl. Like nothing seriously messed up had just happened. I must have looked like a wild animal because Mrs. O'Malley approached me cautiously and said, Sit at the table, dear. I'll get you some breakfast. Just like that, didn't she know who I was? What I had done? I felt like someone should be arresting me."

"O'Malley came into the kitchen and told me to sit so I did. He said Ryan was asleep in the other room. A bowl of Lucky Charms cereal appeared in front of me—real Lucky Charms not the Happy Shenanigans generic brand."

"Across the table, Jenny had milk dripping down her chin, and she said, If you find a gold star, you get to make a wish."

"I lost it then, flinging my cereal across the room. How could I make wishes after everything I had been through? I threw up all over the table and passed out. When I came to, O'Malley was sitting in a chair next to my bed. I didn't like him there. I didn't trust him."

"He said, Sheridan, you've just had one of the most terrifying experiences anyone could ever face. We'll get to what you saw when you're ready to talk, but until then know this, none of it was your fault. You are one of the bravest young ladies I have ever known. Because you had that cabbie make a call, we were able to get fifteen girls out of that building all because you were brave enough to go after your sister. Now you just need to decide, will you be a victim or a survivor?"

"I told him, two people are dead because of me. He explained my mother was found dead of a heroin overdose and that was the end of her story. I persisted, willing to take the blame, but he cut me off and said, Do you think I don't really know who was responsible for you being in that hospital bed a few years ago? That story your mother concocted never made sense but since you agreed, we had to go with it. Don't allow her to have any more control over your life. She's gone."

"I shook my head saying I didn't want to go forward. I didn't deserve it. This made him angry. He told me I was stronger than that. He said, I'll be here to help you. I know you have no reason to trust me, but someday I hope you will. Right now, I suggest, you learn from what you've lived through and use it to move forward every day. Survive and thrive. I live with that motto. I saw what you saw tonight. The body of a little girl whose life ended in that pit of hell. I looked into the faces of fifteen girls who will never be the same. I've seen so much in my years on the force Sheridan, and I get up again, each day. I survive, I thrive and I turn to those around me for help when I need it. You must choose to do the same."

CHAPTER 33

Mouth once again dry and tired, so very tired, Sheridan finally faced Clayton. During the telling, she'd kept her gaze trained on the stark, leafless trees outside the window, remaining apart. Distant.

He sat with his head bent and his hands folded together between his legs.

"O'Malley helped me through the following days and months. Allowing no blame or self-pity." Shivering, she wrapped both arms around her body, holding herself together. Her stomach churned as she remembered those girls. Their emaciated bodies, the sound of the gunshot, and the fear, the absolute terror her father would somehow take Jenny again—a terror that remained.

"O'Malley is the reason I work so hard, why I strive for success, because I want to give back to him. I need to believe that if another little girl is living in a nightmare, she can turn to the police for help. That's why I support law enforcement. Why I'll never be able to donate enough." She shook her head. "But money doesn't erase the dark mark on my soul. I have to live with blood on my hands."

Clayton crossed to her, handed her a couple tissues, and then wrapped both arms around her. "Thank you for telling me."

The floor creaked above them, and then the shower turned on. Jenny was awake, and Sheridan didn't want her sister to see her so upset. "I need to go back upstairs. Jenny doesn't know any of this."

"All right, but just listen a second." Clayton tipped up her chin. "You did what you had to in order to survive, I'll never fault you for that. In war, I did the same thing. I understand why you feel so conflicted."

"Clayton, please don't excuse what I've done. I-I'm...I'm a murderer." A wave of nausea struck, and she fell to her knees, clutching her stomach.

He fell with her and then braced her head between his hands. "Sheridan, that's not true."

"Let me go."

"Stop it." He shook her a little. "That little girl's death is on your father's hands, and as for your mother...what's done is done. Consider it assisted-suicide if you have to, but don't take full blame."

Sheridan sniffed then released a shaky breath. "I pray for forgiveness, but deep down, I'm still that monster. I want my father dead, and I want to pull the trigger. I've planned his death, dreamed of it. Revenge is this dark pulsing blood inside me. I don't want to be a monster anymore, but until my father is gone, I have no choice. I can only defeat him by letting the darkness reign."

"I'll help you." He kissed her forehead. "You won't fight him alone."

"You'll stay, even now?"

"Yes, Sheridan, even now." Lifting her into his arms, he carried her back upstairs to her bed and settled beside her. "Is there more news about your father? Have you heard from him?"

"No." Sheridan narrowed her brow. Why was Clayton asking about her father? Just moving on as if she hadn't just told him she'd committed matricide. Maybe he'd think about what she'd done and change his mind about their relationship. He'd been a cop. Cops arrested murderers. Dramatic, maybe…but still…she'd be uneasy around him for a few days, waiting for him to break out the handcuffs.

He cleared his throat. "The next time you see your father, you should contact the FBI."

She stiffened. Why was he bringing the FBI into this? Had he spoken to them? "Their agents contact me all the time. There's this Agent Denver who's in it for himself, and he doesn't care about collateral damage. Keeping my family safe isn't his priority. Plus, he has to work within the boundaries of the law, and he can't stop my father that way."

Clayton gripped her chin. "Understand this. We will work against your father together. If we need to bring in the FBI, we will. None of this lone wolf stuff. I investigate bad guys for a living, remember?"

"So because you're an ex-cop, I'm supposed to do as you say?" Sheridan straightened against her headboard. "I've prepared for my father's return for a very long time. He's mine to deal with. Not only that, *you* are in his rifle sites now, and he'll use you to get my money." She jabbed a finger against Clayton's chest. "Do *not* think for one minute I'll allow that."

Clayton gripped her finger. "I can take care of myself. This isn't a movie set where you can get hurt and walk back to your cushy trailer at the end of the day. I have been in dangerous situations before. I appreciate the sentiment, but don't think for one second you're protecting me from anything. We are in this together. If I have to lock you down somehow, I will. Am I clear?"

Sheridan closed her eyes and shook her head. Hadn't he listened? Didn't he understand the danger he was in? "When Jack Bennett comes into my life, he hurts those around me. He physically abused Laney, tried to traffick Jenny, and murdered a child in front of me. There's no line he won't cross. I'm capable of following him across that line. I don't want the same for you."

Clayton kissed her quick and hard. "Slim, when it comes to you, I crossed that line a long time ago. We'll track him down."

"I don't want the FBI involved in this. The more people involved, the more chance the story gets leaked to the press. I don't want people digging through my personal life. I don't speak to reporters, and I'm sure as hell not talking to Agent Denver again. He seems to think I'm just like my father." She laughed. "Maybe he's right."

Clayton grimaced. "Whether you like it or not, the FBI *is* involved."

"With what?" Her heart raced a little, what was he saying?

Clayton sat on the edge of the bed. "They're involved in this case. Your father is on their most wanted list. You have to know that, right?" He stood and combed his fingers through his hair. "I'm sorry, Sheridan, but I just can't keep this—"

"No! You said you wouldn't leave." Heart pounding, Sheridan wrapped her legs around him, anchoring him in place. "You promised."

"No, that isn't what I was going to say."

She'd told him too much. He seemed so unsettled. "I don't want to talk about my father anymore."

Her relationship with Clayton was so tenuous at times, and expecting him to accept everything she'd told him was asking a lot. She should make him go. Let him think.

He sighed and then settled beside her. "Are you going to be okay?"

"I don't know. I've never told anyone that story before, so I don't know how I'll feel later. Right now, I'm a little numb."

"If your case had gone to trial, you would've gotten off."

She laughed. "Oh, that's funny. No, I don't agree. People from my side of town can't afford fancy lawyers, so yeah, I'd have ended up in prison or juvie."

"I doubt it." He took her hand and fiddled with the ring he'd placed there just last night.

"Yeah, well you grew up in a lakeside mansion. Sorry, but people on my side of the tracks are guilty the minute they step into the courtroom."

"So cynical."

"I have every right to be."

"I thought I was bad, but damn you have me beat."

"I like to be a winner." She grinned.

He kissed her lips. "You are, baby. You are."

Shaking her head, she physically moved him to lay half on top of her. "There. Lay right there."

He yawned and patted her shoulder "Everything's going to be all right."

"Mmm...hmm." Why argue? Yawning herself, she used the tip of her index finger to make deliberate marks on his back.

After a moment, he peered up at her. "What are you doing?"

"I'm writing letters on your back"

"What letters?" He plopped back against her chest.

"Try to guess which specific letter I'm writing." She couldn't hold back a smile, which was fine because he couldn't see her anyway with his head buried half on her shoulder and half on the pillow.

She drew a squiggly line.

"S, right?"

"Yes."

Next came a slash with a half-circle.

"It's a P?"

"Good job." Sheridan rubbed her nails gently up and down his back as if clearing a chalkboard.

He shivered. "That tickles."

"Be still." She slapped his shoulder. "Now, those were practice. This time you'll have to put all the letters together." Unsure why she was telling him this now, she took a deep breath and wrote out the next letter on his smooth back.

"H," he said.

"No, it's a vowel." She traced the pattern again.

"Oh, an I."

She nodded then ran her nail in a straight line with a little jut at the end.

"L"

A circle.

"O"

He had to know what she was writing by now, but she kept going and traced out the next letter.

"V" He rose up his forearms.

She arched a brow.

"It's not going to be that easy. You have to say it."

"Say what? I was just drawing letters on your back."

"Say it." He pleaded, his eyes all puppy-dog-sad.

"If I say it out loud then the words lose their magic. They become real, and I can't hide anymore."

"You can't hide now." He kissed her cheek, and then whispered in her ear. "Say it."

She trembled as his lips brushed across her neck. "You keep pushing me, making me feel things, experience things that I never thought I could. I need to be an empty shell to make it through the coming days, to face my father, but *you* won't let me. My heart won't let me. So, if you want to be a stupid son of a bitch and stay after everything I've told you, after reaching in and digging out the worst parts of me then…you get me. You get my love." She lifted a hand and caressed his scruffy face. His gorgeous face. His imprinted-in-her-heart's-coloring-book-forever face. "I love you, Clayton Kincaid. And I will love you until the day I die, so thanks a whole hell of a lot for turning me into a love-sick sap."

His grin practically split his face, and his bright blue eyes held a bit of a cocky twinkle. "A stupid son of a bitch?" He burst out laughing.

"Oh, seriously, fuck you." She rolled out from under him

and headed for the door. "I'm making myself breakfast. You can go forage in the forest for all I care."

"Oh, come on, Slim. Don't be like that. You're a love-sick sap, remember?"

As she walked out of the room, she lifted a hand and flipped him the bird, but she did so with a stupid—and yes, sappy grin on her face.

CHAPTER 34

Shivering in the chilly early-morning air, Sheridan clapped her glove-covered hands together. She faced Scotty who was bundled in jeans and a brown Carhartt coat. Appropriate attire for a horse farm. Except he had on tennis shoes instead of cowboy boots. Too bad she had no wardrobe trailer to dress him properly. "My instructor and I are riding bareback again today, and I'm attempting some jumps. By the time she's finished with me, I should look like a natural on-screen." She nudged Scotty's shoulder with her own. "You need some boots, cowboy."

He sipped from his thermos. "Too open out here."

"Already had this argument with Clayton."

"He's thinking with his dick." Scotty scanned the area. "Only reason he's letting you out here like this."

"Maybe he just trusts you."

"One guy isn't enough."

"He's getting more."

"We'll see. Go on in and get done so we can get out of here." His words come out with puffs of steam. Anger and cold air didn't mix.

Scotty wouldn't spoil her enjoyment of the day. She was in love. Preparing for a film. A light dusting of snow covered the grass. And she was about to see her favorite animal. She'd never had a pet, so taking care of her horse was a new experience.

Chuffing and snorts came from inside the barn.

Hmmm….a lot more noise than usual at five a.m.

Leaving Scotty on watch, Sheridan walked toward the back stall that housed her Irish Sport Horse, Chance. She'd loved him the moment she'd seen his golden brown beauty, his dark ears and tail, and his big brown eyes. His forehead had a splash of white down the center. Gorgeous beast. Apparently she was falling in love with all kinds of creatures lately.

Each time she entered the barn, she stopped and breathed in the plethora of scents that brought about a sense of a time long past. Hay, leather, a hint of molasses, and manure, which made the experience more…earthy. But today another scent mixed with the others. Something foul. Like a dead skunk. The owners were very meticulous about keeping the barn as clean as possible, so it seemed a little odd.

At Chance's stall, Sheridan noted that the horrid smell only got stronger. She pulled a bag of apple slices from her coat pocket.

He whinnied, but not in a, I'm-happy-to-see-you way.

Unease crept down her spine.

His ears were rapidly swiveling—flicking back and forth. His head was raised high and his upper lip curled as he breathed in and blew the air back out. Her trainer had called that action, flehman. A horse pushed scent particles through this thing in their noses to detect pheromones or when they smelled something unusual.

"What's the matter, Chance?" On her tiptoes, Sheridan peered into the stall and gasped, tumbling back and falling on her butt.

No wonder Chance was skittish.

A body was propped along the back of the stall, half covered in straw. Dried blood dirtied the woman's face and purple bruises covered her arms and neck. Her clothes were ripped, but most disturbing of all, her eyes were open in a terror-filled stare. Her cheeks were sallow, and her body was a light gray-blue.

Sheridan pinched her nose as the smell reached her nostrils. "Oh, dear God. Aunt Vera, what did he do to you?"

And had whoever done this stayed? Were they waiting?

On alert, Sheridan backed into a corner, pulled her gun from its side holster, covered her nose with the crook of her elbow, and reached into her jeans pocket for her phone. Why couldn't she have three hands? Blocking the smell while holding a gun wasn't standard practice and the stakes were too high to miss the target.

She pressed O'Malley's number.

He answered on the second ring.

"Lieutenant, I've found Aunt Vera." Sheridan slowly opened Chance's stall. Gently cooing, trying to calm the frightened horse. She led him out and wrapped his reins around a stall across the way.

"Sheridan, are you still there? Where did you find her?"

"At the stables." Sheridan patted Chance's neck. "It's okay, boy."

"Is the area secure?"

"I'm not sure. Sh-she's d-dead." Sheridan briefly closed her eyes against the visual burned into her retinas.

"Do you have a gun?"

"Yes."

"Good. Stay where you are and don't move your aunt. I'm sorry, Sheridan...I'll be there soon."

She needed to notify Clayton. "Oh, my God. Scotty." He had to be warned. He could be sitting in the crosshairs right now.

After peering around Chance and not seeing anything suspicious, she sprinted back to the stall and checked her aunt one more time, just to be sure.

In the straw, a speck of white screamed look-at-me. Glancing over her shoulder first, Sheridan pinched her nose then entered the stall and picked up the sheet of notebook paper. Her heart pounded like a caffeine-induced hummingbird. This close to her aunt's corpse, she breathed in short intervals to control the wave of nausea due to the horrid stench. She could guess what the paper would say and who it had come from.

Dearest Daughter,

Recent events have forced me to no longer play so nice. You see how I deal with people who defy me. Cash at the homestead. Tonight. Or Jenny is the next body you'll find beside a pile of horseshit.

Sirens wailed in the distance. The law was on its way.

The law. The FBI. Likely Clayton.

She should let them handle everything, but the darkness inside her stirred and adamantly disagreed. Clayton had tamped it down for a while, but her father had once again threatened her sister. Had once more dropped a dead body at her feet. No law could stop him. He'd been free to create chaos for eight years now. And she'd had those same years to prepare.

Clenching her jaw, she crammed the note in her coat's front pocket, pulled up Clayton's number, and...finger poised above the green phone symbol, she released a slow breath, holding back all the tears that would come.

But not now. Now she had to make a choice.

Scotty hollered her name.

Cars doors slammed outside the barn. Blue and red lights flashed.

"I'm sorry, Clayton."

She swiped Clayton's name aside and called Jenny instead.

Her sister answered at the end of the first ring.

"Jenny."

"Hey, Sheridan. What's—"

"Plan A. Go."

CHAPTER 35

Hanging up, Sheridan prayed that all the emergency preparation she and her sisters had done would pay off. She had to trust that Jenny would get Laney and make it to the safe house.

Scotty rushed to her side, gun drawn. "Oh hell." He covered his nose.

"Vera's in the stall." Sheridan jerked a finger behind her and staved off any show of grief over her aunt's death. She'd have to call Ryan, but again...not now.

Her primary focus was on the police cruisers outside the barn. Second was on meeting her father. An assignment she didn't plan on sharing with anyone.

Scotty grabbed her arm. "Sheridan, the area isn't secure."

"My father isn't here."

"How can you know?"

"He wants my money before he kills me."

"Stay by my side." He led her out of the barn, walking so that her back faced the stalls and he crept forward at her front.

Once outside, Agent Denver pulled up in his familiar sedan, dust flying as his car skidded to a halt.

Clayton shot out of the passenger seat, raced forward, and then wrapped her in his arms.

"I figured O'Malley would call you." She didn't return his

embrace. Staying numb emotionally was crucial for the coming hours. No weakness. No mercy. Only vengeance. "Vera's dead."

"I know. Are you all right?" He pulled back, and placed his shaking palm against her cheek, searching her eyes. "Damn it, Sheridan, I didn't want you coming here, and I about lost my mind when the Lieutenant called."

"My father destroyed her." Sheridan closed her eyes as visions of her aunt's battered body surfaced again. "I planned on calling. Why are you with Agent Denver?"

"We were in a meeting when I got the call." He tugged loose the knot in his tie.

Mr. Kincaid was dressed for a meeting—black dress pants and jacket, white shirt, and light blue tie. Business attire. Meeting-with-the-FBI attire.

Alarms sounded in her head, breaking through her icy barrier. *Clayton and Denver were meeting?* "What do you mean 'in a meeting'?" She lifted her chin and met his gaze.

When she tried to yank away, Clayton secured her in his arms. "Sheridan, we'll discuss that later. Right now, we need to get you to a secure location."

"No." She held up a hand. "Let me go. I need to think."

"Sheridan—"

"The only thing you would have to discuss with Agent Denver would be me. That's the only thing that makes sense." She fought to breathe as all the air left her lungs. "What did you tell him?" Oh, this was worse than death, because she'd told him everything. Her heart skipped a beat, and she swallowed past the lump in her throat. "Answer me."

"Calm down, Ms. Bennett." Agent Denver approached her, hands raised. "We've been working together to locate your father. And based on today's events, it's a good thing, because you can't keep out of trouble."

She poked a finger against the agent's chest. "How dare you go behind my back and get Clayton involved in this! You really will stop at nothing. Do you realize the danger you've put him in? Not only him, but his entire family. Everything and everyone that has anything to do with me is a target."

"Sheridan, helping the FBI was my choice." Clayton reached for her, but she shoved him away.

"Your choice." Brow furrowed, she clasped a hand against her chest. Seeing her dead aunt, receiving a letter from her psycho father, and fear for her sisters, was now topped with Clayton's duplicity. "I don't even know...how could you keep this a secret when I trusted you with everything? Oh my God...everything. And what does that even mean? Your choice?"

"I agreed to help them."

"You agreed to help them." She enunciated each word, slowly processing the meaning. He'd met with the FBI. The sharp knife of betrayal sliced open her chest, cut out her heart, and the bloody mass tumbled to the ground.

She regretted every word, every kiss, every glimpse into her soul. Staring at the ground, she tried to see past the haze of absolute devastation. And she'd thought she was broken before, but this...

Sirens whirled, lights flashed, and voices bounced in her head. A trickle of sweat ran down the side of her face. Dust filled the air and the scent of hay and horse shit mixed with the pungent scent of her aunt's decaying body almost brought her to her knees.

"Why?" She barely choked out the word before she lifted her head and met Clayton's gaze. "All this time you've been working with the FBI to catch my father. Is that why you're with me?" She clutched her middle on the verge of losing her tea and toast. "Why would you do that? I trusted you."

Clayton clutched her shoulders. "Sheridan, they approached me after we met. They knew we were friends and asked me to notify them if your father contacted you. I agreed to cooperate. That is all."

"Oh, you've been cooperating all right." She tried shrugging him off. "Don't touch me."

Clayton gave her a small shake. "Whatever you're thinking, stop."

"You don't get to tell me what to think. *You* are a liar." She shoved him with both hands. "I revealed parts of myself that I've never shared with anyone and you went and used this information t-to…to what…further yourself with the FBI? Why?" Throwing up both hands, she leveled him with an icy stare. Had he used her? Had he taken her body and soul as a way to prove himself to these men? He'd had plenty of opportunities to tell her the truth, so why had he lied? "Was fucking me all a part of getting your information? Was each touch a way to make me fall? Well, great job, asshole. I've hit the pavement."

"Sheridan, that's enough." He clenched his jaw. "We'll discuss this…"

She reared back and hit him in that tight jaw with a right cross. "We won't discuss anything. We are done." Sobbing, she shoved his shoulder. "You've betrayed everything."

Rubbing his jaw with one hand, he gripped the back of her neck with the other. "I did what I had to in order to keep you safe."

Sheridan laughed. His naivety had her borderline hysterical. "You think Denver gives a shit about keeping me safe? They don't even care if they get my father at this point. They just want Korzakov." She swiped her wet cheeks. "They use everyone Clayton, and they sure as hell used you."

"Stop." He kissed her hard. "Right now I need you to focus. We have a murder on our hands, and we need all the information we can get before your father strikes again."

Using the back of her hand, she wiped his kiss from her mouth. Her father *would* strike again, and those words were the only thing that semi-jolted her from her red haze.

"I'm sorry. Didn't you and Agent Denver the Dick work out my father's next move in one of your meetings?" She sneered.

"What no one seems to understand is my father is already ten steps ahead. He's been a player his whole life. A couple of green FBI agents and a deceitful private eye won't stop him." She shook her head. "I'm such a fool. Here I thought *I* was a good actor, but no, you're the one with the golden statue this time. Un-fucking believable."

#

Clayton had to play this carefully.

Sheridan's wide eyes, tears, and anger were understandable. He deserved most of what she was spewing...but not all. Finding a dead body would push anyone over the edge, make them irrational. Not that he'd say any of that right now. His jaw already ached. He couldn't focus on their issues, because regardless what she believed, her safety was still paramount. He'd raced out of his office the minute O'Malley had called him, more frightened than he'd ever been in his life, and he'd been in some sticky situations during his time in the Rangers and as a cop. Sheridan Bennett apparently trumped them all.

"Slim, we will discuss us once we get through today." He gripped her hand and squeezed. "Right now, I need you safe, so let's get you home with your sisters. I'm sure the detectives will want to speak with you, but I'll feel better if they do so in a car or at your house."

"Well, by all means, let's do what makes *you* feel better." With a stone-cold glare, she flicked both hands in the air before stuffing them back in her coat pockets.

Her blue eyes were rimmed in red. *Damn it.* Perhaps he'd pick up a pair of kneepads because a ton of groveling was in his future. She loved him so she'd forgive him. He had to believe that. "I realize you're upset and for now, I've let you vent, but I will have my say." He tugged on her arm and led her to Denver's car.

"Don't touch me." She jerked her arm away, knocking a

piece of paper out her coat pocket.

Her eyes went wide and she dived for the scrap.

He covered it with his foot. "What's that?"

"It's nothing." She shrugged then sniffed. "Just a phone number for a guy who asked me out the other day. May I have it back, please? I have a call to make."

Frowning, he bent to pick it up.

She shoved him, almost knocking him off balance as she reached for the paper. "That's mine."

"Stop." He held her at arm's length as he tugged the paper out from under his shoe.

Sheridan's entire face went red. "If you read that note, I will *never* speak to you again."

"The threats are getting old, Slim."

"No threats. I'm way passed those."

"If you say so."

She huffed out a laugh and shook her head. "We are *so* done."

"No." He whipped his tie from around his neck and shoved it in his pant's pocket. "You don't walk away because you're pissed and hurt. Love doesn't work that way."

"Oh, okay, you're gonna talk about love now? You're throwing that word around like you've ever known what it meant. Give me back my note."

He opened his mouth to retort, but decided not to give her any more ammunition and read the note instead. "What does this mean? Where is the homestead?"

"Now you want my cooperation?" Arching a brow, Sheridan cracked her knuckles. "So sorry. That opportunity passed the second I saw whose side you're really on. I don't want a liar in my life. I got on fine without you, and I'll do so again."

"Try it." Done with her theatrics, Clayton drew her against this body and kissed her.

She struggled, but he only drove deeper. Roughly exploring

her mouth. Holding her still for the brutal drive. The evidence that she wouldn't walk away.

Wrenching out of his arms, she shoved against his chest. "How much of *that* did you discuss in your meetings? Stay away from me." She turned in her black cowboy boots and stormed off.

Clayton let her go but only because her furious self was heading toward O'Malley. Plus, she needed time to cool off…and so did he.

"Well, Kincaid, that looks like it went well." Denver slapped him on the back.

Scowling, he ground out, "Let's get back to it." His phone vibrated with a call from Rachel. "What is it?"

"I have something." Rachel responded.

"What?" Clayton moved away from Denver.

"The sister's cell phone has been off-line for about a half hour. No calls, texts, nothing. It's still at the house. Sheridan made one call to her sister then her line went dark, too."

"They are probably using disposable phones. Track Jenny's car and get back to me." Tapping his phone against his open palm, Clayton searched the area for Sheridan. She'd always said she had a plan. Had she alerted her sisters? And where the hell was she?

"Hey Kincaid." O'Malley waved him over by the barn.

The Lieutenant stood beside to two people dressed in jeans, boots, and flannel shirts, likely the stable owners.

Clayton stopped and introduced himself.

After working with them on how to remove the horses so the forensics people could properly search, O'Malley thanked them and waited until they were out of earshot to continue. "Kincaid, run Sheridan back to her house. We'll wrap up here then I'll bring the lead detective by." He removed his stocking cap and ran a hand through his hair. "I'm a tad worried, son. I haven't been able to get through to Jenny."

Clayton searched for Sheridan's blonde head in a sea of crew cuts and silver sunglasses. "Where is Sheridan now?"

"Last I saw, she was looking for you."

A patrolman rushed to O'Malley's side. "Sir, my car is gone."

Clayton spoke through clenched teeth. "I'm going to kill her."

CHAPTER 36

"Well, you've done it now, Bennett." Sheridan whipped the police cruiser into her driveway. "I've got good lawyers…maybe I'll only get ten to twenty years." She pulled up to her front gate, mentally repeating her plan. Go in. Get rucksack. Head to barn. Get truck. Meet father. Possibly die.

She would not walk into her father's "homestead" unprepared. "Not like I did with stupid Clayton and his stupid lies. Jerk ass men thinking they can just come into your life and take over and seduce you into loving them." She swiped at the tears on her cheeks. "Stupid, stupid, stupid. I don't have time for this."

After rolling down the window, she punched in the gate's code. She'd left her main cell phone back at the barn, which had the remote access app to the gate.

An engine revved behind her.

Next thing she knew, her neck snapped forward from the impact of a vehicle ramming into the back of the squad car.

Jarred back in place by her seat belt, she glanced in the review mirror and saw blond van-man.

Using his heavier vehicle, he pushed her car through the gate.

"I don't think so." She slammed on the brakes, threw the car in reverse, and pushed the pedal to the floor.

Smoke billowed up from the tires as she tried to stop his

forward advance.

Locked together, steel on steel, Sheridan released a raw scream before throwing the car in Drive and racing up the driveway.

Coming to a stop, she flung open the car door, ran to the side of the garage, flipped open the panel, punched in the garage door code, and prayed the door would open quickly.

"Damn it." The black box's red light blinked. *Incorrect code.*

Hands shaking, she entered the code again. "I don't have time for this. Stupid code. Work this time, please!"

Van man gunned his engine and barreled straight for her.

He hit the edge of the police cruiser, lost control, and slammed into her front porch. She could hear him cursing as he tried to open his door. The fractured pillar blocked his way.

He scooted over to the passenger side to the unhindered escape route.

"Don't look. Move, move." Sheridan rolled under the garage door's slight opening.

Van man grabbed her hair.

"Get off." She slipped away, but left a chunk of her hair in his hand.

He rolled in behind her.

Racing to the front of the mustang parked in the middle bay, she stopped and peered over the hood.

Shadowed by the light from the mid-morning sun, psycho blond stood in the now fully open garage door. "Father sent me."

Flinching at that reveal, she straightened and looked him over. "I see." And she finally did. The kid was a young version of her father. Blond, yet a slightly heavier build, and crazy blue eyes. Now she knew why he'd always seemed so familiar. "If you're my brother, then why are you trying to kill me?"

His upper lip curled, and he spit on her floor. "He may be *our* father, but you are not my sister."

"What is the game plan here? Where is Daddy by the way?"

Keeping her breathing steady, Sheridan cursed O'Malley's detective that had taken her gun, telling her he had to run it "just in case." She didn't think baby brother had a shred of sanity. Another victim of Jack Bennett's evil blood.

Considering her options, she strolled to the side of her car. Her heart was back at the barn, so the only thing left was her wit and she had no doubt she could outsmart this man.

Baby brother had a gun in his hand, but depending on his accuracy, she could try to drive off but—no keys.

Plan B then.

He ran the gun's barrel across her car's hood.

A chilling scrape that grated across her already frayed nerves and quite frankly pissed her off. "Do you know what kind of car you're scraping? What the hell?"

"You and I are going to the bank."

"They'll have my bank covered. Stupid move if you ask me."

"No. No. No." His mask began to slip, wide blue eyes locked on hers. "You saw what happens to people who don't follow the plan. When Vera told the Korzakov's where we were staying, we made her pay. Just like you will pay. It didn't take long for Vera to die—pity, as I'd just started having fun." He ran a hand over the front of his jeans, shifting his cock in his pants.

Sheridan shivered. "You're disgusting."

He laughed, full-on, head cocked back and everything.

"Wasn't funny."

"Yeah." He wiped his eyes. "Yeah it is, because I had to make the beating look worse. Couldn't have anyone knowing I'd killed her with just one punch."

A sneer lit his face. If he thought that could shock her, then he didn't know her at all. It would take more than one punch to knock her out.

"Father doesn't make senseless moves." He took a step forward. "The note we left was a decoy. We're changing the plan."

"Sorry. Not playing his game." Spinning on her heel,

Sheridan darted off to the side of the garage, to a room she'd had built as a storage area for garden tools. Slamming the steel door shut behind her, she grabbed garden rakes and shovels off the walls, leaving a trail behind her. Baby brother fired off shots, each bullet striking the door with a loud crack. Moving quickly, she worked her way to the corner to the escape hatch in the garage floor.

Her brother yanked open the door behind her and kicked aside all the garden tools.

Sweat pouring down her back, Sheridan lifted the small metal ring from the tunnel's lid before dropping, legs first into the underground tunnel. By design, the opening was very narrow and one her hefty brother couldn't possibly fit through without getting stuck. Stretching, she eased the lid down behind her, taking a moment to catch her breath and acclimate herself to the dark, confining surroundings. This tunnel was nothing like her high tech shelter in the basement. This was only meant for escape—and claustrophobia.

Crouching at the bend in the tunnel, she reached for the flashlight and the key fob to her home's alarm system she kept in a cubbyhole. She pushed the panic button, knowing that the system would immediately notify the police.

The muffled sound of her alarm's sharp shrill sounded even down here. Any criminal who could stand that eardrum piercing sound could steal her TV's with her blessing.

The narrow passageway yawned ahead, a pitch-black tube leading to a wider cement opening further down. The flashlight's beam helped narrow her focus.

Then the tunnel's hatch squeaked open.

Her breathing stopped. *Don't move. Don't make a sound.*

The house's alarms screech became louder but didn't drown out her brother's curses as he attempted to fit into the opening behind her.

"You stupid bitch." He stopped, grunted, and then fired

256

round after round into the tunnel.

Adrenaline rocketed through her. Bullets were raining down. *Move. Move. Escape.* She covered her ears, scrambled onto her hands and knees, and crawled away.

Bullets pinged against the metal walls and whizzed past her body.

As a stinging sensation struck her left calve a few inches above her ankle, she hissed. Ignoring the pain, she moved on until she could stand upright.

The temperature dropped as the tunnel angled down and farther away from the spray of bullets behind her. The flashlight highlighted a wallpaper of webs, and she saw a creepy centipede scurrying away from the chaos. She tried not to think of the bugs taking up residence in her hair.

"Breathe, Sheridan. You can do this."

The throbbing pain of her wound reminded her to move forward. Time had no meaning as she limped along in the dark—a single flashlight beam to light her way.

A damp earthy scent filled her nostrils as well as a slight copper tinge. Blood. Her blood was spilling out all over this tunnel. Were opossums meat eaters?

A scurrying sound came from behind her.

"Oh shit. Be a mouse and not an evil vampire raccoon. Please God. I don't want to die by vermin. Or maybe I'd be half coon, half human, transforming by the light of the moon." Rolling her eyes, she laughed. "You're insane. Gone crazy. And it's all Clayton's fault. Although I should lay some blame on my psycho brother and my insane father." She shivered. "It's frickin' freezing down here, and I'll likely bleed out before I reach the surface."

Her skin dampened from sweat and the moisture in the air as she limped down the corridor. She had traversed this path many times while living here, checking for leaks or cave-ins. In time it would crumble, but not today, she had an appointment to keep.

Fear for her sisters niggled at her nerves, but she held back her worry. She focused on reaching the end, on survival. She would not feel the heavy weight of her pant leg soaked in blood. She would not give in to the searing pain, or the dizziness in her head.

Finally, a set of metal stairs appeared at the end of her flashlight beam. "Thank, God." Wincing as her ankle took her weight on each rung of the ladder, she halted for a moment and glanced down the tunnel. Had her brother squeezed through? Was he following her even now? Doubtful, but he could be searching the area around her house, that was if he was smart enough to figure out she would not exit in the same place she'd entered.

Willing to take the chance, she twisted the hand-wheel on the hatch, using all her strength, to force it open.

Breathing in the fresh air, she took a moment to send a prayer of gratitude that she'd made it to the end.

"Still got a long way to go, Bennett." Head just out of the hole, she glanced around her old barn. Sensing no immediate danger, she turned off her flashlight. She let her eyes adjust to the sunlight, piercing through the worn wooden slats.

Detecting no intruders, she levered herself out of the tunnel. Once out, she forced the lid back down.

"Okay, heart, time to stop pounding. Come on leg. We can do this." Standing, she kept her weight on her right leg before brushing herself off, trying not to think about how many eight legged creatures had escaped the hatch with her.

Hobbling to her truck, she bit her lip when her left sock squished with each step.

"I'll get the first aid kit and wrap up my leg." Upon arriving at her vehicle, she leaned against the side for a moment to catch her breath. Much to her chagrin, she thought about Clayton, about everything she'd told him. Bracing her hands on her knees, she fought past the pain pulsing through her body. "I think he hurt me worse than the stupid bullet." She hissed out a sigh. "Stop it, Bennett. You don't have time to bleed from your heart or anywhere else."

Her father and his malicious son had a date with her gun, which was stowed in the emergency bag she kept in her truck.

This time she wouldn't be the only one left wounded and bloody. This time they'd see what happened when you left a woman broken and she'd welded everything back together with vengeance and barbed wire stitches.

Because so far, she still hadn't won. Her father still held every Ace.

Him holding the winning hand had to end, because she couldn't keep losing. She couldn't.

CHAPTER 37

Once they'd tracked the stolen police cruiser to Sheridan's house, Clayton shoved O'Malley into the Lieutenant's sedan and hightailed it to her house.

On the way, O'Malley's phone rang. "O'Malley...I see...we're on our way there now." He punched off his cell and tossed it into the cup holder.

Clayton glanced over and arched a brow.

"Panic button was deployed at Sheridan's home two minutes ago. Police have been dispatched."

"Any sign of her?"

"No. And I know you're in a hurry son, but let's not put other lives in danger because one foolhardy girl decided to take off on her own."

"Foolhardy is too kind a description. I need to check with Rachel to see if she can pinpoint Sheridan's phone, however, our escapee has all those pre-paid phones so she's probably using them instead."

Clayton's phone buzzed in his pocket. He didn't dare read the text while driving, not when O'Malley was in the passenger seat. The call was likely from Rachel, telling him Sheridan's house alarm had been triggered. He brought his speed down to forty-five while weaving through traffic, lights flashing.

His woman had, once again placed herself in harm's way after everything he'd done to keep her safe. Talk about betrayal. Her actions today were exactly why he hadn't told her about assisting the FBI. Regardless of everything she'd said, he did not believe she could kill her father in cold blood. He didn't want her to make that choice, but now she was off, raging with emotion, and likely planning to do something stupid that would ruin her life forever.

"Did she ever mention her escape plans to you?" O'Malley thrummed his fingers against his leg.

"No. But we know the last call Sheridan made was to Jenny. They'd both know to drop their main phones since they can be tracked."

"I do know they went through safety exercises every couple of months."

"Do you think Sheridan will go into hiding with her sisters? Or do you think she's gone rogue?" Clayton sped up as they hit the road in front of Sheridan's house.

"Unfortunately son, I don't believe escape was ever in her plans. I've always feared her father would back her into a corner again, forcing her to make a choice."

Clayton studied all the police cruisers in front of Sheridan's house, the bent gate, and the van crashed into her porch.

"Looks like the kid crashed through the front entrance."

"Right...the front entrance...wait a second, the truck. Shit!" Clayton whipped the car around.

O'Malley cursed and gripped the side panel's handle.

"We need to check for a back entrance." Clayton shot back down the drive then stopped and dug out his phone.

He pulled up his location in his map app, looking for back roads behind her house. "Let's check this one." He pointed to road marked County Rd. 400. Handing O'Malley his phone, Clayton made a sharp left then travelled about a mile. He caught sight of a dirt road just before the turnoff and stomped on the brakes.

"Kincaid, are you trying to kill us?" O'Malley braced a hand against the dash.

"This is it, not the other road. This one."

The car bumped along the rutted road. A faded red barn was up ahead.

"Slow down, son. We need wheels if we're going to catch up with her."

The old barn had vertical wood slats. The two windows on the front and the wide, sliding door, created the vision of a happy face. The roof was weathered steel. Brown grass, lightly covered in snow surrounded the barn. A tree had sprouted along the side, its stark limbs a reminder that winter was here. A few remaining leaves blew in the slight breeze.

"I'm guessing this is it." Slightly hopeful, Clayton threw the car in Park, hopped out, and headed inside. "Sheridan!" He raced through the open door and searched the area but saw no signs of her. The truck wasn't inside either.

Clayton fought back the urge to punch a hole in the old wood. Instead, he punched in Scotty's number. "Hey, remember when I had you pick up Sheridan's truck from the grocery store? I need you to give the truck's details to one of the patrol officers and put out a BOLO. Got me."

"Can do, buddy." Scotty agreed. He'd stayed behind at the crime scene in case Sheridan returned.

"Clayton, I've got something." O'Malley waved him over. "Blood drops here. And a flashlight with dried blood." He pointed to the flashlight. It was beside a square steel opening, like the ones Clayton had seen in movies that led to bomb shelters.

Stomach churning, Clayton closed his eyes. He had no doubt the blood was Sheridan's. He tortured himself for a moment considering all the places she could've been hit with a knife or gun—both equally horrific. Yet, someone had driven off. Her? Or had the van driver caught up with her and taken her captive?

Clayton rubbed his aching forehead. "We know someone is driving a Ford F-150. Scotty's got the details and is giving them to one of your guys." He glanced at O'Malley and saw his same fear in the old man's eyes. He'd tan her hide for putting that look there. Not to mention all the other reckless shit she'd done.

While O'Malley checked in with his deputies, Clayton opened the hatch and hollered for Sheridan. When she didn't respond, he climbed down the metal steps. At the bottom, he bent over to fit in the space. So, this was how she'd escaped the night she'd gone to the store. "Sheridan! Are you down here?" His voice echoed down the corridor and received no response. A thin trail of blood went from as far as his eye could see to this exit. He'd have O'Malley's deputies check hospitals and drug stores. Maybe she'd gone there, but the more likely scenario was her following the directions on her father's note.

"The homestead." Clayton braced his hands on his hips as he stared down the metal enclosure. "That has to mean the apartment they lived in when Sheridan was little." He had no time to investigate this tunnel, so he climbed out, besides she wasn't down there. He couldn't hear anything but his own thundering heart.

O'Malley helped him to his feet. "Escape tunnel?"

"Yes." Clayton shut the lid. "Sheridan used to live on Sixteenth Street, right? Since her father hasn't been back in years, he'll go to familiar places like their old home. The other option is the hotel where he took Jenny."

O'Malley eyed Clayton. "Sheridan really let you in on some secrets, didn't she?"

"I should have handcuffed her to my side. I swear if she goes off and gets herself killed..." He huffed out a breath, shaking his head. "We've fought through so much, and then she pulls this stunt. I don't know what else I was supposed to do. I've already lost one person I loved. Now I'm supposed to lose another? I can't let that happen."

"We'll get to her, son." O'Malley clapped a hand against his shoulder. "She's running on autopilot. She didn't wait for me either, but she sees running as keeping us safe."

"She's wrong." Clayton clenched his jaw. He'd get her back and never let her go.

"I take the blame for this." O'Malley studied the bloody flashlight in his hand. "I've told her to stand strong for so long, I guess she really took my advice to heart. I never meant for her to face her father again, not after what he did last time." He met Clayton's gaze. "I understand what she's doing, and I have every intention of being by her side at the end, whether she likes it or not."

"Me, too." Damn it, if the old man brought him to tears, he'd really hit something...someone...a fucking tree. Going all heart-to-heart wasn't what he needed now, nor did he wish to listen to an "understand-Sheridan's-motives speech." Right now he needed guns and a clear target.

"Keep your focus clear, Kincaid."

"I'm trying."

"Good. Let's see what they've found up at the house."

On their way back to the sedan, O'Malley's phone rang.

"I see...in the garage floor you say? She's not in there now?...Gather the rounds as evidence and cordon off her entire house. The media will congregate soon, and we need everything locked down before her house gets swarmed. Got a blood trail out here in a barn on the south end of the property. I'll need someone to take a look."

O'Malley hung up, shaking his head. "The entrance to her hidey hole was in her garage floor. The lid was up and shell casings were all around the surface and at the bottom of the opening. It appears she made her escape through there. They said the opening was very narrow, so I doubt the blond kid could follow her down."

"I wonder what other secrets are in that house. Hell, her

sisters could be locked in some panic room and we'd never know."

"We could use heat sensors."

"True." Clayton rubbed his chin. "We need to move on to the old apartment."

O'Malley nodded. "I'll call for backup, and if she isn't there, we'll hit the hotel."

Clayton opened the driver's side door, eased into the seat, and waited for O'Malley to get settled.

"You ready?" Clayton faced the Lieutenant.

"For the first time in my long career, I'm having trouble remembering I'm a cop. We can't shoot first, Clayton. That's not how it works no matter how much we wish it different."

"I hear you, but right now all I can think about is what Sheridan's walking into. She's injured, scared, and most likely armed. She's heading into a trap, and I'm afraid she won't escape."

"Then let's find her."

Clayton nodded and hit the gas. This whole situation was a train wreck waiting to happen, and instead of pulling the brakes, he worried he'd be standing alongside and watching as everything crashed and burned.

CHAPTER 38

Icy air blustered through Sheridan's damp hair, cooling her heated face and likely adding pneumonia to her list of ailments. She was perched on an apartment building's rooftop directly across from where she'd grown up—the homestead. Blood loss had her teeth rattling with chills while at the same time, she felt as though her leg was stuck in an inferno. She leaned against the brick chimney, breathing deeply, trying to think two steps ahead, but struggling to focus when her entire being was narrowed on the pulsing pain coming from her leg. Four Advil hadn't done anything but make her sleepy.

Over the past couple of years, she'd driven by this old apartment in order to ground herself after all her fame. She'd even purchased the building and considered having it torn down. If those walls could talk, she'd be in worse trouble than she already was. "Instead, you've become a landlord." She rolled her eyes. Two apartments sat above a barbershop and pizza place. As a kid, her clothes had always reeked of burnt cheese. Not a pleasant scent in the classroom.

Sheridan searched for binoculars in the backpack she'd stored in her truck. Finding them, she raised them toward the lower level of the red brick building that encompassed so many bad memories.

A freckled-face kid was working behind the pizza counter, taking an order from a mother and her son. An elderly man, with a white towel over his shoulder was staring out the barbershop's window.

Keeping vigil from her rooftop roost, she waited to see if anyone entered or left the building from the side stairs. Her father had requested this meeting, yet he hadn't made an appearance. She'd be damned if she would walk in first. She scanned the streets below. Hopefully no one could see her up here, dressed entirely in black. Her hair was tucked under a black cap, courtesy of her bag.

Cursing, she ducked as two black SUV's appeared down the street. Both crept past the building before moving on. The vehicles then drove down the block before backtracking. Even knowing they likely couldn't see her from her rooftop perch, she stayed low as they came to a crawl in front of her building.

She barely breathed while the vehicles parked along the street two blocks down. The passenger of the second vehicle got out, along with another man from the first. Then a woman emerged from the back of the second SUV.

Her stylish red suit stood out in the drabness of the neighborhood, where the only bright colors came from spray-painted graffiti.

Maria Korzakov had found her ex-lover's hiding spot. O'Malley must have a leak in his department or else how would she know to come here. Unless someone in Agent Denver's office had squealed, maybe even the man himself.

Standing beside the vehicle, the woman conferred with her men. They shook their heads and waved their arms as they glanced at the apartment building. She snapped her fingers—a move that silenced them. *Nifty trick.* More men spilled from the vehicles and surrounded her as she walked toward Sheridan's old apartment. Each click of her heels seemed a death knell.

They all went up the stairs to the apartment, the woman leading the way.

Seconds later, a late model Cadillac pulled in front of the

pizza joint.

Her brother stepped out of the driver's side, glanced up at the apartment building, put on a baseball cap, and jogged down the sidewalk toward the parked SUVs. He paused there then lifted a closed hand toward the building.

Sheridan bit back a scream. What was he doing? What was in his hand? Heart racing, she shot to her feet.

A Jeep with a loud muffler barreled down the street, screeching to a halt at the curb next to her brother.

Her father was at the wheel.

Once her brother hopped into the passenger seat, they sped away, careening around the block.

Why would they leave the Cadillac and take off in that dilapidated Jeep?

Oh shit!

Instinct took over as she ran toward the roof top door.

The blast from the exploding car knocked her off her feet.

Chunks of brick and mortar blew past, striking her body and face.

Dust filled the air.

Sheridan blinked, wiping particles from her eyes. Coughing, she lifted onto her hands and knees.

Car alarms sounded and fire raged in the building across the street. Had anyone escaped? Dizziness threatened when she lifted her head to see if anyone was running from the building.

Blood from a head wound trickled down her forehead. Her arms and hands were covered in cuts, but one thought came crystal clear—she had to get off this roof.

Ears ringing and eyes burning from the smoke, she stumbled as she pushed to her feet.

Get to the door, and then the truck.

She limped her way down the stairs as the inhabitants ran out of their apartments and joined her on the journey down. Crying and muffled questions rang in her ears as she followed the rush out of the building.

Blending with others, she spared a glance towards the building—nothing but broken bricks. The entire upper level had collapsed and flames engulfed the remains.

She staggered back to her truck, sounds popping in and out of her left ear as the right rang with a deafening hum. Entire body shaking and her hands slick with blood, she fumbled as she slid the truck key into the lock. After opening the door, she wiped both hands across her ragged jeans before working the key into the ignition.

Police lights flashed. Sirens erupted from all corners. People gathered outside the building, searching for survivors.

She needed somewhere to stop and assess the damage to her body. After wiping the blood off her forehead, she closed her eyes, slowly breathing in and out. The pain in her leg sent shafts of fire up her entire body as if a mechanical contraption clicked on a brain sensor that discharged more agony straight back down. Injured but not out, she considered her next move. Playing out the end game

Dear old dad and baby brother would likely be surprised she hadn't died in their trap.

"Time to move on, Sheridan." She wouldn't think of Clayton. Or worry about her sisters. Not now. Instead she coughed out the dust and smoke she'd inhaled, threw the truck in Drive, and barreled down the alley, passing an oncoming fire truck. She turned away from the blast site. Away from all the trauma and death.

A tear fell from her eye.

"No! You don't get to cry." With a fist, she slammed the steering wheel, raging over the lives her father had taken. More innocents added to Jack Bennett's death tally—and embedded into her soul.

She'd failed, because once again she'd never seen it coming.

CHAPTER 39

Lights from the police cruisers and fire trucks lit up the macabre scene. Clayton stood beside a fire truck, watching as the firemen finally turned off their hose. Eyes watering from the smoke, Clayton wiped his cheeks then wrapped his suit jacket tighter against his body, staving off a cold chill from the winter air and from the uncertainty of Sheridan's whereabouts. They needed information and all they had was rubble and death.

Denver and his cronies had arrived but had no answers. Yet, somebody knew the exact moment to blow this building. Someone had shared information. Clayton wouldn't get bogged down in investigating that thought now, not when Sheridan could've been inside. If she was dead, injured, or if one hair was out of place on her head, he wouldn't stop until he discovered who had betrayed their plan.

O'Malley shuffled up beside him. The press had arrived with their cameras and microphones a few minutes ago, and the Lieutenant had given a cursory statement.

"Clayton, we don't know if Sheridan was in the building. Focus on what we do know. Maria Korzakov's purse was in the SUV up the road. *Her* body has been found. From what the EMT's tell me, a few of her men will survive. We'll question them to see who was inside." He shoved his hands in his front pockets.

"Let our guys do their jobs."

"Any evidence Jack Bennett was inside?" Clayton stared at a stretcher being loaded into an ambulance. One of many he'd seen in the past half hour. "Anyone see anything?"

In this area of town, no one could afford security cameras so that was off the table. But patrolmen were pounding on doors. People from the building across the street were milling around outside. Why they'd want to stand outside in this cold was beyond him.

"With everyone looking for Jack and Sheridan, it's only a matter of time before they're found." O'Malley braced a foot on the fire truck's shiny steel running board. "The entire town is on lockdown. He has no way out. And she's one of the most recognizable people on Earth."

Rage, fear, and sadness warred within Clayton's heart, threatening to break loose. She couldn't be dead…if he lost her…

Shouts came from a cop, standing at the entry of the building across the street. Denver raced over.

The Lieutenant's cell phone pinged. After he read the text, he stared at the screen a moment before wiping a tear from his cheek. Then he handed Clayton his phone.

I witnessed the explosion at the apartment tonight. I left a statement at this house's mailbox - 108 14th St. Jenny and Laney are safe. I'm waiting outside the hotel where Jack took Jenny. Once more, I'm calling for backup. In ten, I'm going in. Sorry and thanks for everything. Love, Sheridan

Squeezing the phone in his hand, Clayton closed his eyes. "She can't do this. What is she thinking?" He paced in front of the fire truck. "Is she insane? She could have died in that building, but no, when she doesn't die there, she goes to find her death somewhere else."

O'Malley removed his phone from Clayton's grip. "She's alive. Let's take that for now and focus on keeping her that way."

"Oh, I'm focused. Let's move."

Hustling to O'Malley's car, Clayton paused when Denver

flagged them down from the building across the street.

O'Malley jogged along at his side, and they stopped in front of the agent.

"A slight blood trail leads from the top of the building, travels down the stairs, and goes out a back exit." Agent Denver stood with both hands on his hips.

"It's most likely Sheridan's." O'Malley glanced at the building.

"How can you be so sure?" Denver narrowed his brow.

O'Malley powered on his phone, swiped the screen a couple times, then handed it to Denver.

Clayton finally took a moment to be grateful Sheridan was still alive, though she had to be close to going into shock based on her continual blood loss.

After reading Sheridan's text, Denver handed O'Malley his phone. "What's the hotel's address?"

Clayton snapped around and faced Denver. "Here's the thing." Clenching both hands into fists, he widened his stance. "This building was either blown up to kill Bennett, or the more likely truth, is that Jack concocted this entire scheme to kill Sheridan and got lucky when Maria showed up. Thing is, someone leaked this location to Korzakov. Maybe it was you, maybe it was some cop on the take, either way, I don't trust you or anyone else. That being said, O'Malley can give you the address, but I don't have a lot of faith that another Korzakov contingent won't show." Clayton jabbed a finger in Denver's face. "Maria Korzakov was killed in that building, and if her brother is aware of that fact, he'll be looking for payback. And he'll find it."

"Kincaid." O'Malley stepped between him and Denver.

Clayton narrowed his eyes at Denver. "I know Sheridan isn't your priority, but she *is* mine. You deal with the Korzakov's, and I'll deal with her."

#

Her father would be where it all began. The confrontation would likely end with both of them dead. Those things happened when someone in the family killed a Russian mobster's sister.

Outside the seedy hotel, Sheridan studied the flurries as they landed against the truck's windshield. Her entire body was one big ache. Woozy from blood loss and half deaf in one ear, she slapped her cheeks a couple time to keep from passing out. O'Malley would come and so would Clayton. Her ten minutes were up. She would walk in alone just as she'd done eight years ago, but this time she had a gun and a steely resolve.

Jack Bennett wouldn't leave this building alive. Living in constant fear and worry for her sisters—and for Clayton, would end today.

Easing out of the truck, she landed on her good leg then ignored the pain shooting up the other as she revisited the same path that, years ago had led to her sister's rescue but not her escape.

Once inside, Sheridan noted the faded numbers still visible on the doors. She choked down bile at the thought of what those numbers meant.

Her father hadn't chosen the same hallway for their showdown. She'd hoped to erase her nightmares with a better memory—one where he hit the floor instead of the tiny girl.

What sounded like a newscast played deeper within the building.

"Jack Bennett, mega-star Sheridan Bennett's father is wanted in connection to an explosion that occurred on Manchester's southeast side today. Authorities haven't released the names of the victims and firefighters are still on scene."

Typical. Bring in the movie star to drum up ratings. No one had covered the story eight years ago when an innocent girl had died, but because she was "Sheridan Bennett" apparently everyone needed to know.

Her father was likely toasting the chaos he'd created, reveling in his name on the big screen. *Sick bastard.*

Drug needles and empty bottles lined the hallway. A pungent smell, most likely urine mixed with the nasty twang of vomit, filtered through her nose.

She turned the corner and took the wide stairs to the lobby.

Her father lounged in a ratty couch set by the check-in desk, a laptop on a short end table was in front of him. The newscast sounded from the screen where an explosives expert was giving his thoughts on the day. Talking heads that believed they held all the answers. If only...

"I see you're enjoying the show." Sheridan stood with her back against the wall, gun in hand, her gaze focused on the target she'd mentally drawn on her father's head. "You've completely screwed yourself. Blowing up a mafia leader's sister...not smart. Plus, you'll never get out of his city. If Korzakov doesn't find you, the cops will."

"And your detective, of course. The game isn't complete without his presence. This is all on you of course. All the death." He kept her gaze. "All I asked for was a couple dimes to rub together, but no, you had to hold out, and then...as you see, more people have died because of your inability to cooperate."

She refrained from flinching because his words were true in a sense. She'd held out and now this...

"That imperious bitch, Maria walked right into my trap." Jack chuckled, shaking his head. "I'm surprised her fat ass made it up the stairs." Gesturing at the screen with one hand, he placed the other hand upon his chest. "Warms my heart to know I had her on her back one last time."

Fury rose at his indifference, though she wasn't surprised. "Unfortunately I was unable to join her."

Frowning, her father rubbed his chin. "Yes...well that is indeed unfortunate because we both know who inherits your money when you die. Jenny will be a much easier target. In her grief, her guard will be down, and I'll swoop in and get what I need."

"Wrong thing to say." Straightening, she aimed her gun at his chest. All the pain today, yesterday, years ago coalesced and hardened her heart. This was it. "I'm through talking."

A bottle clanked behind her, sending a cold chill down her back.

She didn't dare glance over her shoulder. If she died, so be it, but she'd still get a bullet off.

"I thought I taught you better." Her father stood and brushed off the front of his dress pants. "Always have a plan B." His gaze shot over her shoulder before he flicked a wrist. "I believe you've met your brother."

Cold steel pressed against the side of her temple.

Sheridan shrugged. "I'll go but you're coming with me."

"Not likely." Her father sniffed. "A bullet through the brain tends to end any hope of that. How enraging to always lose." He crept closer, smiled, and then slapped her face. "I'll get your money, and your sweet sisters will both die."

The taste of copper filled her mouth. She used it to fuel her fire. All she had to do was pull the trigger. She opened her eyes and lifted her hand.

"Do it and I'll end you." Her brother's rank breath whispered across her face. Then he kicked her leg.

She screamed in agony and fell to one knee.

"Oh, are you hurt?" Her father stood on her injured leg.

Sheridan cried out in pain. Why hadn't she just shot him the minute she'd entered?

Her brother ripped her gun from her hand. "Shall I kill her with her own gun, father?"

"That'd be poetic, Sheldon, but I don't think we have time today. I believe I've proven my point once again. She'll deliver the money now." He stomped on her leg again. "Won't she?"

Sheridan blinked as a wave of nausea struck and black dots

lined her vision. "No," she gritted out. "I won't."

"Looks like we'll be killing your sister after all. We'll get the money from Jenny then finish her off, too." He laughed. "Give me the gun. I'll finish this."

Sheridan waited until her brother held out the gun then she shot to her feet. Using her momentum, she shoved her father over. Arms flailing, she tumbled to the ground with him.

A deafening crack ripped through the air.

Sheridan jolted to attention, scanning the area for the shooter.

Her brother wobbled for a moment then hit the ground, landing right beside her.

The bullet hole between his eyes dripped blood onto his brow.

Sheridan screamed and shuffled to her feet.

Clayton stood about twenty feet away, his weapon trained on her.

No...not on her—on her brother.

He'd shot her brother.

A wave of dizziness had her clutching at the wall behind her.

Agent Denver and men in blue uniforms trailed in behind Clayton, guns raised.

Ears ringing, and likely on the verge of shock, she couldn't distinguish between the voices.

Where was her father? Her gun? She searched the floor beside her brother.

There! A hint of metal under her brother's hand.

She turned back to Clayton and noted his gaze was focused directly behind her.

She dove for the gun and spun with it in her hand, pointing it at her father.

He sneered and shouted something before pointing his weapon at Clayton.

"No!" Rising to her feet, she stood between her father and

Clayton.

The trigger's cold steel pressed against her index finger.

Next thing she knew, her head snapped to the side as someone rammed into her, knocking her over.

Landing with a grunt and pain sizzling across every nerve, she kept her gaze on her father and lifted her weapon again.

Clayton kneeled in front of her and fired.

The loud boom reverberated through the room.

Her father's body jolted backwards as Clayton's bullet hit him square in the chest, creating a red blossom on his white dress shirt.

She screamed but it was soundless and more than likely endless.

Clayton lifted her and carried her behind a wall of police. They were crouched behind chairs, pillars, and old tables as they fired shot after shot.

Who are they firing at?

The tinning in her ears kept everything slightly muffled.

Locked behind Clayton, she peeked around his side.

At the lobby's entrance, she saw a group of men in suits and some in jeans and dress shirts firing back at the police. They were popping off bullets as they retreated out the front door. Had to be Korzakov's men. Who else would have the balls to fire at a room full of police?

Coughing from the dust filling the air, she turned to look at her father. This time his blood seeped out onto the carpet. This time it was his eyes open in terror and staring straight at her.

Clayton wrapped both arms around her chest and shouted in her ear. "I am going to tan your hide when we get home. Do you have any idea what you put me through today?"

"Too tight." Sheridan shoved against his chest. "Can't breathe."

"Well, now you know how I've felt all fucking day!"

Sporadic pop, pop, pops sounded from outside. A few

officers had followed the mafia men out.

Clayton stood then shook her shoulder. "You will stay right here until the ambulance arrives. Do you understand?"

Eyes narrowed, Sheridan nodded.

He held out his hand. "Give me your gun."

"No." Her entire body started to shake as adrenaline left her system. No way would she leave herself unprotected in this state.

"Gun."

"I-I n-need i-it."

"Right now I could care less what you need. Give me the gun. Now."

She slammed her gun into his palm.

He jabbed a finger in her face. "Stay." After giving his directive, he stormed over to O'Malley.

Her old friend just looked at her and shook his head.

Great. His disappointment hurt almost as much as her leg. She lifted it a little, check that, nope, nothing hurt as much as her leg.

Agent Denver marched over to her father and bent to check his pulse before nodding at an agent who came to his side.

Sheridan swallowed past the lump in her throat.

Dead.

Her father was dead and she hadn't ended him. Clayton had. He'd taken two lives—for her.

Catching her stare, Denver barreled over to where she rested against pillar.

"Sheridan, are you injured?" Agent Denver bent to check her bloody pant leg.

"Can we just cut it off?" She tried to smile but failed.

Denver straightened. "I'm taking you in for obstruction of justice, stealing a police car, destruction of police property, concealing a fugitive, and every other offense I can come up." He got right up in her face and yelled, "Who do you think you are coming here on your own? Your father had the entire Korzakov contingent looking for him. Do you realize what would've happened if we hadn't shown up?"

Sheridan peeked over to where Clayton stood by the main doors talking to the men who were lining up the dead bodies.

One of which was her brother.

"Is that…the blond…he said he was my brother?" Sheridan slumped to her side onto the floor, clutching her stomach.

"Is that what he told you?"

"Yes, I don't know if it's true, though." What kind of blood ran in her veins? Her father and her brother were both psychopaths so what did that make her? "Agent Denver, I need to get to my sisters, so when can I get out of here?"

"We'll send an agent after your sisters. You aren't going anywhere, as I believe I just mentioned."

Sheridan sniffed. "I won't tell you where they are."

"I don't care. They'll eventually come out of hiding."

"No, they won't. We've trained too long and too hard. No one will ever find them. I need to know they're both safe. After that you can do whatever you want with me. I don't care."

"You don't get to make decisions on how this all plays out, Bennett."

"You're sure as shit right about that." She huffed out a laugh.

"Stay here."

For defiance sake, she stood then hobbled over to where her father lay face down on the ground.

How many policemen had they lost tonight? Would those men still be alive if she had just given her father the money? But if she'd done that, she would have set a precedent, and he'd have drained her dry.

Aching with despair, she erected a mental shield once more. She'd deserved to die as punishment for her mother's death and the little girl's death, but that hadn't happened. So, now she had to live with more blood on her hands.

She sucked in a breath. Too much. The burden on her soul

too heavy.

Overcome, she dropped to her knees, tears rolling down her cheeks. An inhuman scream rose from deep within and poured out her mouth. Enraged at all her father had put her though, and what she'd become because of him, she hit him once, and then again—then over and over. Her curses ringing in her ears and her fists hitting dead flesh as she released years of pent up rage.

Strong arms wrapped around her from behind, pulling her away. "Hey, hey, stop, Slim. He can't hurt you anymore."

"No. Let me go. I hate him, and I hate you. Don't touch me." Struggling to be free, she knocked her injured leg against a coffee table. Pain fired along the side of her body, sending a punch to her brain and knocking her straight into sweet, dark oblivion.

# # #

Sheridan woke to find Clayton asleep in a chair beside her hospital bed. His fist propped under his chin.

Mouth dry. Eyelids heavy. Leg throbbing. Why hadn't they just chopped it off as she'd suggested to Denver? He probably wanted her to keep it so when he arrested her, he could cuff her hands and her legs.

Closing her eyes again, she said a silent prayer for her sisters—and for Clayton. He'd been forced to take two lives. For her.

What did you say to someone after that? He'd also taken her chance at revenge, which didn't set right. How would she define herself now that she was no longer a protector?

Clayton stretched his arms in front of him and released a loud yawn.

"Clayton?"

"Hey." He rubbed his eyes then scrubbed a hand over his face. "You okay?"

"My sisters. Are they okay?"

"Jenny called last night. They're with the O'Malley's. She saw the news and figured it was safe to reach out."

A small portion of the heavy weight lifted from her heart. "Good." She fiddled with the stark white sheet. "I'm so sorry for what you had to do…ending my father's life…and my brother's. It wasn't for you to do."

His brow furrowed. "Sheridan, that's where the problem lies. You think it's all up to you and that others shouldn't be involved."

Grumpy from the pain and mental trauma, she struck back. "You are no different. Running around with the FBI and excluding me from your plans."

Clayton sighed. "I don't think either one of us is ready to have this conversation."

"What conversation is that?"

"Do you have any idea what you put me through? What you put O'Malley through? How horrified we were when we saw that building and thought you were inside."

She kept her gaze on her sheet, because she didn't want to see the emotions raging in his eyes when she couldn't figure out her own. "I'm sorry."

"That's doubtful."

"That's not fair." Sheridan clenched the sheet in her hand. "I had to keep you safe and that meant keeping you far away from me."

"I wasn't safe racing across town hunting you down, and you were this close"—he pinched his thumb and forefinger together— "from getting shot in the head by your brother."

"What the hell do you care? I was just a job anyway."

Clayton slammed both fists against the arms of his chair. "You *are* a fucking job—a full time one, and I signed on a long time ago knowing you were trouble. But if you think I'd do anything different, you're wrong. I protect what's mine."

Jolted to attention by his words, she risked a glance into his ocean-blue eyes. As she'd suspected, she glimpsed his steely resolve and a hint of hurt in their depths. Time to change the subject. He was right. They weren't ready for this conversation. "How long have I been in here?"

"About a day and a half. They removed the bullet from your leg and cleaned up all your scrapes."

Worrying her bottom lip, she closed her eyes and settled back in the bed. "You should go home and get some rest. I'll be fine by myself."

Clayton released a bark of laughter. "You still don't get it, do you? You're too banged up and drugged up for me to explain everything. Or for me to yell, which is what I'd really like to do. So *you* get some rest, and I'll be here when you wake up."

"Why?"

"Because when you love someone you stick by their side."

She opened her eyes and shot him a glare. "There's a lot I could say to dispute that statement, but I'm too tired to argue with you right now. All I want is hot tea and sleep."

"I'll get you something decaffeinated. And you won't be disputing anything." He stood and stretched that long gorgeous body. "Be back in a few."

After waiting for the door to shut, Sheridan curled up into a ball and burst into tears.

CHAPTER 40

Standing in her kitchen, Sheridan leaned against the counter, waiting for her peppermint tea to steep.

Clayton had given her space for a few days after dropping her off from the hospital. Maybe he'd needed a break, too. They'd avoided deeper discussions during her recovery. A good thing since she didn't know what to say. They were forever connected now, but she wasn't sure if they were linked by death or by love.

Her phone buzzed in her hand. For two days, costars, reporters, her publicist, her agent, even her stylist had all called to get the "real" story.

Jenny couldn't go to school. Laney couldn't work. Her agent, Bobbi, wanted her to come up with a statement, but how would she encapsulate into a few paragraphs the culmination of her life? How would she express her feelings now that her father and brother were dead? She couldn't, so she hadn't written anything.

This morning she'd had a long discussion with her lawyer. The Manchester police did not take kindly to "stealing" a police vehicle even though technically she had just borrowed it for a time. In recompense, she agreed to purchase a new vehicle. After dealing with Agent Denver and more legal jargon than she ever wanted to hear again, she still believed the worst had come from O'Malley. He'd lectured her for an hour at the hospital then left her to contemplate the consequences of her ill planned actions.

Her physical wounds were healing but the emotional wounds seemed leashed, almost feral, snapping and snarling with a wish to break free.

Her father no longer posed a threat, so did that mean she could relax her guard? Her driving purpose in life had ended far too abruptly. And now too many people wanted answers. Wanted her to dig through emotions far too raw.

Magazine covers printed fallacies. Photographers ran unchecked through her backyard. Jenny and Laney wanted their lives back. Questions came from every direction. But only one thing broke through, what now? That question was a ceaseless drum pounding in her head and in her heart.

What now?

# # #

"This is the end. My only friend, the end." Rachel stood in her usual spot in his office doorway.

After a jaw-cracking yawn, Clayton rocked back in his leather office chair. "Why are you quoting The Doors?"

"You've been stomping around here for a couple days, and I've been patient, but now you need to spill."

"You don't need to know anything."

"As your employer I'm very concerned about your health."

"No, you're nosy and likely looking for book fodder."

"Moi?" She rested a hand against her chest then plopped into the chair. "Talk to me."

"You're not my mom."

"Do I need to be?"

"That's creepy as hell." Clayton ran his fingers though his hair. "You're not leaving until I talk, are you?"

"No, buddy. I'm not." Rachel smiled. "I kind of love you. And I know that…well…things with Sheridan are difficult right now. Plus, the whole shooting—"

"All right. Stop." Clayton groaned before scrubbing a hand over his face. "I killed people during my time as a Ranger. I divorced myself from the guilt because it was my job…but this time…I suppose…maybe I should feel weighted down by two deaths, but I don't. I kept Sheridan safe. Was there another option? Another choice? I've considered the scenario countless times, and I don't see it ending any other way. I never want to take another life, but I'm trained to assess and act…so I did." Words were easy, but the truth was he hadn't slept or ate much in days. The police had taken his gun and were reviewing the scene. No charges had been filed against him. He had no doubt they'd rule both shootings were clean. He was still worried about any possible remaining threats to Sheridan by the Korzakov's in retaliation for Maria's death. He planned on reaching out to Erik soon, but didn't want Rachel to know.

Rachel propped her feet up on his desk. One of her tennis shoes was untied.

"Fix your shoelace before you trip and fall as you leave." He flicked a finger at her tennis shoe then turned back to his computer.

"So speaking in movie terms—"

"Trying to work here, Harris. I spilled now let me be."

"The hero saved the girl in a blaze of bullets, so what's the issue?"

Clayton shoved away from his desk and crossed both arms over his chest. "She wanted to pull the trigger."

Rachel nodded then sipped her coffee. "Makes sense."

"No, it doesn't."

"Why not?"

"Why would it?" Clayton arched a brow.

"Revenge. Sheridan's father caused her a lot of pain. She wanted retribution."

"So she needed his death on her conscience? I don't think

so."

"It's better that it's on yours?" Rachel tilted her head.

"Yes. Absolutely."

"Why, because you're the big man and can handle it?"

"Pretty much, yeah. You know, the whole, I'll take a bullet for you, well…"

"You *didn't* take a bullet." Rachel's feet ticked back and forth on his desk.

"Took it. Gave it. I protected my woman. That's what matters."

"Yeah, well she wanted to protect you, too."

Clayton sighed. "I know. I get that. Right now she's angry because she feels I betrayed her. I guess I did. I knew all along I should have told her about working with the FBI, but I just rode it out instead."

"You'll work through this. You love her and that'll move mountains and shit."

"Eloquent as always, Harris." He huffed out a laugh.

"I have my moments."

"Have one in your office then."

"Fine, I'm leaving." She blew him a kiss and headed out his door.

He dropped his forehead against his desk and sighed. "I need sleep and a huge steak, but first I need to see Sheridan."

Well…speak of the she-devil. His phone rang with her ring tone.

He pressed the phone to his ear. "Hey, Slim. What do you need?"

"Clayton, listen I'm going to California for a few days…maybe a week. I need some time away. From this town. The memories. The media."

"What makes you think going to California will be better? The scrutiny will be worse out there." The woman kept running, but he'd wait. And if she didn't come back, he'd camp out at her house. Jenny and Laney would let him in. They weren't afraid of him—unlike their sister.

He'd promised to stick by her side and none of the events over the past couple months had changed that fact. "We can talk about this trip tonight. I'd actually planned to call you just now. You must have read my mind. Plus, I didn't think you were cleared to leave town."

"I'm already at the airport. O'Malley knows. He wasn't happy...that seems to be the consensus with him lately...but anyway, I'm boarding in fifteen minutes."

"Why would you go to the airport alone? How did you even get there?" He shot out of his seat, considering how long a trip to the airport would take. "Damn it, Bennett. Leaving doesn't solve any problems, nor does the fact that, once again, you've made a decision without me."

"That's the thing." She sniffed. "I-I don't know what my problem is, so I can't solve it. I need to go away to figure it out."

"Is that supposed to make sense?"

"I wish it would. I'd like someone to scrape out the insides of my brain, analyze the entire mess, and then put everything back together again." She sobbed into the phone. "Oh hell, I have no idea what I'm saying. You're right, as usual, I *am* running away, and you need to let me. I don't know who I am or what I want. I don't know myself. These thoughts I'm having aren't...normal." She heaved a sigh. "I need time to find answers."

"Don't go." Clayton closed his eyes. "Stay here. We'll work it out together."

"Clayton, I...they're calling my section."

He opened his eyes and stared at the screen saver on his computer. Neon lines spinning and twirling. "I'll be here when you get back."

She was quiet so long, he'd thought she hung up. "Sheridan, you still here?"

"Why?" She whispered.

"Because I love you."

"But I don't even know who it is you love."

"That's okay, Slim, because I do."

"I have to go."

"Then go."

The line went silent. This time she was gone.

He stared at the blank screen for a moment before leaning back in his chair. The corner of his gym bag caught his eye. Boxing. He'd round up one of his trainer buddies and hit the ring. Because regardless of what he'd said to Rachel and to Sheridan, everything was coiled tight in his gut.

Just as Rachel said, he'd fought for the girl, so why didn't he feel like he'd won?

CHAPTER 41

Two days into her trip, Sheridan missed him. That's what stupid love did. The overwhelming emotion made one path clear and it led straight back to Clayton Kincaid.

She'd stayed two weeks with friends out of sheer stubbornness and worry that the answer couldn't be that obvious—but it was.

So now, two weeks later, she stepped out of the airport and into the cold December morning with only one destination in mind. In disguise as Scary Sherry, she grabbed a cab and directed the driver to Clayton's office.

He'd kept her together. Made her stronger. Put her first and she'd thanked him by walking away. While true many issues remained unsettled between them, she'd stop whining about things she couldn't change and focus on a future she'd dreamed of for years. The major threat to her life was gone all due to Clayton's vigilance.

After paying the cabby at the curb of Clayton's office, she hopped out, grabbed her bag from the trunk then tipped the driver. He gave her an odd look then drove off.

Taking a deep breath, Sheridan approached the front door and hit the intercom's button. "Clayton?"

The intercom crackled and then she heard his voice.

"Sheridan? Just a sec."

The door buzzed, and then the lock popped free.

He stood at the top of the stairs looking far too handsome in jeans and a red polo. "Why didn't you call?" He stuffed his hands in his pockets. For the first time, he seemed hesitant. Even distant.

Stomping the snow off her boots, she removed her gloves and placed her foot on the bottom step. "It's cold down here. Do you mind if I come up?"

"Sure." He waved her up.

"I came straight from the airport." At the top of the stairs, she caught her breath then walked into his office.

When he passed the threshold, she tugged him in, shut the door behind him, and shoved him against the wall. "I'm sorry, and I want you back." She leaned up to kiss him, but he stepped to the side. Frowning, she met his gaze. "I'm confused. Last I knew you wanted to work things out. What's going on, Clayton?"

He turned on his heel and situated himself behind the desk. "Sit down."

"All right." For some reason, she believed so much more than the desk sat between them. But what? Well...besides him killing her father and brother, her running off all the time, and him coordinating with the FBI behind her back. Sure, those things existed, but this seemed like something else.

He pressed both index fingers under his chin, looking like a principal dealing with a bad student.

"What did I do?" Flutters erupted in her belly as she took in his stoic expression. "I told you I just needed time."

He still didn't speak, just tapped a yellow file folder against his desk.

"I knew the minute I accused you of betraying me that the words weren't true. Is that what you want me to say? I didn't mean for my absence to create this divide." She waved a hand over the desk. "Why aren't you talking to me?"

"You know why?"

She swallowed past the lump in her throat. "You say that like I should know, but obviously, I don't, so what? I want to understand."

Clayton opened the folder and tossed a couple photos across the desk. Eight by ten photos. Taken through a window. Of her and a man she'd never seen before. A nude guy. In the top photo, she was sprawled beneath him, her mouth open in ecstasy.

She laughed. "What are these?" Shaking her head, she looked at the next one. This one had them lying in bed together—after. "They should've put a cigarette in my mouth. These are ridiculous." Rolling her eyes, she threw the photos back on his desk then looked up and caught his gaze. "Wait." She leaned back. "You don't believe these pictures are real, do you?"

At his non-answer, she felt her stomach go from flutter to nasty flip. She'd come here today to discover if they had a future, and now she knew. If he wanted to believe those photos were real, then she'd let him. Hadn't he always represented a dream she could never have? A dream that now crashed to pieces, emptying her insides to the point where she would never breathe again without pain piercing her heart.

She'd let the fantasy become real, and that was her mistake. After having her past collide so violently with her future, she should've known better than to believe in a happily ever after.

She called on all her acting skills to deliver the word she had always known would come. "Goodbye." Biting her lip, she opened his office door and headed for the stairs.

Just as she was about to take the first step down, she stopped when he grabbed her shoulder.

"Where are you going?"

"I-I don't know." She stared at the floor.

"Why would you leave when you just got here?" He tipped up her chin.

"You think…" She waved a hand toward his office. "The photos…you think I was—"

"No." He growled out a heavy sigh. "Stop trying to think for me. I'll admit upon first glance, I got a little…angry. But then I put a few things together in my head."

"Okay." Her heart raced, and she slumped against the wall. Boneless and quite sure she was on the verge of a stroke.

"Constance has been calling a lot lately, and then I get these photos. Come back into my office. Rachel will interrupt us if we're out here too long." He took her elbow and settled her into his office chair. Leaning against his desk, he tapped his chin with his cell phone. "I recalled something Constance said weeks ago when we were looking at those photos your brother taped to that board game."

"The Operation game?"

"Yes."

"Oh. What did she say?"

"She said she could do better."

"At what?" Sheridan pursed her lips. "I don't understand."

"The photos. She said she had a program that could do better."

"I see. So…Constance sent these." Sheridan picked up the photo again, studying it. "They do look pretty real."

"Yeah, they do." He frowned. "I had a slither of doubt, but then I realized you'd never do something like that to me."

"So, why the silent treatment? I sat here thinking we were over after I came home ready to try again."

"You left for weeks then just show up here. Give a guy a minute to catch up. One minute I'm looking at you naked with another man, then you're at my door."

She took his hand and placed it over her heart. "This has only ever been yours. Only yours."

"You done running?"

Sheridan kissed the inside of his palm. "Yes."

"Damn straight you are." He yanked her out of the chair and pulled her between his legs then captured her lips in a dominating kiss, growling as his tongue swept inside.

"Right now." She tugged on his shirt. "I want you right now." Shoving him back, she unzipped then wiggled out of her pants. "Take yours off."

He shrugged then complied. "Rachel and Bronco are always having office sex. I guess it's my turn."

She ran a hand up and down his thick cock. "Yes, it is. I know we have a lot to talk about, but I want this first. I want the connection. I need to know we're okay."

"We are, but, I'm with you, we better make sure." With a deep chuckle, he plopped into his chair, settled her on his lap, and—"Oh, shit. Wait. Grab my jeans."

She groaned but did as he asked.

"Hand me my wallet." He flipped it open, grabbed a condom, slicked it on, and then met her gaze. "You ready?"

In answer, she rose up on her knees and settled him at her wet core. "I need this. Take me." Hands on his shoulders, Sheridan wiggled until he was balls deep. "Oh, I missed this." She flashed a wicked smile then rolled her hips.

Raspy breaths, deep kisses, and loving murmurs lifted away all the uncertainty and pain as they raced toward that peak of pleasure.

Clayton's deep kisses turned carnal, his breathing stuttering out in short bursts. His strong hand was clamped tight against her hip, guiding her up and down. "Now, baby, I need it. Give me everything."

What choice did she have? She tumbled into bliss. Exploding in waves that crashed and washed over her heart, healing fears and insecurities while giving intense pleasure.

Clayton thrust deep once, twice then buried his deep moan in a kiss that allowed no doubt of his ownership, of his belief in everything they were together. Soft kisses followed then he wrapped his arms around her. His heart beat heavy against her chest, forgiveness and understanding in each thump that echoed from his body to hers.

#

Minutes later, Sheridan brushed her fingers over his strong jaw. "What now?"

"How about we begin with you understanding I will do whatever it takes to keep you safe. I'm sorry, but I wouldn't do anything differently." He slapped her hip. "Let's get dressed before Rachel barges in."

Sheridan grabbed her pants off the floor and pulled them on. "What will you do about Constance?"

"I'll ask her about the photos, but she'll lie. Doesn't matter."

"Matters to me," Sheridan scoffed. "She tried to break us apart."

He wrapped her in his arms and kissed her. "Didn't work."

She untangled from his hold and leaned a hip against his desk. "She and I will have words someday."

"Doubtful."

Sheridan punched his arm. "If anyone is going to screw with our relationship, it's me. Not her."

"I'd rather not discuss Constance right now. I think we have bigger issues."

Nodding, she took his hand. "For so long, I only cared about one thing, destroying my father. If I didn't have that, then who was I? Once I arrived in California, I realized you knew the answer all along. I am a woman who was looking for safety in all the wrong places. Safety is with you. It isn't in death or in revenge. It's sitting in the basement with you at my side. It's in your kiss. It's letting my sisters find their own way. It's letting go of my past and embracing a future. I can stand on my own, I've done it for many years, but now I'd like to see how much better I can be if I find the rest of the answers in my life with you." She leaned her forehead against his chest. "Thank you for protecting me. This whole experience has been a nightmare for you, and I didn't make it easier. I'm so very, very sorry."

"Not everything's been a nightmare." He nudged her with his hips.

"I'm trying to have a serious moment here." She grinned and looked up into his aqua-eyes. She should've known from the first moment she gazed into that deep blue, that she'd be lost like a freaking mermaid in the Aquaman Triangle.

She hadn't believed this kind of love was possible, but his feelings were evident in his look, his touch, and his smile. All along, he'd patiently waited to put a broken girl back together, easing each piece into place so easily she hadn't even realized it was now complete.

She'd likely fall again, but this time she wouldn't have to pick up the pieces alone. This time she had her own super hero

"Sorry. Didn't realize I wasn't following the script. I'll set my face to serious moment." He straightened his shoulders, raised his left brow, and pursed his lips. "How's this for serious face?"

"Not winning any awards with that one." She laughed. "And I have no idea what you're talking about, we haven't followed a script since we began. If we had, we'd be in bed with you doing unspeakable things to me over and over again."

He rocked her back and forth in his arms. "Unspeakable? Hmm....maybe you should whisper a few ideas in my ear."

"I could, but I'd rather show you. I'm much better at acting things out. I am a famous actress, you know."

Clayton tugged on a strand of her hair. "Our life won't always follow a script, Slim."

"Oh, I don't know." She batted her lashes a few times. "I think I'd like you sitting in the director's chair."

"Thought we were being serious."

"Nah, let's just be."

He met her gaze and nodded. "So, you want to *just be* back at your place or should we test out my desk?"

She trailed a finger down his chest. "Hmmm...I feel we should discuss payment for all your hard work over the past few months."

"Oh, honey. You'll be working that off for a long time to come."

"I certainly hope so." With a sly grin, she took his hand, led him to the stairwell, and then stopped and gazed up at him. "I'm no longer broken. You've shown me that the brightest stars only shine when lit from within. I've got so much love for you in my heart, I could light the world."

"You've always been my star, Slim." He ran his thumb across her bottom lip then kissed her.

"Took me a while." She grinned.

"It did, but we're where we need to be."

"No, not quite." She licked her lips then raced down the stairs and out the door, knowing he'd catch her.

And when he did...her star would really shine. With pleasure. With love. And with hope.

EPILOGUE

"You agree to my terms?" Otari Korzakov held out his hand.

"I agree." Erik Pavel steeled his nerves and shook the man's hand.

Sitting across from his greatest enemy in this run-down restaurant, Erik didn't flinch or show any sign that he was the least bit worried. The old man believed Erik had once again sold his soul to the devil. Not quite.

His soul belonged to a vow he'd made long ago. Today's meeting was set up to guarantee the Korzakov family would leave Sheridan Bennett and her family alone in exchange for Erik coming back into the fold.

"You no longer wish for vengeance in your mother's death?"

"My mother is still alive." Eric shrugged.

"Yes, your *birth* mother."

Erik stood and buttoned his jacket. "I belong with this family. I have given my word I will work in your interests. Now, I have another meeting across town. If you'll excuse me." Erik waited by the table, because this could go either way.

"You're excused." Otari nodded. "I will need you later this week. I have a new man who needs to learn the ropes. His name is Ted McCord." Otari flashed a wide grin, and met his gaze with a too-sure twinkle in his eye.

Erik inclined his head. Did Korzakov expect him to know that name? He didn't, but he couldn't show any doubt or confusion. "I'm at your service."

He stepped away from the table, waiting for a bullet in his back. When it didn't come, he hit the bathroom before he left, washing the man's filth from his skin. He stared at the man in the mirror. "Your friend's woman is now safe. And I'm one step closer to my revenge." He grinned, pulled the gun from his holster, and made his way to his car.

Six months later

Walking into the master bedroom after a long day at work, Clayton heard coughing coming from the bathroom, so he followed the sound. He'd moved into Sheridan's house right after she'd returned from California. They'd weathered the initial media storm after she'd taken him to a movie premiere a few months ago. Each step in their journey wasn't always easy, but they did it together.

"Sheridan?" He didn't see her in the bathroom, but he swore...

"Go away."

He found her lying by the toilet, all scrunched up.

The smell of vomit wafted in the air.

Sheridan peered up at him. "I don't like you very much right now."

He squatted next to her and brushed a sweaty strand of hair from her face. "Can I get you something? Some peppermint tea?"

"No, this illness came from you."

"And how did I give you this bug?"

"You gave it to me, buried it in there deep, and now it's making me sick."

Clayton blinked. "I gave it to you?"

"Yes, it's your fault."

"I see." Bug. Illness. Vomit. Didn't take much to deduce what was wrong with his superstar. He took a moment to absorb the fact that he would be a father and accepted it easily. Smiling, he closed the toilet lid and sat down. "Guess you'll have to marry me now."

"I knew it," she groaned. "I knew that was the first thing you'd say."

"Well, we can't have our little bug running around without my last name now, can we?"

"Fine, fine, we'll go to Vegas and do the Elvis thing. Now go away, I need to get cleaned up."

"This weekend?"

"If you say so." She flopped a hand in his direction.

"I love you like crazy. Come lay down with me so I can hold you."

"Now there will be two of us." She rested her head against his leg. "Are you happy about the baby?"

He ran his fingers through her soft blonde hair. "No words exist for how I feel. I love you, Sheridan Bennett soon to be Kincaid, and I'm ready to take this next step, are you?"

"Yeah, time to put the Bennett curse behind us."

"Slim, we already left that behind."

"You promise."

"I promise."

Thank you for reading *Clayton's Star*. I hope you enjoyed Clayton and Sheridan's story. If you did, please leave a review at your purchase site. Reviews are appreciated by the author.

Available Now

Book #1 in The O-Line Series, *Ember's Center*
Book #2 in The O-Line Series, *Rachel's Guard*
Book #3 in The O-Line Series, *Maude's Score*

Book #1 in The Elementals Series, *Water's Threshold.*
Book #2 in The Elementals Series, *Fire's Field.*
Book #3 in The Elementals Series, *Air's Vision*

Please enjoy the following excerpt from *Water's Threshold*, Book #1 in The Elementals Series.

Since arriving in Wyoming only a few months ago, Maya had experienced a strange energy pattern that interrupted her sense of peace. A consciousness never felt before, as if something attempted to anchor her in place—a pull unlike anything she had experienced since starting this new life nearly one hundred and fifteen years ago.

This internal strife was because of him—Terran Forrester. Mother had warned this would come. He was part of her purpose in being in this place at this time. Her orders were to guide him, because their destinies were entwined. Having Mother Nature set her up on a "fate date" left her feeling like a contestant on a game show. During her human life, Maya strove to control her own destiny, never handing over power. As an Elemental, she remained determined to give her all to their cause, but it chafed when Mother asked for more—to open her heart. Why now? Why was this burden of love thrust upon her with a mate she had not chosen?

Mate. What a ridiculous word.

Maya blew out a breath, causing a bevy of bubbles to dance their way to the surface. She couldn't have children so Mother using that specific word made the whole idea more ludicrous. Yet, Mother's wishes had come to fruition and that fact rankled. When spying on Terran, Maya experienced emotions surfacing she'd thought buried in a deep well long ago.

Her duties included watching him as he went about his daily human life. She enjoyed observing his frequent visits to the banks of the Snake River where he filled little glass vials. A soft hum raced through her body each time she spied him doing ordinary things, like working up a sweat at the gym or grabbing a cup of coffee at the local café. Since her last sexual adventure occurred in the free-love laced 70's, she was more than overdue for male attention. Terran would, no doubt, approach sex with the same care he did his experiments—meticulously and thoroughly.

That trickle of lust thrummed especially strong tonight at the gas station, when he'd touched her shoulder, all concerned citizen, seeking to offer assistance to an unfamiliar woman. Her waterlogged heart had pumped like a steam engine traveling uphill.

About the Author

In the spring of 2013, Jillian Jacobs changed her career path and became a romance writer. After reading for years, she figured writing a romance would be quick and easy. Nope! With the guidance of the Indiana Romance Writers of America chapter, she's learned there are many "rules" to writing a proper romance. Being re-schooled has been an interesting journey, and she hopes the best trails are yet to be traveled.

Water's Threshold, the first in Jillian's Elementals series, was a finalist in Chicago-North's 2014 Fire and Ice contest in the Women's Fiction category.

Jillian is a: Tea Guzzler, Polish Pottery Hoarder, and lover of all things Moose.

The genres she writes under are: Paranormal and Contemporary romance with suspenseful elements.

Connect with Jillian Jacobs online

Website: www.jillianjacobs.com

Twitter: https://twitter.com/GreenMooseProd

Goodreads: https://www.goodreads.com/JillianJacobs

www.ingramcontent.com/pod-product-compliance
Lightning Source LLC
Chambersburg PA
CBHW070000200626
46811CB00021B/2487